THE MARS ANOMALY

JOSHUA T. CALVERT

ACRONYMS

AI – Artificial Intelligence
API – Application Program Interface
AxEMU – Axiom Extravehicular Mobility Unit
BIN – Badan Inelijen Negara (Indonesian National Intelligence Agency)
CME – Coronal Mass Ejection
CNC – Computer Numerical Control
CNN – Convolutional Neural Network
CNSA – Chinese National Space Administration
CT – Comp (Compensation) Time; mandated coffee or lunch break
DNA – Deoxyribo Nucleic Acid (genetic makeup of living organisms and many viruses)
DRACO – Demonstration Rocket for Agile Cislunar Operations
ESA – European Space Agency
ESOC – European Space Operations Center
EVA – Extra Vehicular Activity (spacewalk)
GPS – Global Positioning System
GPT – Generative Pre-trained Transformer (AI component)

GSFC – Goddard Space Flight Center

FOMO – Fear Of Missing Out

HiRISE – High Resolution Imaging Science Experiment

HR – Human Resources

HUD – Head-Up Display

ISS – International Space Station

LEO – Low Earth Orbit

LIDAR – Light Detection And Ranging

LtCdr – Lieutenant Commander

ML – Machine Learning

MRO – Mars Reconnaissance Orbiter

NASA – National Aeronautics and Space Administration

Orch-OR – Orchestrated Objective Reduction

PMT – PhotoMultiplier Tube

SDO – Solar Dynamics Observatory

SOC – Science Operations Center

SOHO – SOlar and Heliospheric Observatory

SPDC – Spontaneous Parametric Down-Conversion

STEREO – Solar TErrestrial RElations Observatory

UHF – Ultra High Frequency

VHF – Very High Frequency

VR – Virtual Reality

PROLOGUE

She stretched a hand upward, examining it. It felt cold. A tingling sensation ran along her arms and up to the back of her neck, as if a swarm of ants were running over them and assembling under her hairline.

Rachel felt a pang of guilt over what she was about to do. Was it selfish? Heroic? Or neither, a mere impulse sparked by her intuition, the guidepost of her life that had never let her down.

Was now to be the first instance? It would be a bad time for fate to leave her hanging.

In the background she heard voices over the radio, familiar, but also strangely confused because they were distorted by intense interference. Snatches of words filtered through to her. Here and there she caught her name, sometimes a 'not' or a 'back.' But scratching and static swallowed up almost everything and marginalized the sounds to mere disturbances at the edge of her perception.

Strangely enough, she saw nothing above her but this foreign sky, which looked like a particularly hazy day at home when the ground fog arose.

All she had to do now was stretch upward to discover the truth, possibly even to become the truth. Forever. She wasn't doing it for herself, but for all those who would follow, who wanted to reach the end that everyone was striving for in their hearts.

Did she have any choice? She thought of Christer. Would she see him? Or would it no longer matter, because there would be no Christer as she had come to know him?

Out of the corner of her eye, she saw the others approaching. She had no more time. Either she solved the mystery for posterity, or she backed off now due to emotions. Masha was constantly present in her thoughts and heart. She had to do it for her, too, even though it meant the end for herself.

Isn't there a beginning in every ending?

1

Goddard Space Flight Center (GSFC), Science Operations Center, Greenbelt, Maryland

"I think I've got something here," Rudy said, repeating louder, "I think I've got something here!"

"From the SDO?" asked his colleague Samantha, who was already on her second night shift with him. Unlike himself, she was no longer a doctoral student, but had already been here at the SOC for ten years – which had surprised him after he took up his post. Normally, the newcomers were given the most unpopular and boring shifts. Perhaps she had messed things up between herself and the boss.

"Yes," he replied with a nod. He turned the right-hand one of his three monitors toward her and pointed to the diagrams and data blocks.

"All right, then, take me through the measurement data and interpret it for me," Samantha prodded him. The solar physicist scooted over to him in her chair and gave him a wave to get started.

Rudy felt like a student who'd been called upon to recite something in class, but he certainly wasn't the first doctoral student to feel that way.

"On the left are the UV and ultra-UV images from the AIA – the Atmospheric Imaging Assembly – expressed in wave diagrams showing the solar corona and its structural dynamics. On the right are the curves for the last forty-eight hours."

He made a few entries on his keyboard and the data sets were superimposed as differently colored curves. The deflection was now clearly visible.

"Considering the time component, I'd say that this," he held a finger directly over the skyrocketing curve, "is an incipient coronal mass ejection."

"A CME," Samantha said thoughtfully and moved closer to the screen. "That's a really good catch."

"What do we do now?"

"We'll send the data to ESOC and the STEREOs tomorrow." The physicist suppressed a yawn.

"Uhh ...?"

"European Space Operations Center in Darmstadt, and the STEREOs are over at their Science Center."

A little embarrassed, Rudy cleared his throat. It was late. Of course he knew where the data from the solar observation satellites was collected and interpreted, but he was tired. Unlike the Solar Dynamics Observatory (SDO), which was positioned as a satellite at Lagrange point 1 between the Earth and the sun, the SOlar and Heliospheric Observatory (SOHO) and the Solar TErrestrial RElations Observatory (STEREO) orbited and were monitored by other colleagues.

"Sure, I get it," he finally said, and his gaze returned to the real-time data coming in from the SDO. The color-coded curve continued to grow, like the wave of a storm front that was gradually building up. "Those are pretty big spikes in almost all ultraviolet wavelengths."

Samantha rubbed her eyes and pulled Rudy's keyboard toward her to make a few quick entries, whereupon the parameters of the y-axis shifted as if they were zooming out. The deflection now stood out even more clearly from the data of the previous days and weeks.

"Please call up the spectrograms."

Rudy switched to the middle monitor and went through the different tabs of the program until he found them. They showed the distribution of solar radiation at different wavelengths and presented red, yellow, green, and blue peaks, with the red ones clearly dominating in the upper frequency range. They silently compared the x and y axes with those of the UV images from the SDO interpreted as a wave diagram.

"Call Darmstadt. I'll go over to the STEREOs."

"Now?"

"Yes, the early shift has probably just started in Germany. That could be a coronary mass ejection on a scale I've never seen in my ten years here."

She got up and left the office while Rudy was still looking for the phone list in his drawer. When he found the right number, he grabbed the receiver and dialed.

"ESOC, Martin Scherinski," a gruff voice announced.

"This is Rudy Longstone from the SOC," Rudy said nervously. "We're getting data in here from the SDO that looks suspiciously like a CME."

"We were just about to call you guys," Scherinski replied. "We've already carried out several runs with the 3D models and the color-coded image analyses to rule out measurement errors. Have you started calculating yet?"

"What am I looking for?" asked Rudy.

"You should take a closer look at the position of the mass ejection and compare it with the sun's rotation and Earth's movement around the sun. I'll send over everything we have. If you come to a similar conclusion, please get back to us immediately. Then we should wake a few people up."

"All right, thanks." Rudy hung up and took the calculator out of his drawer. Then he looked at the incoming data from Darmstadt in his inbox and began making computations.

When Samantha came back, he had just finished and felt like he was going to throw up.

"The STEREO has made similar measurements and the boys can ... What is it?" the physicist asked when she saw his pale face.

"Darmstadt has also confirmed and sent over data. A massive coronal mass ejection," said Rudy in a strained voice. "If the initial calculations are correct, the plasma cloud is moving at around twenty-four hundred kilometers per hour."

"That would be one of the fastest we have ever measured."

"Yes, and it could hit Earth."

Samantha frowned and took the piece of paper he'd held out to her. On it were the corresponding figures, which he had calculated and compared with those from Darmstadt. They were identical.

"That's a problem," she muttered. "This thing is huge."

"And fast."

"We have to wake them up."

"Who?"

"Everyone! I'll start with the director's office."

2

RACHEL

" ... joining us now from Houston is Roger Myers, physicist and astronaut, veteran of three ISS missions," said the Good Morning America moderator, turning to the display showing the face of the popular astronaut, who, atypically, was not smiling from ear to ear. On the contrary, Myers looked somber, and his eyes expressed exhaustion. The time '6:33 A.M. PST' was superimposed on the image. "Hello, Roger."

"Good morning, Andy."

"Roger, what is known so far about the solar storm that is heading our way?"

"First of all, we need to clarify the terminology. It is a so-called coronal mass ejection, or CME, which means that the sun ejects plasma consisting mainly of protons, electrons, and the atomic nuclei of heavier elements, such as helium, oxygen, and iron. Most such ejections are entirely normal and are related to changes in the sun's magnetic field lines. Ejections only become a solar storm when the plasma hits the Earth and our magnetosphere is disturbed."

"Okay, but the Department of Homeland Security has announced that this plasma cloud is very likely to hit us and potentially cause disruption to power grids and internet connectivity," the moderator declared with the worried concern of someone who barely understood the situation because he was usually covering Los Angeles potholes or the latest weird eating contests.

"That's correct," confirmed astronaut Myers. "NASA and the Pentagon are busy preparing our satellites. Some will have to change their orbits, while most will be temporarily shut down for safety reasons. Modern satellites have shielding for such events, especially the military ones, but we don't want to take any risks. The disruption to GPS and internet systems will only be temporary."

"How long will the storm last?"

"According to our current calculations, about three hours. Auroras can occur throughout the southern hemisphere when the charged particles of the plasma cloud hit our magnetic field. This is no cause for concern, as the protons and electrons merely collide with gas molecules, resulting in photon emissions. Nevertheless, we recommend that everyone, including those of us in the northern hemisphere, leave all electronic devices switched off."

"So no souvenir photos of this spectacle?" joked the presenter.

The astronaut's expression remained serious. "No. It's safest if we all go to bed like normal and sleep through this event instead of worrying about it."

"There are already rumors that the government is worried about possible looting, as there may be disruptions to the internet, power supply, and radio communications. Can you say anything about this?"

"No, you'd have to ask a government employee. But I think that's unlikely. The forces of law and order are preparing for everything and we've warned them well in advance. So everyday life should go on as usual, as much as possible. We're lucky in our time zones that it's happening at night, when most of us would normally be asleep."

Rachel switched off the television and stuffed the Tupperware containers of food for lunch into her bag, her routine every morning while watching breakfast TV. Then she took the keys from the kitchen table and went into the hallway.

"Masha!" she called up the stairs, "Are you coming?"

"In a minute!" sounded from above.

She looked at her watch and sighed, "I'm leaving in five minutes."

"I'm tired," her six-year-old daughter complained, coming down the stairs with disheveled hair and rubbing her eyes. As always, Masha's backpack looked far too big for her delicate frame.

"I can understand that. I am too."

"But you don't look tired." Her daughter looked at her reproachfully and yawned while Rachel finger combed her straw-blond hair at least halfway into shape.

"That's because I've been up for an hour preparing this." She picked up the last of the Tupperware containers and put it in her daughter's backpack.

"I don't like black bread," Masha grumbled.

"You'll like it one day."

"I don't like it."

"Come on now."

Rachel helped Masha into her jacket and nudged her through the door toward the driveway. The sun was already creeping leisurely over the horizon, making the morning dew glisten beautifully on the grass of their small front yard. There was nothing to suggest the elemental force that was supposedly going to break over the Earth tonight. Would the auroras be visible here in California?

"I have math today," grumbled her daughter as they sat in the car and rolled backward onto the road.

"I thought you liked math."

"Yes, but that class is with Mr. Tinnerman, and he has terrible breath." Masha grimaced as if she had bitten into a lemon.

"Remember that you're with your Auntie this afternoon?" Rachel tried to cheer her daughter up, and Masha's little face did indeed brighten up quickly.

"Can I sleep over tonight?"

"Not today, Dear. Not today."

"Why not?"

Because a plasma cloud is hitting the Earth tonight and I'm worried, she thought. Because when 'they' tell you that you shouldn't worry, it usually means now is the time you should worry.

"Because I'm going to watch a movie with you."

"A movie?" Masha clapped her hands, no longer looking tired. "What kind of movie?"

"You're six now. That's the age at which we were all confronted with our first childhood trauma."

"Huh?"

"My Girl, Honey. We're watching My Girl."

"That's stupid."

"How do you know that? Have you already seen it?"

"No, but it sounds stupid."

"You'll remember this movie for the rest of your life," Rachel promised her daughter as she steered onto the street of Longwood Elementary School. She stopped in front of the door. Dozens of pupils were already streaming from the buses and bike racks to the nondescript, prefabricated building, chattering so loudly that even through the closed car windows they could be heard like the buzzing of a beehive. "See you tonight."

"Okay." Masha opened her door and slid off her seat. "Bye, Mom."

She waved and watched as her daughter ran across the lawn to two of her friends who were waiting for her. Smiling, Rachel paused until the three girls had disappeared through the entrance and then drove on to the university.

Today would be her first time teaching in the large lecture hall, which was not normally used by the Faculty of Linguistics. So she turned into a different corridor from where she usually went to introduce the world of linguistics to small groups of 20 to 30 students. When she reached the lecture hall, it almost took her breath away. There were 400 seats and all were taken. Some students were even sitting on the steps in the aisles between the rows of seats, and there was still a quarter of an hour to go before the lecture began.

Before she went all the way through the door, she took a deep breath and steadied herself to face the noise and the oppressive presence of so many people. She had never spoken in front of such a crowd before.

It was quiet for a short while when she walked in, until the initially timid whispering grew louder and louder. Rachel set her bag down on the table in front of the three-part table and the smartboard and began to adjust the fit for the headset that was ready for her.

She tapped the microphone on her cheek a few times and heard the corresponding clatter from the speakers, which quieted the students.

"Good morning, first-year students, and welcome to the lecture on the 'Sapir-Whorf hypothesis.' In this lecture, we will examine the foundations of this fascinating and sometimes controversial theory in linguistics. The Sapir-Whorf hypothesis is named after its main proponents, the American linguists Edward Sapir and Benjamin Lee Whorf, and is concerned with the relationship between language and human thought. The Sapir-Whorf hypothesis focuses on the idea that the structure of a language influences the way its speakers perceive and think about the world. There are two main versions of this hypothesis: the strong version, also known as 'linguistic determinism,' and the weak version, also called 'linguistic relativity.'"

The first hands shot up, a dozen at first, then almost all of them.

Rachel sighed and pushed her script aside. "Any question that has nothing to do with E.T.?"

All the hands went down again.

"Well, let's continue with the two versions of the hypothesis, which will show you that linguistics can do much more than just analyze the emergence and development of languages. Properly applied, it penetrates into philosophy and opens a door to understanding reality in terms of subjective filters – ears and tongue alike.

"Let's start with linguistic determinism, the strong version: it states that language completely determines thought and perception of reality. This means that speakers of different languages experience and think about the world in fundamentally different ways because their languages have different structures and categories. However, this view is considered too extreme in modern linguistics and has little empirical support. And still today.

"Linguistic relativity, on the other hand, in effect the weak version of the hypothesis, is less radical and states that language influences – but does not completely determine – the way we think and perceive reality. In this view, speakers of different languages have different thinking and perception tendencies based on the specifics of their language, but they are still able to think beyond the boundaries of their language and adapt their perception."

As soon as she caught her breath, first a few, then all of the hands shot up again. "Any questions that don't relate to my activities outside this lecture hall?"

The hands went down again.

"Which of you has ever been to Japan?" she asked.

A few hands went back up.

"Which of you has Japanese ancestors, or even grew up there?"

Two hands remained.

"Let me explain the Sapir-Whorf hypothesis using a concrete example."

Rachel went to the blackboard. "Imagine a Japanese speaker and an American speaker sitting in the same room discussing the arrangement of furniture. In Japanese, the spatial relationship between objects is often expressed by particles that refer to relative position, such as ue (上, above), shita (下, below), mae (前, in front) and ushiro (後, behind)."

She drew the characters on the blackboard with chalk.

"Japanese speakers are therefore used to focusing on the position of objects in relation to other objects. The American speaker, on the other hand," she gestured to the auditorium, "speaks English, a language that relies more heavily on absolute directions such as right and left to describe spatial relationships. In this situation, the American speaker is more able to describe the arrangement of furniture in terms of cardinal directions or their own position.

"Now let's imagine that both speakers are asked to decide together where a new piece of furniture should be placed in the room. The Japanese speaker suggests placing it mae – in front of – the window, while the American speaker insists on placing it to the right of the door. Since their languages use different spatial reference systems, they perceive the room design in different ways and have difficulty agreeing on a common solution, even though they are trying to talk about the same objective space and the same objective furniture. Through the lens of their languages, both become something subjective that cannot simply be subjectivized.

"This example thus illustrates that the speakers' different languages influence their perception of reality by using different spatial reference systems. As a result, they perceive and evaluate different spatial relationships while in the same situation. Although this is a very simplified example, it shows the possible implications of the Sapir-Whorf hypothesis for communication and understanding between speakers of different languages."

She paused and sighed when all the hands went up again. She slowly circled the table and sat on the edge.

"All right, then. Let's get it out in the open." She pointed to a young man in the back row who, with his horn-rimmed glasses, looked more like a shy nerd than one of the cheeky surfer dudes further forward. "State your question."

"Uhh, I hope this question is okay, but do you know the science fiction movie Arrival?" the young man asked, earning a storm of indignation from his fellow students as he obviously hadn't asked the most obvious question. Rachel liked him immediately and smiled.

"Quiet, please!" She waited for him to look at her and then nodded. "In fact, it's my favorite movie, and will probably be yours if you decide to pursue a career in linguistics. Many people don't know that the 2016 movie is based on the novella Story of Your Life by Ted Chiang, which all of you should read."

Rachel smiled. "Those of you who haven't seen the movie yet should cover your ears now or I will spoil it for you with my comments. The alien Heptapods from the movie come to Earth, and the linguist Doctor Louise Banks tries to establish communication with them. As you can imagine, there is no greater discrepancy between the language systems of two speakers than when they are from other planets. All reference systems are different. The Heptapods have a unique written language. Their characters, which are circular and complex, represent whole sentences or thoughts, rather than a linear sequence of words or syllables, as is the case with most human languages.

"This written language is non-linear and allows information to be expressed without reference to a fixed timeline. As a result, the Heptapods have a completely different perception of time and causality compared to human language users. Over the course of the film, Doctor Banks learns the Heptapod language and begins to see the world through their eyes, as suggested by the Sapir-Whorf hypothesis. Her perception of time changes dramatically, and she gains the ability to see into the future and perceive past, present, and future events simultaneously.

"This change in Doctor Banks' perception and thinking is a direct result of her learning the Heptapod B language and serves as a powerful illustration of the Sapir-Whorf hypothesis in the film. It is used as a means of exploring the profound effects of language and communication on human thought and perception of the world. The movie shows how learning a completely different language – in this case the language of an alien species – can fundamentally change human perception and understanding of reality."

The young man with the distinctive glasses nodded cheerfully and all the hands went up again. She would probably have to get this over with so that not every lecture ended up the same way. She pointed her finger at a woman further toward the front who looked particularly excited. "Yes, your question please?"

"Ma'am, I've read your book, like probably most of us here, and first of all I want to say that I'm a big fan," the student called out breathlessly and many students rapped their knuckles on their desks. "Did you expect it to be so successful?"

"No, and I'll be happy to sign autographs for you all when the lecture is over, but please focus on questions about today's topic. I'm here to teach you something and make linguists out of you so that we can learn to understand each other and the world we live in a little better," Rachel explained kindly but firmly.

Then she had an idea. "Let's talk about my book Why E.T. Wants to Eat Us. Why is it a stupid idea to want to make contact with aliens? Please refer to the Sapir-Whorf hypothesis in your answers. Yes?" she addressed the same young woman.

"If the Sapir-Whorf hypothesis suggests that the structure of a language influences the mindset and perception of its speakers, it may be that a completely alien language and mindset provides no basis for communication, right? Even if we were able to learn their language, we might still struggle to truly understand their perspective on the world, and vice versa. This could lead to misunderstandings and miscommunication that could have serious consequences. Like with the example of the axe you gave in the book," explained the student she had pointed to.

"Correct. An axe is a tool, in effect, something with which I can extend the functions of my body to achieve an immediate goal. Basically, when we say tool, it's a peaceful-associated word. But an axe is also a weapon, an extension of my body's functions to harm or kill someone," Rachel explained. "If I show another person an axe and they don't speak my language, they will probably think one of two things: This person wants to kill me, or this person wants to cut down a tree, to put it simply. That puts us at fifty-fifty, if we leave out things like body language for the time being. How do you think an alien would react? Could he afford to make the tool assumption and be fifty percent wrong? The stakes could be his life."

"But what if you communicate via a universal form of communication? Something like mathematics, which functions as the basis of the universe, and would be understood by intelligent aliens?" someone shouted out into the lecture hall.

"Good question. It's not the first time someone has asked me that," she replied, smiling knowingly. A few students giggled cautiously. "Who asked that question?"

A dark-haired man in the last row stood up and said, "I did."

"Good. So, you flew to Alpha Centauri as an astronaut and met an alien from the Terralians. He also came in a spaceship and you are facing each other. Let's make it simple: he's bi-symmetrical humanoid like you. How do you start?" she asked.

"I establish a mathematical basis of understanding. Geometric shapes, prime numbers, and that sort of thing."

"Okay, good. The alien indicates that he understands and returns the favor by explaining his numerical system. It's obviously not metric – just like the imperial system here isn't either. It is based on historical quantities that have no mathematical logic. Let's say he calculates in dodecadal units because his world has twelve moons or something like that. That works, and it continues with mathematical operations like addition, subtraction, and so on. What have you gained from that?"

"I know that we are both intelligent beings and could go on to physical quantities such as distances and his home world," the student suggested.

"Good. Now the alien wants to know where Earth is and how far away. Would you tell him?" asked Rachel.

"No, probably not."

"Why not?"

"Because I don't know if he has good intentions."

"That's right. To find out, you have to do what?"

"Learn more about his value system?"

"Right. What forms the value system?"

"His parents?"

"Sure. But let's first stay with the culture as a defining framework within which his values will move. How can you tap into that? Not with math, that's for sure. There is no mathematical measure for values, let alone empathy or compassion. But you still want to try. How do you go about it?"

"I would try to find out what environmental conditions prevail on his planet, because that would influence the type of culture that developed there," said the student.

"Scarcity of resources could be an indicator of increased evolutionary pressure. Ergo violence." Rachel nodded. "But how do you do that?"

"I could try to explain the four seasons on Earth to him using the constellation of the planets in relation to the sun."

"Good idea." She clapped her hands and stood up. "But the alien comes from a planet that has no seasons. The conditions are always more or less the same."

"Okay, then I'll try to explain extreme weather conditions to him. Heat and cold, for example. He should understand that, as it's certainly warmer on his planet than in a vacuum."

"How do you do that?"

"I rub my hands and over my body to signal that I need to generate heat through movement."

"Yes." Rachel nodded again. "You shiver a little to show him that your body can no longer maintain its core temperature. Okay. In Terralian culture, rubbing your hands together is a gesture of aggression that is part of a ritual duel. He suddenly jumps back. Adrenaline shoots through your veins because of his sudden, unexpected movement."

"I let him know that I'm not a danger and put my empty hands out in front of me," said the student.

"No, that could also be seen as aggression, as a defensive posture," exclaimed a fellow student.

"Defense is not aggressive."

"Yes it is," Rachel said. "If I have a shield, it signals that I'm expecting a fight. But let's keep it simple today. You're an astronaut, and you stay cool. You quickly lower your hands and remain inactive to minimize any room for misunderstanding."

The student nodded.

"The Terralian is one of the astronauts of his species, too, and therefore well trained, a defensive team player. That's why he shows you a special feature of his species: the mating crest, a kind of plumage that fans out from his neck in a magnificent bright red."

"Like in Jurassic Park," someone shouted, and everyone laughed.

"Yes, the nasty little beasts that eat the traitor as he tries to disappear with a sample." Rachel smiled wider. "A threat to you, you anticipate an attack from your experience with that kind of body language and run away. The Terralian follows you, trying to convince you that there's no reason for it and that he didn't mean to scare you. But the human flight instinct kicks in and you feel like the hunted."

"But that's a lot of negative assumptions," the student complained.

"Too many positive ones, if you ask me. There are primitive peoples on Earth for whom a grin is a sign of aggression and a willingness to fight. If you try to disarm them with a smile, they'll kill you. And they are of the same species as you. Another example: Intuition. At the beginning of linguistics, many interactions were left to intuition. Do you know why?"

Since no one spoke up, she continued with the answer.

"Many primitive peoples believe that intuition is an insight into past and future lives. That we are connected to who we once were or will be in a spiritual way, and therefore have intuitions based on experiences that we have not had ourselves. At least not at this time.

"Today, intuition is one of the most difficult terms to grasp linguistically because it has such different meanings in different language areas. Here, the connection between terminology and meaning changes fluidly. If you tell an Indian that your decision is based on intuition, he will most likely accept it or even appreciate it. If an Indian tells a European the same thing, he will probably be met with raised eyebrows – just like us, they would dismiss it as esoteric.

"My point is this: It's extremely difficult to come up with a meaning for something here on our planet, even though we can speak the same languages."

3

Muara Karang Power Station, North of Jakarta, Indonesia

"Apa kamu sudah mematikan? Aku bisa melihatnya dari wajahmu, kamu belum melakukannya!" Budi eyed his colleague suspiciously. "Did you, or didn't you?"

"Sure, I've got everything set to shut off. The staff are over in the workers' quarters." Agus pointed behind him, where the complex of the gas-fueled power plant spread out as a sea of lights between scaffolding and smaller buildings. To the south, they had a perfect view over the sea of buildings in the metropolis, which seemed to stretch to the horizon. The night was almost over and the sky was already turning a dark blue. "When are we supposed to leave?"

"Soon." Budi shrugged his shoulders. Suddenly, the lights went out around them. Section after section went dark below them, and then the neighborhoods adjacent to the power plant. "Are you sure we should be standing here when it happens?"

"Everything is switched off, so nothing can overcharge.

And the backup batteries are off now." Agus pointed downward. They were now standing in a sea of darkness, as the rest of the capital was also going without power as a safety measure against solar activity. Even the diesel generators in the hospitals had been switched off so as not to risk the electrical infrastructure.

"Your word in Allah's ear."

They gazed down at the metropolis in silence for a while. It was a strange feeling, as if they were floating in the void, above a structure of shadows that had taken shape.

"It looks ghostly," Agus said. "Kind of surreal. Jakarta is so loud, so garish, so everything."

"Now it's as calm as the sea."

"Not for long, that's for sure."

"Oh, maybe the whole thing is just another one of those government scams to pull something off."

"They're trying to pull off something?" Agus asked his friend and colleague, scratching under his helmet.

"You know, trying to corner political opponents or some shit like that," Budi said vaguely.

"You watch too much television."

"And you, too little."

"I don't think so. I wouldn't have noticed this NASA stuff if I'd just skipped the box, but my wife just can't help herself. She just sits in front of the screen all day like a rat in front of a snake, and ... What?"

"I think it's starting," Budi said in awe and slipped his helmet off his head in slow motion. He turned his eyes upward.

Agus followed his gaze to the sky and his mouth fell open at the awe-inspiring beauty of the spectacle that was unfolding there. The entire firmament, streaked by the delicate fingers of the dawning morning, seemed to be ablaze with pearly flames. Like magical discharges of manna, almost material-looking threads of dancing pastel shades sparkled in the darkness, caught in a dance of particles. The Aurora Australis stretched from horizon to horizon – in every direction. A kaleidoscope of changing shapes. Time seemed to stand still under this mesmerizing light that made everything mortal seem tiny and insignificant.

"My goodness," Agus stammered breathlessly, placing a hand on his friend's shoulder without taking his eyes off the cosmic elemental force that was igniting the sky. When Budi didn't move, he frowned and swallowed to clear the sudden dryness from his mouth. Then he looked reluctantly at him and only now realized that his neighbor was no longer staring upward at the cosmic beauty, but down at the city sprawling in front of them.

It shone in the light of all the light bulbs and lamps, as though they had never been darkened. At first he thought it was an illusion and blinked a few times, but that didn't change anything: every light source in Jakarta seemed to glow with maximum intensity.

"I thought you'd switched off," he mumbled.

"I did, I swear I did," Budi replied hoarsely, turning in circles on his scaffolding. Every lamp in the power plant complex was also shining around them, and they were all emitting a subliminal hum.

"I should have checked," Agus growled and ran down to the control center. He heard Budi's footsteps behind him.

However, every computer in the control center was shut down and nothing could be started. There was no power.

"How is this possible?" He went outside again, this time up to the roof, and looked across the sea of bright lights.

"It's not, my friend," Budi said devoutly. "It's a miracle from Allah."

4

NASA Headquarters, Washington, D.C., Office of the Administrator

"How sure are we that there was no power supply?" asked NASA Administrator Anthony Stevens as he scanned the group of tired faces forming a semi-circle around his desk. The large television on the right wall showed changing images of a brightly lit Jakarta. Sometimes it was streetlights shining brighter than they should, with people standing on the street below and pointing at them. Others showed families in their living rooms, which were at first pitch black, and then suddenly as bright as day when various lamps came on at the same time.

"We are in close contact with the Indonesian Ministry of Energy and our Ministry of Foreign Affairs. We have been assured that none of the power plants were supplying electricity at the time. Every one of them had been shut down," reported Associate Administrator Lagarde. She scrolled on a tablet and kept nodding. "This information is also supported by the fact that there was virtually no damage to the power grid."

"Couldn't that be because the CME only grazed us, and thus it was nowhere near as serious as we feared?" asked Mark Kelley, the NASA Administrator's chief of staff.

"Basically, yes," Lagarde confirmed. "However, the particle onslaught was still severe enough that it destroyed hundreds of transformers in Sumatra and the Philippines in areas that apparently didn't shut down or didn't shut down fast enough."

"So we have to assume that Jakarta had no electrical power being supplied at the time – that's what everything we know so far points to," Administrator Stevens summarized, rubbing his tired eyes.

He hadn't slept a wink that night, not even when the CME was over and he had verified that the American satellite network had remained largely undamaged. Many had been repositioned, others simply switched off. Only a few military satellites had remained active because their shielding had been deemed strong enough, which had held true for most of them. In the images from one of them, he saw Southeast Asia at night in almost complete darkness on the television. Only a few patches of light stood out from the blackness – and Jakarta, a glowing yellow ball in the void.

He noticed that his advisors were still looking at him questioningly.

"All right, then. Any idea what I should say to the president at the briefing?"

"I wouldn't pay too much attention to Jakarta," said Kelley. "The videos may go viral on social media, yes, but ultimately the majority don't believe in fairy tales."

"But this is not a fairy tale," Stevens reminded his chief of staff. He pointed to the television to illustrate his point. "So far, no one has been able to explain this to me. I realize I'm the only one here who isn't a scientist, but how can a city light up if it doesn't have any damn electricity? I need something to work with here when I'm sitting with the president."

"There are a few possible explanations," Lagarde continued. The physicist took a deep breath. "It could be induced electrical currents. The geomagnetic storm triggered by the CME affected the Earth's electromagnetic fields. These fields could then have generated induced currents in the electrical cables to light up the light bulbs. This would also explain why no other devices worked."

"Or," said Kelley, "they were electrostatic discharges. The fact that a lot of charged particles were thrown into the atmosphere could have led to an increased electrostatic charge, which caused the light bulbs to discharge."

"We can speculate here forever," said Jonathan Walters. The physicist and deputy administrator had previously remained silent and twirled his white moustache instead of getting involved. Now everyone was listening to him as if he were some kind of oracle. "It could be exotic particles that we don't yet understand because we've never observed a coronal mass ejection of this magnitude hitting us. Maybe even dark matter that interacts with the matter of light bulbs in a previously unknown way. Or quantum effects of the CME that have caused a change in the quantum states of the atoms in the bulbs."

"But that is – with respect – extremely speculative," said Lagarde, sounding almost offended.

"That's exactly my point." Walters nodded thoughtfully. "We could speculate here forever, and the longer we do that, the more fanciful the whole thing becomes. Let's leave that to the research in the wake of this event. For the meeting with the President, I suggest we focus on the results of our satellite analysis, because this is a matter of national security."

"Good idea," Kelley agreed. "And here's to being damn lucky that the damage was so minimal."

"Minimal?" asked Lagarde, snorting. "The damage to the power grids in Southeast Asia is in the hundreds of billions. Despite everything."

"If that ejection had hit us head on, we probably wouldn't have any satellites left, and the world economy would have collapsed – just before we plunged back into the Stone Age," Kelley reminded them. "We got off lightly."

Stevens's assistant poked her head through the door. "Sir? Your car is ready," said the young woman.

"I'm coming." He stood up and smoothed his suit as the phone on his desk rang. He ignored it and rounded the table. "Thanks, good work tonight, and ..."

He didn't get any further because Lagarde's cell phone rang. Then Kelley's, followed by Walters' phone. They looked at each other, frowning, surrounded by the intrusive warbling of four different phones all vying for their attention.

After a brief moment of confusion, all except for Stevens answered. He looked at his wristwatch and suppressed a curse. There was no such thing as being late for the President of the United States.

As he reached the door, he felt a hand on his shoulder holding him back. "What?"

It was Walters, his deputy. "I think you'll have to cancel your appointment."

"With the president? Are you ...?"

"Yes," the Deputy Administrator interrupted him. "Owens from JPL is already on his way here."

"Owens? Why?"

"I told you that Mars would most likely be hit exactly by the center of the plasma cloud, didn't I?"

"Yeah, so?"

"Our calculations were correct."

"Don't tell me our satellites were destroyed." Stevens felt a headache setting in.

"Two of them. We still have MRO, the Mars Reconnaissance Orbiter," explained Walters.

"Good news, bad news. I'm afraid this will have to wait until after ..."

"It can't, sir. The MRO picked up something on the surface of Mars."

"Something? Can you be more specific?"

"I'm afraid not. Owens' plane lands in a few hours, then he'll show us. I strongly suggest you ask the president to come here."

5

RACHEL

Not even a third of the seats were occupied when she entered the lecture hall the next morning. But she wasn't too disappointed. She had expected a lot more of yesterday's crowd to be pure autograph hunters who were interested in science fiction but not linguistics. The Sapir-Whorf hypothesis was probably the only reason why there were more than a dozen left. She wondered if the student with the math question was enrolled in physics or math?

"Good morning," Rachel said after putting on the headset. "One more lecture and then I probably won't have to use this," she tapped the microphone, "anymore."

A muted giggle answered her.

"How many of you have been enrolled in linguistics since the first semester?"

About ten hands went up.

"And which of you is thinking about enrolling, and is only here because this lecture is about the Sapir-Whorf hypothesis?" she asked.

The other almost 90 hands were raised.

"I see. Now that we're rid of the groupies, I'd like to do

my best to introduce you to other aspects of the Sapir-Whorf hypothesis, and prove to all the fence-sitters among you that linguistics can indeed be a gateway to understanding the world around us. What feelings do you have when you think of the word darkness? Feel free to close your eyes."

She waited, gave them some time, and then called on the first ones who volunteered.

"A bit scary."

"Danger."

"Uncertainty."

"Silence, silence."

"Predators."

"The unknown."

"Crime."

Rachel nodded and called up a picture of Elon Musk. She smiled as she looked at the many wrinkles on his forehead.

"Elon Musk once said that he was afraid of the dark as a child – it's human and woven into our DNA through evolution. Most predators are nocturnal, and we humans don't see very well in the dark. So we fear it, because it makes us seek shelter at night and stay by the campfire. But at some point Musk read in a book on physics that the only difference between day and night is the number of photons that reach the eye. Darkness is merely the absence of photons, in effect, elementary particles. Since then, Musk says, he is no longer afraid of it. The world is still exactly the same, just without light particles."

Rachel pointed to the picture of Musk. "However you want to feel about him as a controversial public figure, his statement is a good example of how language shapes our view of things that, in nature, simply are what they are. Conditions are explained and loaded with meaning through the labeling of language into valued things. This in turn determines how we feel and deal with them."

She now had the students' attention for sure. Some were whispering, but it was the kind of animated whispering that every professor likes to hear.

"Let's make it a little more philosophical. How does time work?"

She waited while the students pondered. Finally, a young woman raised her hand.

"Yes?"

"Linear?"

"Correct. Our logical understanding of time runs linearly from point A to a point in the future. A Buddhist monk, on the other hand, would say that time does not run at all, but is an illusion, because there is only the present moment. Many of you are probably familiar with great spiritual works such as The Power of Now by Eckart Tolle, or Love What Is by Byron Katie. They can show us that we may be misperceiving, because evidence of the past is only in here." She tapped her head.

"But when I see an accident scene, I know that the accident happened in the past," objected one student.

"Where is the proof of that?"

"I see it."

"When will you see it?"

The young man hesitated and nodded. "Now."

"That's right. And the future is a dense fog. Something that the present theoretically moves into. But it also only exists as a thought of the next present. It's similar to the universe, I gave this example in my book: The universe is not infinite, because it has a finite mass, but it theoretically expands infinitely. Not into an infinite space, because space is only created through expansion.

"It is the same with language and the perception of time. Only through language does time become an abstract concept that is not born of nature – even though physicists would argue about it for a long time. But we'll leave that to them.

"So today I would like to explain some interesting aspects of the representation and organization of time in different languages and how they can influence the mindset and perception of their speakers. This phenomenon is closely linked to the Sapir-Whorf hypothesis, which states – a little reminder – that our language shapes our thinking and our perception of the world."

She called up the first slide of her presentation, which showed a group of indigenous people in the Andes gathered around a fire pit. "Let's first look at the Aymara language, which is spoken in South America. In this language, the past is conceptualized as lying in front of the speaker and the future as lying behind the speaker. This is in contrast to most other languages where the future is conceptualized as being in front of the speaker and the past as being behind the speaker."

The students began to whisper.

"Fascinating, isn't it?" asked Rachel.

"Is that even possible?" The question came from a student somewhere in the back of the room.

"For the Aymara, yes. For them, the past is considered something that can be seen and known, while the future is unseen and unknown. So far, it's logical. This spatial metaphor is reflected in the grammar and vocabulary of the Aymara language. One example of this is the use of demonstrative pronouns, which indicate the spatial position of objects or events in relation to the speaker.

"In Aymara, there are three demonstrative pronouns that refer to near, middle, and far positions. When describing past events, the demonstrative pronoun for the near position is used, while for future events the demonstrative pronoun for the far position is used, which is exactly the opposite of our language. In this case, the spatial representation of time in the Aymara language can lead its speakers to view the past as something concrete and known, while the future is seen as less tangible and uncertain.

"For example, when planning and making decisions, they may rely more on the past and past experiences than on speculation about the future, as is the case with us. We also learn from the past – at least we try to – but always against the backdrop of speculation about the future, because we want to work toward something."

Rachel circled her desk and sat back down on the edge of the table.

"So it would be a mistake to assume that the perception of time is something that is universal because it follows a logical thought pattern. It's not like that. The Aymara are no exception. Another remarkable language, for example, is Kuuk Thaayorre, which is spoken in northern Australia. In this language, temporal and spatial relationships are expressed in terms of absolute cardinal points, such as north, south, east, and west, rather than in terms of the speaker, such as in front, behind, right, or left."

Many hands went up.

"You're wondering how that's even possible?"

She smiled as the hands lowered again.

"Well, the Sapir-Whorf hypothesis suggests that such differences in the representation and organization of time shape the cognitive processes and understanding of time in the speakers of these languages. So they really do think fundamentally differently, which is why it will always be difficult to turn this into a communicable concept.

"How would you describe the taste of something that you can see but have never tasted? In terms of Kuuk Thaayorre, this could mean that speakers of this language may be better at navigating their environment and orienting themselves by compass points than speakers of other languages. So the Aboriginal Thaayorre people think a lot about their position in relation to cardinal points and not the other way around as we do.

"There is a study by Lera Boroditsky and Alice Gaby that has received a lot of attention in linguistics. They found that Thaayorre speakers arrange temporal sequences along an east-west axis, corresponding to the movement of the sun in the sky.

"English speakers, on the other hand, tend to order temporal sequences from left – past – to right – future. This is difficult for us linguists to decipher because there are no specific grammatical structures in this language that we can analyze.

"Nevertheless, imagine that a Thaayorre speaker remembers an event that took place yesterday and thinks about an event that will take place tomorrow. He might think of yesterday's event as being to the east of his current position, while tomorrow's event is to the west. The spatial arrangement of these events corresponds to the movement of the sun in the sky and cannot be separated from the temporal component for him.

"We, on the other hand, first separate space and time from each other, and then conceptualize it. The first encounter between Aboriginal Australians and Europeans must necessarily have been a first contact that barely allowed for mutual understanding, even though they were of the same species. Language defines your perception, dear students. It can be a gateway to mutual understanding, or the cause of terrible mass murder, as in the case of the Aborigines.

"The examples are many. We could talk for hours about how there was no concept of land ownership in Native American languages, which is why they couldn't even understand the sale of land to whites. To them, the land was simply land that they were a part of. That a person could own it was simply not part of their language. In this case, language ..."

Rachel faltered as the students began to murmur, her eyes following the gazes of the young men and women. Their focus had wandered to the door, where two men in black suits had appeared. One of them beckoned her with a hand gesture.

"All right, we'll take a ten-minute break," she said into her microphone and switched it off, wondering who the two men were and why they were interrupting her lecture. They waited until the students had left the lecture hall, then signaled to someone in the corridor, whereupon a woman in jeans, a sweater, and an open jacket came in.

"Can I help you?" Rachel asked when the strange team reached her at her table.

"Sorry to disturb you, Professor. You are Doctor Rachel Ferreira – is that correct?" asked the lady, who was dressed like one of the male professors from the Faculty of Astronomy.

"Yes. And you are ...?"

"Lucille Pendergast. I'm the head of the HR department at NASA." Pendergast held out a hand to Rachel while pointing at the two grim-faced men who seemed to be scanning the lecture hall with their eyes. "The two gentlemen behind me are from the Secret Service."

"Secret Service?" Rachel reflexively shook hands and then reached up to scratch her head. "What I wrote in my book about a conspiracy to keep secret ..."

"Don't worry, we're not here because you're on the New York Times Best Seller list," the NASA employee assured her. "At least not only."

"Then why?"

"We need your help. Could you postpone your lecture?"

"For what?"

"For a flight to Washington, to NASA headquarters."

"Excuse me? I can't just ..."

"Yes, you have a daughter. We have a car parked outside her elementary school. Secret Service officers can take her to the airport where we can meet her and fly together," Pendergast explained.

Rachel blinked in confusion and tried to banish the sudden dryness from her mouth. It felt like she'd been chewing on a dusty rag. "What's this about?"

"I can't tell you that until we're on the plane. I'm sorry."

"I need to call my sister. Please take my daughter to her," Rachel said, stunned.

6

RACHEL

An hour later, she was sitting in a government Learjet, watching the fleecy clouds over San Francisco Bay grow smaller and smaller below her.

Rachel felt like she was in a dream. The drive to the airport's private terminal had passed in a daze, during which she'd wondered if someone had secretly drugged her. After a brief conversation with her sister Beth – and Masha, who didn't seem to mind the slight change of plans because her aunt was sure to give her far too many sweets, once again – she had canceled her appointments for today and tomorrow by calling in sick. She hadn't been able to think of anything better in the heat of the moment.

Now she was sitting in a business jet on the way to the capital, together with a woman from NASA who was busy juggling several cell phones the whole time.

"Would you tell me why I'm here? Or wake me up, if you don't mind?" she asked.

"Oh, excuse me, Professor."

"Rachel."

"Oh, yes. Lucille." The NASA personnel manager smiled

absently and put her phones away, which was obviously difficult for her. "Sorry about this, Rachel. It's all going haywire at the moment."

"I guess that's why you pulled me out of the lecture? Did E.T. call and you need a translator?" she joked.

Lucille didn't even hint at a smile while she nodded pensively.

"You know about the coronal mass ejection from the sun that hit us."

"Of course, there was no other topic on the news yesterday, and there isn't today – at least not on Good Morning America."

Lucille nodded again. "Fortunately, we were only hit by the fringes of the plasma cloud, but Mars was right in the center of this monster of charged particles. During this event, the Mars Reconnaissance Orbiter, or MRO, photographed something above the crater of Elysium Mons that shouldn't exist."

"Mars Reconnaissance Orbiter?" asked Rachel.

"One of our orbiters circling the Red Planet. The satellite has been supplying us with data since 2006. It's equipped with a high-resolution camera that is called 'HiRISE' for High Resolution Imaging Science Experiment, and a spectrometer, but that doesn't play a role in this case."

"I see." Rachel didn't 'see' a thing.

"During the particle storm that hit Mars the MRO took strange images, which are currently puzzling us," Lucille continued.

"What kind of images?"

The astrophysicist opened the bag next to her seat and handed over a folder containing a single color photo.

"A large light phenomenon with a diameter of about one hundred and fifty meters, directly above the crater of Elysium Mons on Mars. This is one of the largest volcanoes on the

Red Planet and it may still be active. When looking at the scale, keep in mind that HiRISE records at a resolution of twenty-five centimeters per pixel. That means that one meter is about four pixels – just to give you an idea of the scale of this light phenomenon."

Rachel frowned at the furrowed, pale-brown area on the picture, and the white and yellow pixel sphere in the middle. It didn't look particularly impressive, more like a screenshot from an ancient computer game with horrible resolution.

"The light phenomenon lasted almost exactly three hours, which corresponds to the duration of the CME," explained the NASA employee. "Coronal mass ejections can cause all sorts of phenomena on Mars because the planet has no global magnetosphere to protect it from radiation in the form of charged particles ejected by the sun. This light phenomenon observed by the MRO could theoretically have been caused by the interaction of the charged particles of the CME with the thin Martian atmosphere or the Martian soil. The energy of the charged particles can ionize gases in the atmosphere or cause materials on the ground to glow."

"But you don't believe that, do you?"

"Nobody here believes that. The light phenomenon appears to be perfectly spherical, and only occurred above the crater of Elysium Mons."

"Nowhere else?"

"No, not on Mars."

"What do you mean?"

"Jakarta."

"Excuse me?" asked Rachel.

"In Jakarta, all the lights in the city were on for three hours, even though the city's power supply had been shut down as a precaution. In principle, there could be some scientific explanations for this if it had not been such an isolated event. The other regions of Southeast Asia were affected by the main part of the particles, but only Jakarta experienced this phenomenon. This cannot be explained scientifically."

"Wait. Are you saying that NASA is assuming it was not a natural phenomenon?"

"Yes, that's what I'm trying to say. We don't have any explanations. Not for Jakarta, not for the sphere of light on Mars. But the fact is, both phenomena only occurred under the influence of the CME, which raises a whole avalanche of new questions."

"For example?" Rachel didn't even really know why she was asking, as she'd only understood half of what she had heard, optimistically speaking.

"You'll find out in a few hours when we land in Washington. The President is expected at headquarters and then ..."

"Wait," the astrophysicist interrupted her. "Did you just say the President?"

"Yes. I guess you still don't really understand," Lucille said and sighed.

"Right. I don't understand a thing." Rachel's head was spinning. "Why am I here?"

"Because as Head of Human Resources at NASA, I am one of the first people to be asked when it comes to putting together a suitable team."

"A team?"

"Rachel." Lucille leaned forward and tapped the image in her hands. "This isn't some astrophysical phenomenon that we can study for years using satellite data. This is something we need to investigate now, on the ground."

"You mean ... with astronauts?"

"Yes, that's what I mean. We've been preparing a manned mission to Mars for years, and after the successful manned test flight of Elon Musk's Starship, the hurdle is no longer a big one. Well, at least not too big," said Lucille.

"Okay, I see. But what I still don't understand is why I, of all people, should be on this plane, and be there when the President is being briefed," Rachel replied.

"The President has known about it for a long time. The meeting is to convince her to finance the mission. That won't be easy."

"You expect me to give a pitch? You should have kidnapped a colleague from the marketing department."

"I don't want you to give a pitch, Professor. I want you to be part of the crew."

7

RACHEL

The Learjet's shimmering wings had cut through the pastel-colored sky, which spread in soft shades of pink and blue over the vast landscape. Approaching Ronald Reagan Washington National Airport, the airplane window offered a breathtaking view of the majestic backdrop of the capital unfolding before her eyes like a painting.

The Capitol's silver dome shone like a jewel in the evening sun, while the Washington Monument rose as a proud sentinel of white marble and was mirrored in the still waters of the Reflecting Pool. The Lincoln Memorial, a temple of democracy, was enthroned at the western end of the National Mall, which stretched out as an avenue of lush green trees and manicured lawns.

Beyond the famous monuments the city spread out, a mosaic of red brick buildings and white marble façades, criss-crossed by the silver threads of the Potomac and Anacostia rivers. The Arlington Memorial Bridge stretched across the Potomac like an embrace immortalized in stone, connecting the capital with the states of Virginia and Maryland.

The sun slowly tilted toward the horizon and bathed the

region in warm golden light. The shadows of the trees and buildings stretched across the land like delicate fingers as the Learjet glided smoothly through the air. The clouds, which had previously adorned the sky as floating tufts of wool, gradually turned into fiery splashes of color, as if they had been lifted from the glowing palette of an impressionist painter.

As the Learjet entered the landing phase, Rachel's apprehension increased significantly. What had previously seemed like a dream began to feel more real with every meter of altitude they lost. More tangible.

The wheels finally touched the runway with a soft sigh, and the plane came to a halt as the last rays of the evening sun disappeared behind the Washington, D.C. skyline. At that moment, the heart of the nation was like a silent poem waiting to be discovered and given new meaning.

A black SUV with government plates awaited them on the tarmac. The pilot parked the small jet right next to it after a short drive across the taxiway. The driver – dark suit and sunglasses – held the rear door open for them.

Five minutes later they were leaving the airport. Rachel pressed her forehead against the window, dwelling on her own thoughts and trying to exclude what the NASA employee had told her on the plane.

It might be no more than a dream, right?

Presently, they slowly approached the impressive NASA headquarters. Her fingers played nervously with the hem of her dress as she gazed at the massive building that loomed before her like a symbol of human achievement. The last vestiges of sunlight cast a golden glow onto its windows, which sparkled like jewels in the façade. The streets were lined with lush trees that fluttered softly in the wind, making the path to the headquarters seem like it led to a secret garden. As they got closer, Rachel could see the bustling people scurrying around the glass-heavy building like ants, each with their own mission, their own destination that wasn't Mars.

The car finally rolled gently into the parking lot and came to a halt. Rachel's heart rate rose another notch as she realized the significance of her arrival. She took a deep breath, gathered her thoughts, and smoothed out her dress. Only now did she think about how inappropriately she was attired. Not only was it much colder here in the nation's capital, but she assumed that this was not how people dressed around the President.

Lucille seemed to notice her unease as they walked toward a side entrance, still accompanied by the two Secret Service agents. "Don't worry about it. The President is much more relaxed than she appears on television."

"I look like ..."

"Like a professor from Stanford," Lucille said with a smile. "That's exactly right."

"Why do I feel like I'm playing a role you made up?" asked Rachel.

"You are playing a role, but only yourself. Why do you think I didn't brief you? Why do you think I didn't explain to you why I want to put you forward for the mission?"

"In principle, it doesn't matter. I can't go to Mars, anyway." She snorted and shook her head. "I feel totally stupid saying that out loud."

"I can understand that it feels unreal to you. That will go away when you sit at the table with the President, believe me," the astrophysicist assured her.

Less than ten minutes later, she would know what Lucille had meant. After a brief security check at the entrance and another done by Secret Service agents outside a conference room, she entered a large room with an oval table occupied by four people. One of them was President Elizabeth Whitmer. She was wearing a high-necked dark dress and no jewelry. She had rolled up her long sleeves, as was her trademark. Her long blonde hair was tied back in a simple braid and her wrinkled, yet somehow ageless face was tanned.

"Aha, Lucille," she greeted the NASA personnel manager with a broad Texan accent. "Another five minutes and we'd have opened the beer without you."

"I definitely didn't want to miss this, Madam President." Lucille shook her hand. Rachel cleared her throat and did the same.

"And you are?" asked Whitmer in a conversational tone.

"This is Professor Rachel Ferreira. She holds a chair in linguistics at Stanford University. I've just kidnapped her from there," Lucille explained with a wink at Rachel.

"Pleased to meet you, Madam President. I voted for you."

"Good, then you may stay." Whitmer flashed a knowing grin and sat back down. The four other people introduced themselves briefly and each one shook Rachel's hand while she was still trying to remember the names. "I'm a little surprised to find a linguist here."

"Certainly not as surprised as I am, Ma'am."

"Well, let's be surprised together. Greg?" The president gave the agent at the door a wave. "Nobody comes in or out from now on, understand?"

"Understood, Ma'am."

"Good." She clapped her hands together. "Now in Texas we'd say, 'let's fish or cut the damn bait.'"

NASA Administrator Anthony Stevens, completely gray and with sagging cheeks, straightened up in his chair next to President Whitmer. "Madam President, first of all, thank you for extending us this invitation. I'm sure you've already been briefed on our discovery on the surface of Mars?"

"Yes. Although I couldn't wrap my head around it. I was hoping you could help me out with that."

"I'm afraid not, Ma'am, at least not easily."

"Sounds like you need something from me, Tony." Whitmer leaned back. She was still smiling, but she no longer sounded like she was having a chat in a bar somewhere in the suburbs of Austin. Now she sounded composed but calculating.

"I'm afraid so." The NASA administrator was visibly uncomfortable and rubbed his hands together.

"I don't have much time. So here's my advice: don't rattle your tail until you're ready to strike." The impatience in the president's voice was palpable now, but it seemed to have the effect of making Stevens shrink back. Rachel couldn't shake the feeling that he feared his ultimate boss. The others at the table looked at their superior but said nothing.

"I think I this is about a manned mission to Mars," Rachel interposed, earning a scowl from the administrator. Lucille eyed her with open amusement from across the table. "I honestly have no idea why I'm here, but now I think it's because I don't work for anyone at this table, and I'd like to go home."

Whitmer looked at her and then laughed. "I like you, Doc." Her gaze drifted to Stevens. "Tony, you should know me better than this. If I'm going to smack you down over a stupid suggestion, it's got to be pretty stupid. If you stab me in the back, I'll cut your balls off, but everything else can be talked about. A mission to Mars, then. Sounds expensive. So I want to hear some good speeches before I walk out of here backward." She glanced at her wristwatch. "You've got one hour."

"Adam Morhaine, Madam President. Might I begin?" offered the man next to the administrator, the only one whose name Rachel had not needed to memorize because he was a kind of folk hero – and one of the last shuttle pilots. He was a burly man in his early 50s with a smoky voice and the look of a war veteran – crew cut, thin lips, piercing gaze.

"Fire away, Adam."

"May I suggest a somewhat unconventional way of presenting our concerns to you? We are dealing with a phenomenon that we cannot explain. But we can try. Perhaps you could just listen to our discussion and then decide for yourself?" suggested Morhaine.

Rachel didn't understand where he was going. Administrator Stevens seemed to want to burn his astronaut to ashes with his eyes. The other woman present, Madeleine Kasper, who resembled a computer scientist with her absent look and thick-lensed eyeglasses, seemed to be solving a complex puzzle in her mind. Another man, Emil Kaparov if she remembered his name correctly, nodded thoughtfully, and Lucille's smile widened a little.

8

RACHEL

Adam Morhaine was the first to break the brief silence. "The light phenomenon has left us all speechless. It definitely has something to do with the coronal mass ejection. The only question is exactly how the CME is connected to it."

"It could have been some kind of interference between the electromagnetic field of the coronal mass ejection and the Martian atmosphere," Madeleine Kasper proposed, "similar to a phenomenon known in computer science as 'signal distortion' or 'interference.' This interference may have caused the light to be reflected or refracted in a way that caused the light phenomenon."

Computer scientist, Rachel thought. I thought so!

Kaparov frowned and said slowly, "That's an interesting hypothesis, Madeleine. But perhaps it's a kind of 'quantum entanglement' in which light particles were transmitted by the coronal mass ejection and interacted on the surface of Mars, which then led to the light phenomenon."

"No." Lucille Pendergast shook her head. "That's another interesting theory, Emil, but we ought to consider the possibility that it's a simple atmospheric phenomenon caused by the influence of the coronal mass ejection on the plasma in the Martian atmosphere. Perhaps there was some kind of plasma discharge that caused this light phenomenon."

"A kind of Aurora Martialis, if you like," Adam replied. "But that still wouldn't explain why the light phenomenon was so localized, and so short-lived. It would have had to occur on the entire affected side of Mars. And there's nothing 'simple' about it."

"We should focus on the opportunities of artificial intelligence and algorithms to answer this question, folks," said Madeleine. "Maybe there are previously undiscovered patterns in the data that could help us solve this puzzle. Or it could be an error in the observational data caused by the extreme stress on the MRO during the coronal mass ejection."

"This is true, but it could also be a completely new phenomenon that is beyond our current scientific understanding," said Kaparov, apparently a quantum physicist. "We should consider all possibilities, including those that challenge our previous assumptions. Perhaps there is a previously unknown interaction between solar particles and the surface of Mars that has caused this light phenomenon. Our discussion alone shows that we have no idea."

"That's true," said Lucille. "Not only do we still lack a satisfactory explanation for the light phenomenon, we don't even have a valid hypothesis. Emil, could you elaborate a little more on your idea of quantum entanglement? How exactly could that play a role here?"

Kaparov thought for a moment and then said, "Well, quantum entanglement says that two or more particles that once interacted with each other remain connected in such a way that the state of one particle directly affects the state of the other, regardless of the distance between them. Perhaps light particles from the sun could be entangled by the coronal mass ejection in a way that affects their interaction with the surface of Mars and caused this light phenomenon."

"Sounds fascinating," said Adam Morhaine, "but wouldn't it be unlikely for such an effect to only occur locally, and for such a short time? And, how could entangled light particles interact so selectively that they produce such a specific light phenomenon?"

"We also have to take into account that the distance between the sun and Mars is enormous for quantum entanglement effects," said Madeleine Kasper in a similar vein. "The probability of entangled light particles reaching Mars and occurring in such a concentration that they produce this light phenomenon seems extremely low."

"Given that the light phenomenon only occurred during the coronal mass ejection and was no longer visible afterward, we would also have to explain why, in this particular case, quantum entanglement was only effective during the event. I'm only your run of the mill astrophysicist, but that doesn't seem plausible to me," said Lucille.

Kaparov listened to his colleagues' arguments and finally nodded thoughtfully. "I have to admit that the probability that the light phenomenon is due to quantum effects is very low. It would be difficult to develop a consistent theory that explains all the observed phenomena and is based on quantum entanglement at the same time. I guess my perspective does not offer the best view of the problem here."

"It's important to explore all possible explanations, but it does seem like we should focus on other hypotheses to better understand the phenomenon," NASA Director Stevens interjected, speaking up for the first time. Being the only one at the table besides the president who was a politician rather than a scientist, he apparently wanted to try his hand at moderating so he could get a chance to speak.

"Rachel," Lucille said, giving Stevens an apologetic look that didn't come across as particularly remorseful, "you've been listening so far, but you haven't said anything. From your point of view as a linguist and new science fiction star, is there perhaps another perspective that we've overlooked?"

Rachel cleared her throat at being so abruptly addressed, and then she frowned. "Excuse me – is this a joke?"

"No," Lucille responded. "I don't think anyone at this table is in a joking mood right now."

All eyes were on Rachel, and every facial expression was serious and tense – with the exception of the president, who looked to Rachel as though she was trying to determine whether she had somehow been caught up in an improv sketch. Which precisely described how Rachel felt. "Well, hmm, it's hard for me, as a linguist, to contribute a scientific explanation. However, if we assume that it's not a natural phenomenon, as you're all suggesting here, then perhaps we must at least consider that it's an unnatural, alien phenomenon. Perhaps it is some kind of communication attempt that only became visible during the coronal mass ejection."

The silence became a little more awkward now, and President Whitmer quietly tapped a finger while she waited.

"That is why I'm here, isn't it?" Rachel continued. "Me, being the science fiction author who has been looking into possible communication problems we might have with aliens, and the one who has advocated not sending any messages into space, and not replying if we should receive any."

When no one responded, she shrugged and continued. "I guess I'm supposed to say what no one else dares to say because you're all afraid of losing your scientific credibility or something. I don't have that problem. I just want to get back home to my daughter. So, I'll speak the obvious: If we cannot explain the inexplicable with the probable, then the improbable is the most probable."

The other experts at the table looked thoughtful.

Lucille was the first to respond. "If it really were an alien phenomenon, we could possibly look for patterns or structures in the light phenomenon that indicate some kind of language or communication, don't you think?"

"Theoretically, yes. But for that we'd have to study the phenomenon through the lens of linguistics, and that's hardly possible with muddy images from orbit, especially because the light is gone now – if I've understood correctly?" Rachel replied.

"Correct. That would be a completely new approach. We could try to use algorithms from computer science and artificial intelligence to identify and analyze possible patterns in the data," said Madeleine Kasper, the computer scientist. "A longer observation period would be needed to make the data set as large as possible."

"Exactly. It would take a lot of time to create a common basis for communication."

"If the thing communicates at all."

"Or is a thing."

"You really think it's possible that it's something like an alien life form?" President Whitmer asked, leaning over the table with her arms crossed. "I realize I'm not the sharpest tool in the shed or I wouldn't have gotten into fucking politics, but some unexplained light bulb lit up on Mars ... and that's supposed to be an alien?"

"No, Madam President." Lucille shook her head and looked at Stevens, who gave her a barely perceptible nod. "However, we think it's possible that it could be some kind of signal from an intelligent extraterrestrial species that only became visible because it was under the influence of charged particles."

"That means it was there all along, but we couldn't see it?"

"Yes Ma'am, something like that." Lucille nodded.

"That's why the linguist." Whitmer waggled a finger in Rachel's direction. "Y'all think someone – or something – is trying to communicate with us."

"Yes. No one at NASA agrees on how to explain the light phenomenon, but everyone agrees that photons could be one of the most likely forms of contact media that aliens would use to attempt communication. Nothing in the universe is faster than light," Adam Morhaine explained in the gravelly voice that had made him something of a gruff father of the nation. "And it's hardly disturbed in the vacuum and incredible emptiness of space if it's properly focused."

"But the light is gone. How can light just disappear?" asked President Whitmer.

"Well, photons are elementary particles and quantum units of the electromagnetic field, which also includes electromagnetic radiation such as light," explained Kaparov. "They are particles and waves at the same time, and they move through space. They have no rest mass, only energy and momentum. Photons are only visible to us in wavelengths that our eyes can perceive. The signal most likely only became visible to us because the particle storm from the sun forced the photons there into a different wavelength range that is visible to optical sensors."

"Before we go right back into the mumbo jumbo," the president commented, "I would like a simple answer to this question: Is it possible to make the signal visible again? Theoretically possible?"

"Yes." Lucille looked relieved. Apparently the conversation had reached the point she had been aiming for. "Theoretically, there are tools for that."

"Let me guess: It doesn't work from Earth."

"That is correct."

"So, you want to send someone there. To Mars."

"A Mars mission has been in the planning ... the preparations have been underway for years," Stevens pointed out. "We just want to bring the timetable forward significantly."

"How far forward?"

"About ten years ..."

"Y'all want to start out in one year?" Whitmer asked, her Texas accent having become even broader. "Is that even possible?"

"It would be expensive, but possible. SpaceX has successfully launched its Starship into orbit, in cooperation with us." Stevens pointed to Adam Morhaine. "Adam was in the cockpit. There would still be a few things to sort out, but in principle it could be done."

"We need to hurry," Lucille added. "We don't know how long this local effect will last. The signal could run out."

"Could it also have been destroyed by this solar storm?"

"Theoretically, yes. But that's unlikely," said Lucille.

"Why?"

"Do you really want to hear the explanation?"

"No." Whitmer waved her off. "I need a calculation of what it will cost. And I need a conversation in private." She looked at Stevens, who nodded eagerly.

"Of course, Madam President."

"Good. And bring your HR manager with you."

Rachel needed a break to clear her head before the return flight. She excused herself to use the restroom and instead sought out the nearest stairwell to get to the roof, which turned out to be no easy task. All the passages were blocked except for one door, through which a cleaning lady had just slipped, staring at her with wide eyes. The young woman looked as caught out as one could look caught out.

Rachel took advantage of her uncertainty and grinned. "I won't tell if you don't."

Instead of answering, the young woman merely held the door open for her and winked as she made her exit. A cool breeze drifted into the stairwell from outside, enveloping her with fresh air and the noise of Washington's streets.

Rachel stepped out onto a small corner between a large ventilation system and a concrete monolith. There wasn't much space, but there was a wonderful view over the capital. Most importantly, this place felt grounded, normal, and manageable, not as unreal as the one she had come from.

"Aha, another fugitive," said someone at her back. She spun around in shock.

Behind her stood a tall, wiry man in jeans and a shirt, with curly blond hair and a three-day beard. He had the angular face and blue eyes of a Scandinavian, and the penetrating gaze of analytical intelligence.

"Uhh, I just wanted to ..."

"Find a bit of peace from the crazies, I suppose," he replied, and winked at her. "I come here quite often when things get out of hand."

"When what things gets out of hand?" she asked.

"My assignments usually take me to places I don't really want to go, and into situations that people shouldn't have to experience."

"Are you some kind of secret agent?" Rachel attempted a smile that left open whether she was joking or not.

"Something like that." He spread his hands in front of his chest. "It's complicated."

"It always seems to be that way here in Washington."

"Amen." He dug a pack of cigarettes out of his breast pocket. "Would you like one?"

"I hate smoking," she replied. "It doesn't taste good, makes you restless and sick."

"Exactly." He still held the pack out to her and grinned when she took one. "I smoke one cigarette a year."

"On good or bad occasions?" she asked.

"If I'm not sure." He lit hers and then his. They stood in silence for a while on the parapet of their little corner, looking down on the city.

"Everything looks so normal."

"You were in the meeting with Whitmer."

"And you are from ...?"

"That's all right. We're working on the same project, I think. It's just that I'm being deployed somewhere else and there's no glory for me."

"What's your name?"

"Christer. Christer Johannsen." He held out a hand to her.

"Rachel Ferreira."

"I know."

Now it was her turn to smile. "International man of mystery, eh?"

"Hey, I love Austin Powers. But I'm not as lucky with women as he is."

"You must have a hard time as an attractive Scandinavian," she replied.

"You find me good looking? Are you married?"

"Excuse me?"

"I have to take every opportunity. It could lead to me not finishing this disgusting cigarette because now I know whether it's a good or a bad occasion." He grinned charmingly. When she didn't answer immediately, he turned the subject to something else. "You're a linguist, aren't you?"

"Yes. Stanford."

"Oh. What fascinates you most about speech patterns?"

"That we interpret the same symbols differently depending on which language we have learned. It's like tunnel vision, created by the compressed air of our vocal chords and tongues. It's paradoxical how something so simple, almost rudimentary, can change and subjectivize something as complex as reality," she explained. "That has always fascinated me."

"Patterns," he said. "We follow patterns."

"Yes. Did you know that there is only one symbol that has basically the same meaning in every language and culture?"

"No. The cigarette as a sign for cowboys?"

"It is the circle. In Buddhist cultures, it stands for the wheel of life, the cyclical process of death and birth. Among the Mâori, it stands for the unity of things, beginning and ending in one, which are never final, but only part of circular processes. In English we have phrases such as 'coming full circle,' as the return to a starting point, the closing of a circle. In all cultures, it is a symbol of completeness and eternity. That is why meeting rooms and symbols of fidelity have mostly been arranged like rings; Greek agoras, Norse symbols, wedding rings. We can't agree on much, but we seem to always agree on circles."

"It's also reflected in the math," Christer replied. "All radii are the same, it's the only shape with uniform curvature and even surface distribution. Circles are a pattern that somehow seems to be favored by nature. Like a relic ..."

" ... of creation, which serves as an indication of its nature," she completed his sentence. "I've read that book, too. Devoured it!"

"Then there's the matter of pi. No matter how big or small a circle is, the ratio between circumference and diameter is always identical."

"Pi."

"Yes, and pi is an irrational number. Its decimal representation goes on infinitely without ever repeating itself."

"Isn't it crazy," Rachel said, "that a shape that is so special in nature and culture as a sign of endlessness also appears in mathematics? Mustn't the circle be the most fascinating thing there is?"

"To be honest, I'm almost more fascinated by you," Christer replied, and pulled the cigarette from his mouth. "This is really disgusting, isn't it?"

"Totally."

She grinned and flicked hers away as his cell phone rang and he sighed. Their eyes met for an extended moment.

"I guess I have to go, Rachel Ferreira." He held out a hand to her.

She grasped it and they maintained contact for a few breaths.

"Next time we meet, I'll ask you out."

"Why only next time?" she inquired.

"Because I have a feeling it will be a long time before we see each other again. But then it will be fantastic," Christer promised her with a smile.

"What makes you so sure?"

"Intuition. Pure intuition."

9

RACHEL

"Thank you, Ms. Ferreira," said one student on her way out, and several others nodded to her or murmured their thanks as they passed her. When the lecture hall was empty – she had since moved to a smaller one – she went out onto the lawn between the Faculty of Linguistics and the Faculty of Communication Sciences.

Water splashed from a fountain that matched the time-honored low-rise building in which they were housed. In Rachel's eyes, there was no campus more beautiful than Stanford.

"Hey, who's there?" she asked cheerfully when she saw her sister Beth walking with Masha in her direction from the parking lots. The sun wasn't too high yet and sent a pleasant warmth into her limbs.

"Hi, Mom." Her daughter grinned and reluctantly let her kiss her on the cheek. Rachel hugged her sister and pointed to the lawn. A few students were sitting here and there, chatting or having a drink.

They also sat down.

"What are you doing here?" Rachel asked cheerfully, ruffling Masha's hair.

"We were just out for ice cream, nearby." Beth shrugged and poked her niece in the side. "So much you should be bursting, princess."

"It was only three scoops!"

"Is that your new gentleman friend there?" asked Beth, pointing to a man approaching from the other direction.

Rachel narrowed her eyes and then frowned. She recognized the jacket first – orange with many patches sewn on – and then the grey crew-cut hair and his typical thin-lipped smile.

"This should be interesting."

"Who's that?"

"That's Adam Morhaine," she replied thoughtfully.

"The Adam Morhaine? The astronaut?"

"That's the one."

"How do you know him? Oh my God, he's coming straight for us!" Beth put her hand over her mouth.

"You may be my little sister, B-B, but please don't act like a groupie, okay?"

"Sure, no problem."

"Doctor Ferreira?" Adam Morhaine approached her and nodded politely to Beth.

"Are you a garbage man?" Masha asked, squinting from the sun as she looked up.

"Masha!" Rachel admonished her daughter. Addressing the astronaut, she said, "I'm sorry."

"Haha! That's all right." Morhaine continued to laugh heartily and sat down next to her on the grass. "Actually, you could say that, Masha. I've been up there," he pointed to the sky, "dumping rocket junk. You know, I was just a garbage man, but the pay was darn good."

"How good?"

"Enough to eat all the ice cream I want until I'm an old grandpa." He laughed again, and Rachel was surprised by the sound that came out of his mouth. She had never heard him laugh on television. At most, a thin-lipped smile had crossed his lips. But maybe that was just part of his brand. Who knew for sure?

"I love ice cream," said Masha.

He pointed to a thick red stain on her dress. "I can see that."

Beth had become conspicuously silent.

"Still with the Secret Service escort, I see?" Rachel asked, pointing at the two shadows in suits, who were standing at a distance and trying to keep an eye on every corner of the campus at once.

"Again," he replied. "Doctor Ferreira ..."

"Rachel, please."

"Adam." He nodded. His smile remained, but it grew more serious. "Lucille sent me."

"Did she think I'd run away if I saw her again?"

"Something like that, I think."

"She's quite right. She used me for a political stunt."

"Well, she used you and your current popularity. She knew the president had your book on her annual list of best reads."

"Everyone knows that. That's the only reason why so many copies were sold," Rachel replied.

"And yet you still work here."

"I love my job. I love the university environment, the smart, inquisitive people."

"Do you know who else is inquisitive?"

She sighed. "Astronauts."

"That's right. We need you, Rachel."

"For what? For another pitch? The one two weeks ago didn't work out the way you wanted it to?"

"Oh, you don't know yet," Adam stated and made a gesture around her.

Rachel looked around. The area was mostly empty. She hadn't noticed it before, but at this time of day it was usually more crowded.

"What don't I know yet?" she asked cautiously.

Before he could answer, Beth held out her smartphone, which she had been typing on for a while. She cued up a clip on YouTube that was only an hour old but, already seemed to have several hundred million clicks. It was President Whitmer, who stepped in front of the cameras in the White House press room and laid down a speech script before she began to speak.

"Ladies and gentlemen, fellow citizens. Today we stand on the threshold of a new era of space exploration, an era in which our world is coming together to explore the unknown, to unravel the mysteries of Mars, but also of the universe and the question of extraterrestrial life. In the midst of a time of global conflict and concern, characterized by war, deepening diplomatic rifts, and the threat of artificial intelligence, we present to you a mission of unprecedented scale and significance that will not only push our scientific and technological boundaries, but also serve as a beacon of international cooperation.

"Two weeks ago, we discovered an unexplained phenomenon on Mars that could possibly be an extraterrestrial signal – a beacon of sorts. We cannot ignore the significance of this discovery and we therefore must do everything in our power to unravel its mysteries. That is why we have decided to launch a manned mission to Mars.

"This mission will be the result of unprecedented cooperation between our nation and the European Space Agency, the Japanese Space Agency, the Canadian Space Agency, and the Indian Space Agency. China has also expressed its willingness to participate in this unique endeavor, although terms have yet to be finalized. This mission will cost a tremendous amount of money and energy, and it will require the brightest minds of our time.

"The next window of opportunity to Mars opens in ten months, and we need to focus on the ambitious and the achievable. We firmly believe that this mission will bring the world together, and that it will be worth every penny. It will be our gateway to the truths of the cosmos and the unification of humanity behind a common goal: answering the question of whether we are alone in the universe.

"Whatever we find out, this mission will establish one thing: That we here on Earth are not divided. That we are one species. Of one flesh and blood, and we can achieve more together than divided and at odds."

Whitmer paused for a moment, and the gap was immediately filled with wild shouts and questions from the journalists present. But the President remained unperturbed and calmly continued.

"The official partner of this mission will be SpaceX. Together we will be at the forefront of space technology and lay the foundations for future generations of explorers and visionaries. Today we are kicking off preparations that will take us on a journey far beyond what we have ever imagined.

"Let us accept this challenge, not because it is difficult, but because it is necessary. Together, let us create a future where science and technology know no boundaries, and where the nations of the world unite to reach the stars. The time has come to conquer humanity's next great frontier – Mars. Together we are stronger, and together we will unravel the mysteries of the Red Planet.

"On to new heights. On to new discoveries. On to Mars!"

As the storm of questions broke over Whitmer, Rachel nodded and Beth picked up her phone again.

"She's really doing it," Rachel breathed. "I thought ..."

"We thought so, too," interrupted Adam. "But obviously she didn't just this minute look at her cards. Six places for the mission and you have one of them."

"Excuse me? I already told Lucille that I don't ..."

"Lucille respects that, although she was disappointed to hear it," he interrupted her again. "But it is President Whitmer who insists on your participation."

"The president?" Beth blurted out.

"Mom, you know the president?" Masha asked.

"She knows me better."

"You would move to Houston. With your daughter, of course, and your sister, if that's what you want." He pointed at Beth, who merely smiled pensively.

"How long?"

"Astronaut training normally takes years. We would have to teach you everything in three months."

"No, I mean how long?"

"Ten months until it starts."

Rachel looked him dead-seriously in the eye. "How? Long?"

"Possibly nine months. The window for a return flight opens every two years when Earth and Mars are on the same side of the sun and approach each other on their orbits around the sun to their closest point," Adam said. "But we will use a newer maneuver to reach Mars in three months, stay for three months and fly back for another three months. We'll then sort of catch up with Earth again."

Masha looked up at her with curiosity rather than fear. "Are you going to fly to the stars now, Mom?"

"I ..." She had come to terms with it after the meeting in Washington, convincing herself that it had all just been a very strange dream.

"You said yourself that we should consider the inexplicable as the most probable," Adam said. "I've been told by several people that you're the best in your field, Rachel, and also one of the few linguists who has done a lot of work on the question of what communication with aliens might look like and how it might work."

"I wasn't exactly optimistic in my assumptions."

"All the more important that you are there to make sure we don't make any stupid mistakes and put ourselves in danger."

She understood what he meant by 'ourselves' and shuddered involuntarily. Did she even have a choice? The mission would take place, that much was certain, otherwise the President would not have made the press statement that was undoubtably going around the world. Someone would take her place if she refused. Someone maybe much less careful than she was? Someone perhaps less good at their job? Could they as a species afford to take that risk?

"I will be the commander of the mission," Adam said. He plucked a blade of grass from the lawn, which he looked at almost reverently, as if it was the first time he had ever seen anything like it. "I saw you in Washington, I've watched recordings of your lectures on the Sapir-Whorf hypothesis, and yes, I have read your book. I don't want E.T. to eat us, I want to make peaceful contact if this is indeed an attempt at communication. I know what you're leaving behind and that my request is not a frivolous one."

Rachel looked at the ring on his finger and wondered how many children he might have.

"Are you at least thinking about it?"

"I already have," Rachel murmured wistfully and pulled Masha close to her.

"Are we moving to Hooston, Mom?"

She smiled sadly and kissed Masha's hair. "Houston, Dear. It's Houston."

10

RACHEL

She felt the water's coldness as she slowly slid down into the NASA neutral buoyancy pool. Although she was sealed in her spacesuit, which enveloped her like a second skin, she got goosebumps. But maybe it was just her imagination, because she knew how cold the water was. The buoyancy provided by the pool simulated a gravity-free environment – not as perfect as the real gravity-free state she had experienced in recent weeks during her seemingly endless parabolic flights in Florida, but she was able to work here for much longer time periods in similar-enough conditions.

Floating in the water, Rachel moved her limbs carefully so as not to give her body too much impetus. In NASA's 'vomit comet,' she had learned that movements that were too energetic had major consequences in zero gravity. Besides, with the heavy suit and the effort required to lift her arms, she would tire quickly here in the tank. Over time, she gained more control and felt more confident in her movements as she slid toward the submerged Starship below her.

The NASA employees watching her gave her instructions and cues through the communication system in her helmet.

Rachel concentrated on completing her assigned tasks, which included minor repairs to the spacecraft's hull and fitting spare parts inside. Her hands, encased in the spacesuit's thick gloves, moved slowly and deliberately as she used the tools and instruments attached to her belt. Each closing of her hands felt like she was bending a piece of metal.

In between, Rachel kept glancing at the displays in her helmet to make sure everything was okay. She checked her life support systems and adjusted the light on her helmet to see her surroundings better as she was sent deeper into the neutral buoyancy pool. There, the training leaders had turned off the lights. After a few tries, however, operating the light functions seemed familiar and intuitive, and darkness had never frightened her. Darkness was merely the absence of photons in the visible spectrum. There were no shadows in the night.

During the training, Rachel also worked with other astronauts who were practicing in the neutral buoyancy pool. They communicated using hand signals that they had practiced beforehand. Non-verbal communication was crucial to avoid misunderstandings and ensure the efficiency of their collaboration. None of these people would go on the mission with her. They were experienced astronauts from previous missions who were only there to help her practice and simulate problems. Her actual colleagues for the trip to Mars were training for mission-specific things, as they had long since mastered all this and had to use their little remaining time to prepare for tasks that had never been done before.

In the silence while they were being pulled up again after hours, Rachel looked up and saw her own reflection in the helmet of a colleague, Juanito. She looked at her distorted image and thought of the countless astronauts who had gone through the same training before her. In this environment of advanced technology and science, she still felt strangely out of place.

When the session in the neutral buoyancy pool came to an end, she pushed through the surface of the water on the lifting platform and immediately the weight of the spacesuit was on her again – dozens of kilograms pressing down on her shoulders and legs. She felt exhausted after the last few hours, drained and, above all, brain fried. The amount of concentration she had to muster for every step of the work was enormous. The lighting conditions, the constant passing on of work steps, the interpretation of radio instructions, the solving of problems that the trainers simulated for her and then the actual work, in which she had carried out some very complex repairs with various tools.

The line of NASA employees nodded in satisfaction as she left the pool, and cleared the poolside to return to their offices.

After changing her clothes, she picked Masha up from the school that had been set up for employees on the NASA site in Houston. No one here still lived at home, because no one was ever off. The project cost $20,000,000,000 a month and everyone involved worked around the clock – only the necessary sleep was not marked by work.

They ate together in the canteen, then she took Masha to after-school care. Later that evening, she picked her up after another tiring hour of working through her spaceship's life support data. Her daughter told her about her day with the excitement of a completely exhausted child – apparently the caregivers did a really good job of providing variety – and then fell asleep between one moment and the next.

Rachel left her apartment again and rode one of the many electric scooters that could be found everywhere, heading to the Starship, which had been set up in the small park between the large, prefabricated buildings. The 50-meter-long spaceship, which stood there like a miniature skyscraper, was covered with the flags of all the participating nations in the project and the signatures of all the employees here in Houston.

A simple gas barbecue had been set up by its landing legs, which looked far too narrow and fragile for this monstrosity of a spaceship, and nearby was a table with a plastic tablecloth and a few lawn chairs around it. Once again, she was the last one.

"Hey, Rachel," Adam greeted her from the grill. He waved at her with the tongs in his right hand, holding a small bottle of beer in his left.

"Evening," she replied, stifling a yawn.

At the table were Raphael Brandt, the German quantum physicist who represented the Europeans, Madeleine Kasper, the computer and cognitive scientist who'd been at that fateful meeting, and Yuki Tanaka – the Japanese woman who would be their on-board doctor during the trip.

"Has he arrived yet?" Rachel asked the group.

"Nah, just landed," Raphael said and held out a beer to her, but she declined with thanks. If she drank even a hint of alcohol now, she would fall into a deep sleep on the spot and possibly never wake up again. "Hey, even I've gotten used to the beer-flavored water."

"I already feel like a walking zombie," she explained. "Remember? I'm a lecturer, not an astronaut."

"If you feel like a wrung-out rag and like your head is going to explode," Madeleine said, toasting her, "then you're well on your way to becoming one."

"I just wish I had that behind me already. The first flight into space, I mean."

"Oh, it's not that wild. Just imagine you're on a leisurely roller coaster that's shaking a bit." The computer scientist with the cocoa-colored skin and mighty corkscrew curls grinned. "And then, nothing wobbles at all."

"I'll probably sleep through the whole trip. Three months of doing nothing," Rachel said enthusiastically, and sat down between Yuki and Madeleine.

Yuki wore her black hair short, and her expression was always cheerful – even as she slid Rachel steaming tea in a cup without handles.

"Jasmine, the way you like it," the Japanese woman said with the expected accent.

"Arigatô."

"Another half hour and then we'll be complete," said Raphael happily. The former ISS commander reminded Rachel of one of those men who adorn the covers of outdoor magazines: weather-beaten, tanned face, cropped hair, and an intense gaze.

"Is that a good thing?" she asked.

"Do you mean because all Chinese people who are even remotely involved with the government are communist spies?" Adam came from the grill and delivered a round of corn on the cob that smelled delicious.

"Well, there are probably more reasons to come to that conclusion than would argue against it."

"China is contributing four billion to this project – every month. That's as much as the Europeans," Raphael pointed out. "I don't think you would jeopardize your own investment."

"It's not even about the money. It's more about coopera-tion. Since the announcement of the joint mission, every-thing has eased politically, at least between the West and China. That alone is worth getting a Chinese colleague."

Yuki suddenly changed the subject. "Is there any news from the MRO?"

"No." Adam shook his head and Raphael handed him the

salt, which he sprinkled generously over his ear of corn. "No activity since the CME. Everything looks the same as before."

"Do you ever worry that it won't be there when we get there?" Rachel asked.

"All the time," Madeleine said, looking grim. "It's probably something like scientist FOMO."

"Yeah, 'fear of missing out' is part of the job for us. Otherwise we might never have become astronauts," said Raphael.

"It's still there," Adam assured them.

"What makes you so sure?"

"I don't know, it's like I can feel it somehow." The engineer and pilot shook his head. "The thing in Jakarta, that won't let me go. The two things must be connected, and it doesn't seem it would all happen, and then just disappear."

"You're not going to join all those TV critics who say we should investigate Jakarta instead of taking the risk of a hasty mission to Mars, are you?" Raphael asked their colleague.

"In Jakarta, all kinds of companies and universities are turning half the city upside down. So far, they have nothing."

"What gives you hope, Adam, that we'll find something on Mars?" Yuki asked curiously. "Our options will be much more limited there."

"That's true, but there aren't people scurrying around everywhere. We have a controlled environment, free from background noise. Hardly any atmospheric influences."

Rachel could think of an endless list of disadvantages, but she kept them to herself. She had been doing so since her arrival a few weeks ago, and she was sure that each of her colleagues had a similar list buried deep in their minds.

"The signal is still there," Adam repeated, standing up and looking around. "Believe me, it's still there. And we're going to decode it."

"Amen." Raphael raised his beer and toasted the others.

Half an hour later, their last team member arrived. Liu Hwang was a small, well-built man with relaxed features but the gait of a big cat. He was wearing denim trousers and a white windbreaker with patches from the Chinese National Space Administration.

"Good evening," said the taikonaut with a bow. Rachel stood up just like the others and shook his hand.

"Welcome to Houston."

"Thank you, thank you."

After they had introduced themselves to each other – of course they already knew almost everything about each other – Liu Hwang took the last remaining chair.

"We have you to thank for this, did you know that, Mr. Hwang?" Adam asked, making a gesture that encompassed the table, the grill and the Starship that towered high above them.

"Please, why don't you all call me Liu?" the newcomer suggested in an almost American way. "What do you mean?"

Adam smiled one of his rare smiles, and a little relaxation – or normality? – spread around the table.

"They would never let us barbecue here late at night if it wasn't a special moment."

"You're welcome." Liu grinned. "I see you've already started without me."

"Sorry, we really had ..." Madeleine mumbled with her mouth full.

The Chinese man waved her off. "Have you at least had the trust-a-Chinese-talk yet?"

There was a sudden silence as they exchanged concerned glances.

"Yup," Rachel said, putting the moment of tension behind her. "Done well before your arrival. No need to tell us you're a communist spy."

"Phew, then I've been lucky. Can I have a beer, too?" Liu

pointed at Raphael as he sat next to the cooler where the bottles were submerged in the ice water. "I thought I'd start my spy report with a review of your beer."

The German grinned broadly, and the others also chuckled comfortably.

"I think we're all going to be good friends, Liu," Adam said, toasting him from the grill. "How do you want your steak?"

"I am a militant vegan."

Silence fell again.

"A joke." Liu waved it off. "You must have heard the saying: a Chinese person will eat anything with four legs as long as it's not a table."

11

CHRISTER

Night had spread is dark velvet cloak over the world as the Air Asia passenger jet approached Jakarta. The twinkling stars in the sky seemed to be reflected in the lights of the metropolis as the mighty Airbus broke through the clouds and the city's contours emerged below.

Christer Johannsen pressed his forehead against the window and soaked up the view. He didn't know much about the city, but on the way there he had worked through all the information he had been given on his tablet.

The majestic Monas, Jakarta's landmark, loomed in the distance. The slender, 132-meter-high obelisk stood proud and lofty in the middle of Merdeka Square, as if it embodied the pulsating soul of this metropolis.

Indonesia's capital, Jakarta, is a melting pot of cultures. Located on the northwest coast of Java, the most populous island in the world, Jakarta is the political, economic, and cultural center of the country. Its significance extends far beyond the borders of Indonesia and makes the city an important hub in Southeast Asia.

The aircraft's turbines roared as the jet flew on through

the clear night. The passengers gazed in awe at the enormous city skyline, which radiated something magical in the darkness. The many canals and rivers shimmered like liquid silver in the glow of the streetlights, crisscrossing the sea of lights like an intricate mosaic.

The wheels gently kissed the runway's tarmac at last and the plane came to a halt with a soft sigh. When the aircraft door opened, the passengers were greeted by the muggy, tropical air and the stench of exhaust fumes and waste.

Christer Johannsen went down the front steps and onto the bus that was waiting to take him and the other passengers to the terminal. The warm, humid air filtered in through the open windows as the bus chugged slowly across the airport grounds. The terminal lights shone like beacons in the distance, welcoming those returning home and visitors alike.

It was humid and cramped inside the bus. The atmosphere was characterized by a palpable tension and excitement that went far beyond what was usual at an airport. Since the phenomenon – or miracle, depending on which country you are from – occurred, Jakarta was no longer just a gigantic city. It was the one place in the world onto which humanity seemed to project all its fears and hopes.

Now that he was there, Christer sensed that there was fear all around. It was palpable in every fiber of his body and weighed on him like a heavy veil of vaporized anxiety.

After a short drive, they reached the terminal and got off the bus. The hustle and bustle of the airport enveloped the passengers as Christer weaved his way through the crowd to get to passport control. A light film of sweat already covered his forehead as he waited patiently for his turn.

When it finally came, Christer placed his passport on the counter and looked the control officer in the eye. His passport was stamped and his fingerprints were taken on a sensor panel, and after a brief nod, he was waved through with an impatient gesture. He took a deep breath and walked through the glass doors into the passenger arrivals terminal.

An elegantly dressed local woman wearing a gray pant suit was waiting for him at the exit. She wore a friendly smile on her lips and held a sign with his name on it. She lifted it slightly to attract his attention and Christer approached her with a grateful smile.

"Selamat datang di Jakarta, Doctor Johannsen," she greeted him warmly and held out her hand. Her voice sounded melodic and inviting, like a gentle breeze blowing through the palm trees.

Her polite gesture told him a lot. She was probably a moderate or even secular Muslim – or not a Muslim at all – as she wasn't wearing a hijab and she'd reached out to shake his hand as a man might, although that was not necessarily customary here. Perhaps she came from Hindu Bali?

Christer took her hand and thanked her before making his way to the exit with her. A large but otherwise unremarkable SUV was waiting for them. After the driver, a beefy guy with meaty hands, had taken his suitcase from him, they got into the back of the pleasantly air-conditioned vehicle.

"You're a contact?" he asked as the SUV started to move. "Which is your first name and which is your surname? I don't speak Indonesian yet."

"I was warned about your humor," she replied in near-perfect English.

"It was more at the expense of my bosses, who remained rather vague when it came to my assignment." Christer shrugged his shoulders. "And the contact person."

"Actually, I haven't even identified myself. I could be someone who wants to kidnap you."

"A funny Swedish geophysicist?"

"We both know you're more than that."

"If we both know that, then I haven't done my job properly," he replied.

"We are supposed to be like chameleons," said the Indonesian.

"Then I wouldn't look like a piece of melted chalk next to you. Could I see your ID?"

"Don't you want to guess first?"

"You are in your mid-thirties, Balinese, hate Jakarta, miss Bali and the atmosphere there. You hate big cities but love your work, which is a vocation instead of a job. You probably belong to the domestic intelligence agency Badan Inelijen Negara, BIN, and were selected by the president herself. Your specialty is counterintelligence, I assume," he enumerated his thoughts and she began to smile appreciatively.

"Wayan Suryani is my name. I have the rank of Kepala Operasi with the BIN," she held out her hand to him again and he shook it once more.

"I'm delighted. So I was right, then."

"Right enough."

"Then you should tell your superiors that a field agent is not necessary for counterintelligence. I'm a United Nations research specialist, not a foreign agent here for espionage purposes," he replied.

"Then think of me more as a babysitter and door opener, and forget about my area of expertise," Suryani suggested. "If you don't want to peek behind the wrong doors, at least."

"I don't know if a paranoid nanny is the right thing for me."

"You must understand our situation, Doctor Johannsen. Since yesterday we have been bombarded with requests to allow foreign investigative teams. In addition, there are requests for permits from every university in the world because they all want to investigate what the mysterious event is all about. The rush for tourist visas is so great that our government websites have collapsed. How many of these people do you think are not tourists?"

"I think a lot of them are tourists," he replied. "You know how it works. If a volcano erupts somewhere, all the flights are booked out shortly afterward. Sensation-based tourism is the new beach vacation."

"This makes it all the more difficult to filter out state actors who are too curious," Suryani insisted. "We are a country that is torn between many much stronger players, namely China, India, and the United States, who all have an interest in our shipping routes and natural oil and gas reserves. Industrial and political espionage is taking place here on a level not seen in Europe, even though they consider themselves the hub of the world there."

"I see." He sighed. "In any case, I'm not a spy, I can promise you that."

"Wonderful. That will make my job much easier."

"What is your job, then?"

"Babysitting." Suryani beamed her opaque smile, only it widened a little more. Christer had to admit that she was extremely attractive – dark almond-shaped eyes, black hair, and nut-brown skin – a fact he would have liked to avoid.

He changed their conversation to a chatty tone as their driver struggled to make his way through the sprawling traffic of the metropolis. "I can imagine that you've had a lot of work in the last few weeks." Everywhere he looked through the tinted windows, cars crept forward, surrounded by hordes of scooters, some of which magically accommodated entire families.

"You could say that. We weren't prepared for Jakarta to become the center of the world."

"That situation must have improved considerably since the preparations for the international Mars mission began, am I right?" he asked.

"Yes. A rampaging mountain river has now turned into a tsunami. Still not the situation my colleagues and I would wish for, but we're slowly coming to grips with the situation since the public's eyes started to get bored with the Miracle of Jakarta. Houston is now more exciting."

Suryani took one of the water bottles from a holder between them, opened it, and sipped. "But don't let that fool you. There's a reason we've only now agreed to the United Nations' request to let a special envoy in. Things have gone utterly haywire here."

"What do you mean?"

"The public may no longer find Jakarta particularly interesting. Most people have probably dismissed the light phenomenon as a fake or a fluctuation in the energy grid, as have most of the supposed experts on the talk shows, by and large," she explained. "But that's not true for the intelligence agencies of other governments. They still want to know what happened here, and they are looking for answers where they should not be looking."

"In your ministries and authorities, I suppose," said Christer.

"Yes. We have arrested two hundred foreign spies in the last few weeks, most of whom have already been expelled."

"So, why did you agree to me coming here?" he asked. "I guess there's a strategy behind it?"

"You're right about that. We've given up trying to unmask foreign actors. We can't do that in these numbers. It overwhelms our capacities," she replied. "Besides, we don't know what the Miracle of Jakarta is all about. So, let's concentrate on finding out – with your help – and making sure that what we do from now on stays between us."

"I am required to send regular reports to the UN's secret committee," Christer reminded her.

"Yes, I know, and that's how it should stay. As agreed. But

we'll have the information immediately – information that we couldn't obtain ourselves because we simply don't have the expertise. Any idea where we should start?"

"Yes. With the basics. The power plants. I already have a list of all the power plants in and around Jakarta and the companies involved."

"You really believe that this can be explained by the fact that someone didn't shut down their power plant even though they were told to do so?" Suryani asked doubtfully.

"If you're in the dark, start with the most likely and work your way outward from there," he explained with a shrug.

"All power plants are under government supervision. The relevant officials would have immediately reported such blatant disregard for official instructions."

"Are you sure that none of these officers would hold out their hand if someone waved an envelope?"

"All right, then. Where do you want to start?"

"At the Ministry of Energy. We'll start with the data there. Is there a chance that it will be digitized?" Christer asked without much hope. He could already see himself rummaging through mountains of paper files, just like in Germany or France.

"Of course," said Suryani, looking a little irritated. Then she patted the driver on the shoulder and spoke to him in Indonesian.

"I hope you've allotted plenty of time for our collaboration. The beginning is usually the toughest," he explained, sighing as he looked out of the window and muttered, "Before the bullets start flying and everything happens far too quickly."

12

RACHEL

In the weeks that followed, she spent a lot of time in a Starship brought to Houston, which the engineers had laid on its belly and completely furnished. That's where they lived now, with the difference that Rachel slept at home with Masha every other night to make the most of her precious time with her. Their work, however, took place almost exclusively in the Starship so that they could all get used to their new home and gradually familiarize themselves with each system.

Around her, of course, the world was not standing still, even if it felt like her world and that of her colleagues was shrinking down into a spacious but still manageable spaceship.

The NASA complex in Houston remained a buzzing beehive that never stood still.

In the factory halls, engineers and mechanics painstakingly checked every detail of the mighty Starship, several versions of which were in the hangars. From the powerful Raptor engine units to the delicate and extremely precise control electronics, every component was carefully examined and tested to ensure that it would withstand the enormous stresses of space flight.

At the same time, scientists and researchers in the adjacent laboratories were working on the development of high-tech instruments and analytical equipment to help the astronauts unravel the mysteries of the strange light phenomenon. Experts in geology and astrobiology developed methods to efficiently collect samples and analyze them on board the Starship, while climatologists worked on predictions for Martian weather and prepared corresponding CubeSats. They would be flying to the Red Planet because of a possible extraterrestrial signal, but as they would have to spend at least three months there, other experiments and sample collecting were another part of their job profile.

In another wing of the complex, the communications specialists dedicated themselves to the challenge of maintaining the connection between the Starship and Earth. They developed robust systems that could withstand even the most adverse conditions, and ensured that data streams would flow smoothly and reliably in both directions.

The mission specialists and space physicians took care of the future well-being of the astronauts, including 'prescribing' daily schedules to prevent psychological problems. They developed nutrition plans that met the special requirements of space travel, and researched ways of counteracting the negative effects of weightlessness on the human body. Training equipment had to be as space-saving as possible and yet ISS-tested. They tested the AxEMU spacesuits, modified for Mars to combine protection and mobility, and prepared them to withstand the extreme temperature differences and dangerous radiation on the Martian surface.

They themselves spent a lot of time outside the Starship in their new suits and gave the designers important feedback, which often only became apparent after many hours of continuous work. In the afternoons, when they were too physically exhausted for strenuous activities, they studied maps and satellite images of Mars to familiarize themselves with the geological features and potential dangers of their landing site. A total of four landing sites were planned, three of them in alternative zones in case the wind and weather were unfavorable when the time came.

The logistics and planning teams worked tirelessly to ensure that all resources and materials were available on time and in the right place. They coordinated the transportation of equipment between various NASA facilities that assisted them and industry partner factories, the construction of the launch pad, and for the safety measures for the launch at Boca Chica, Texas. They carefully planned the supply chain for fuel, food, and spare parts, always balancing efficiency and safety.

In the shadow of the gigantic Starship and Super Heavy rockets, the software developers worked on the on-board computers and automation systems. They wrote code that would enable navigation and control of the spacecraft and, together with OpenAI, developed AI systems optimized for the mission to help the astronauts solve unforeseen problems during the journey and on Mars.

The experts for environmental protection and energy supply worked on advanced solar technologies and the efficient use of resources such as methane to make fuel available for the return journey. They researched the possibilities of using the natural resources of Mars and thus minimizing the payload with which they would take off from Earth.

Despite the enormous pressure and the short time remaining until the start of the mission, there was an atmosphere of determination and optimism that became increasingly infectious. In the corridors of the control center and in the factory halls, ideas were discussed, plans forged and solutions found. Even the press, which was omnipresent outside the security areas, seemed to be taken in by the cooperative spirit, and so the project became ever more deeply integrated into contemporary pop culture, spawning television shows, talk shows, and whole stacks of books and cult-like fan groups. Not even the growing tensions with Russia, which was still recovering from its failed campaign, took up much space in the reporting.

And with each passing day, the window of opportunity for their departure drew closer. They were only given the exact date two weeks beforehand – for security reasons: June 1, 2025. Rachel felt a mixture of melancholy, guilt, and excitement when she thought about setting off into space in the near future. Melancholy because she would be swapping the beauty of Earth for a tin can flying through the most hostile environment. Guilt at having to leave Masha behind, even though Beth had been spending more and more time with her daughter for months to get her used to it.

Her excitement felt like a betrayal.

She was especially anxious about the dangers that awaited her. She had expected to be excited about the signal and the possibility of contact with extraterrestrial intelligence. But in all the work and exhaustive preparation, so much information had poured in on them that hardly anyone was still thinking about the light phenomenon – apart from the theorists all over the world who were researching it and constantly coming up with new hypotheses. She would have time to work her way through them when she and her crewmates were in flight for three months.

During training, they simply had no more free brain cells for this – the focus was on everything that could go wrong. The list was so long that Rachel could hardly believe that there could be a safe option apart from destroying the spaceship.

The mission's international leadership shielded their team from the outside world as best they could, which was both relieving and strange at the same time. On the one hand, it was the only way they could still think and learn clearly, and on the other, it felt surreal. Sometimes she woke up at night and thought her current life was some kind of cosmic joke, something unreal that a screenwriter had made up.

A trip to Mars to communicate with aliens who had turned on some cosmic lamp? It sounded too absurd. Without the cultural feedback from the public via television, radio, and social media, everything remained abstract and somehow small. But perhaps that was exactly what kept them going, working 20 hours a day until they collapsed from mental and physical exhaustion. At the beginning of the project, they had been told that they would sit with a psychologist for an hour every other day, but nothing had come of it. There was simply no time, and perhaps that was a good thing.

The only bad thing was that she already missed Masha, even though she hadn't flown off yet. The fear of dying during the trip and leaving her daughter motherless was almost unbearable in her moments of weakness. But her colleagues also all had children of their own and were struggling with the same demons, which gave her the strength to bear it somehow. By the time Masha was older, she would surely understand and not hate her for it. She hoped.

The evening before the mission started, she lay in her bunk in the Starship that had also served as their accommodation after their move to Boca Chica, to the Starbase, in order to change as little as possible, despite the change of location. Masha lay next to her, pressed close. The other astronauts were with their families, taking the opportunity to escape the ship one last time before it would be their only home for the next nine months or more. But Rachel found a certain strength in being here once more, alone with her daughter.

"Do you think you'll find E.T., Mom?" Masha asked against her chest.

"No, Dear. I rather think I'll find something like E.T.'s bicycle bell. At least I hope so."

"His bike bell?"

"Whoever wanted to make contact with us is obviously not on Mars themselves."

"So this is like a phone?"

"That's what we want to find out," Rachel explained, looking up at the ceiling of her bunk. "I'd be happy if it's just a bell. 'Hey, we're here. We're here.'"

"Are you scared, Mom?"

"Yes." She had once sworn to herself never to lie to her daughter, and she never considered breaking that promise.

"But you seem pretty calm."

"Because I have made a decision. At some point, you will understand that making a decision about something is the most reassuring thing in the world."

"I'm going to miss you." Masha began to cry quietly. When Rachel tried to comfort her, she resisted. "It's okay, Mom. I've been crying a lot, but it doesn't feel so bad anymore. Beth says it's healthy."

"She's right," said Rachel, trying not to let her voice break. "We can talk on the phone quite often when I'm first out there. And when I'm further away, we'll send each other video messages. Then you can make fun of my hair without me being able to pinch you."

She ran her fingers over the fresh stubble on her head and began to tickle Masha.

"But only after tomorrow!"

When Rachel fell asleep, she did so with a firm optimism, unaware that death would be knocking at the door in just a few hours.

13

CHRISTER

The work was tiring. Day in, day out, scrolling and clicking through documents from the Ministry of Energy until Christer worried about getting carpal tunnel syndrome. His right arm tingled from his wrist to his elbow, and his eyes watered not just in the evening, but as early as midday. They scanned, top to bottom, through thousands of documents from the last few decades. Thanks to powerful AI assistance, they were translated surprisingly well, although it was evident here and there that the programs did not correctly interpret every subtlety of language, even one as simple as Bahasa Indonesia.

Most of it was boring bureaucratic lists, orders, requests, and other everyday documents from a huge authority that had produced vast amounts of paperwork. When he thought about how many trees had been felled in the past to make all the sheets of paper for things that were being digitized today, he felt sick. Not just because of the overexploitation of nature, but because of the largely senseless overexploitation of nature.

Wayan turned out to be surprisingly patient and didn't

complain that they were basically doing nothing – or at least it seemed that way. She followed his instructions to look for something that caught her attention, although he could imagine that didn't sound like much help. But it wasn't meant to be. She was just his door opener for the Ministry of Energy's files.

Either she was aware of this and that was why she was so relaxed, or she trusted him, which he thought was impossible.

Until the day he finally found what he was looking for, even though he hadn't even known what it was that he wanted to find. Which was precisely the nature of his job.

Wayan had just arrived in front of the large white building with a yellow logo emblazoned with the words 'Kementerian Energi dan Sumber Daya Mineral.' The architecture reminded him a little of Japan, and thus of some of his best years before working for the UN. As she did every late afternoon, she had brought coffee with her, handed him a cup and nodded to his two bodyguards from her unit who then made their way back to his car.

"Today is the rocket launch," she said, glancing at her wristwatch. "In a few hours."

"I heard about it," he replied laconically as they walked toward the entrance to the Ministry of Energy – against the flow of dozens of officials leaving for the day.

"Don't you want to watch the livestream like everyone else?"

"No." He shook his head. "Too stressful."

"You don't seem like the emotional type," Wayan said.

"Because you've never seen me when there's a major event like this where there's no room for anything to go wrong. There's no plan B – scary." Christer shook himself. "No, I'd rather wait for the good news and then be happy about it. Besides, we have a lot to do."

"I know." She let out a sigh. "Do you really think we'll

find anything? We've only gotten through fifteen years – we've only reached the eighties. If this keeps up, we'll reach retirement before we've worked our way through it."

When they got down to the basement and opened the door to the cramped office space, the musty, damp, moldy old-paper smell hit them like it did every time. There were six monitors on a simple wooden table – three on each side – connected to computers. Christer put down his bag and took a seat after taking a big sip from his coffee container.

"What are we doing here?" Wayan asked as they silently booted up their computers. He had just placed his right hand on his mouse, a part of the silent ritual that they had been repeating for weeks now. He was surprised that the agent had not yet gone mad from boredom. It was also a little impressive and showed her strength of character. He had respect for that.

"I've been wondering why you hadn't asked that before now."

"I asked," she replied.

"Yes, and I answered: We go through all the data to look for anomalies."

"That's about as helpful as 'I don't know.' Do you even have a strategy? A suspicion?"

"Yes and no," he replied somewhat cryptically. "My suspicion is that there is a simple explanation for the alleged Miracle of Jakarta. I'm a data scientist and I don't believe in hocus-pocus."

"And since it was an energy phenomenon, start with the Ministry of Energy." Wayan nodded. "I can follow you that far. But why not the public utilities? Why not industry?"

"Have you ever investigated them?"

"No, why?"

"Companies hate all documentation that is not legally required or that could ever possibly implicate them at some point – in effect, contracts. We wouldn't find anything there that could indicate any wrongdoing."

"Because they would have made it disappear."

"Exactly. It's vastly different in ministries. Here, documents pass through too many hands, and after every change of power at the top, a large part of the staff changes and the old one is required to hand over everything and give an account if something is missing. There are two fears in the public sector: the fear of the next election, and the fear of doing something wrong. Politicians can be extremely vindictive." Christer lifted his hand from the mouse and glanced between the monitors.

"So you don't suspect a problem at the Ministry of Energy," she stated with a quizzical expression.

"We'll, here's the time for that, 'I don't know,' you mentioned. But if there ever was a problem, whether here or in the industrial energy sector, we'll find the evidence here."

"And the UN sent a special envoy whose past is so secret that even I couldn't find out anything about him?" Wayan raised an eyebrow doubtfully. "I could have put a gaggle of secretaries on the job and they'd be done by now."

"No, they wouldn't be," he contradicted.

"Now let's get to the part where you actually answer my question about what we're doing here?"

Christer smiled. "I have a talent that may soon no longer be needed: I recognize patterns where others don't see them – connections that are hidden but obvious to me." He shrugged his shoulders. "I recognize them as soon as I see them."

"Isn't there an AI solution for this?"

"They do exist, but they are – still – spitting out too many false positives. These are patterns that are not really patterns, at least not for us humans. Imagine a program that specializes in correcting text. Programs can do this extremely well because the data basis is clear; just follow the rules. But if you have a poem, it fails because poems follow certain rhythms, but not necessarily grammatical rules. Poems can only be edited by humans."

"I understand," Wayan said, but she didn't act particularly convinced.

"Come here," he said, and waved her over when she hesitated. She hesitated a bit and then stood up, smoothed her pant suit, and walked around the table to stand beside him. She smelled of a subtle, almost indecently seductive perfume.

He pointed to the monitor on his left, which showed exploration tenders issued by the Department of Energy between 1982 and 1988. Then he moved his finger to the middle monitor, which showed the visas issued by the Immigration Department between 1982 and 1988, adjusted to filter out any foreigner who did not have a doctorate at the time the visa was issued. On the right-hand display were permits for mining exploration during the same period, which had also been issued by the Department of Energy.

"Do you see a pattern there?" Christer asked her, and Wayan narrowed her eyes.

"Where did you get the data from the immigration authorities?"

"I asked."

"But not me."

"No."

Her expression darkened and he felt a brief stab of guilt.

"You went over my head."

"Just for this," he said, but the brief flare of disapproval in her expression had already been shut down by an unreadable one.

"I understand," she replied coolly.

"I'm sorry, I'm not very good at this diplomacy stuff ..."

"That's all right. You use your resources as you see fit."

Christer couldn't shake off the impression that he had just gambled and lost, but she simply pointed to the displays.

"I don't see a pattern there. What do the immigration authorities and exploration tenders have to do with each other? Were foreign specialists hired?"

"That's my guess, yes," he explained, relieved that the unpleasant part of their conversation was apparently behind them. "In the 1980s, there were several mining companies looking for uranium deposits. Nothing ever came of it because the environmental and safety concerns were too great."

"Nuclear energy wasn't particularly popular with our citizens, neither back then nor today." Wayan shrugged her shoulders. "It also required too much foreign know-how, which was far too expensive to buy. At that time, my country was much poorer than it is today."

"Most of the exploration areas from back then are located around the Pangrango. That's not far from here, is it?"

"Sixty kilometers."

"The mining concessions for the exploration of uranium deposits were awarded for five years. Officially, however, according to the companies involved, all operations were stopped after less than a year. The area was then declared a national park, but the concessions were not withdrawn."

"Because they were invalid. Drilling is not permitted in national parks," said Wayan.

"Mm-hmm," Christer said, pointing to the visa allocations. "Next, look here. In 1982, several drilling specialists from the United States entered the country, and a year later, nuclear physicists from Germany, Russia, France, and the United Kingdom."

"So? That fits in with the explorations."

"It does. But here comes the anomaly." He tapped on his

keyboard and called up another document that showed old passport copies on various tabs. "They've all disappeared."

"What do you mean?"

"Not one of them ever took a return flight. They had ninety-day visas, but never left the country – at least not by legal or visible means."

"Maybe they were poached and stayed?"

"A total of twenty scientists and engineers who had families at home?" Christer shook his head. "That doesn't seem credible to me. Besides, they would have made appeals to the authorities. Maybe there would have been a family reunification program."

"Do you believe it points to a crime?"

"Possibly. But above all, I believe in a pattern." He called up more files. "By 1988, over three hundred more scientists, engineers, and researchers had entered the country and, apparently, disappeared. Many were in Indonesia on business, employees of large international companies, but most were on vacation."

"Can I make a guess? Nuclear physicists?" asked Wayan.

"Not in particular. Every field. Materials researchers, radiation technicians, physicists, radiologists, geologists, geophysicists, surveyors – the list is long."

"Where do you see your pattern? Every year, an incredible number of people disappear around the world – including in Indonesia. Usually the simplest explanations are the most likely; a love affair, an accident while hiking, escaping from a tax investigation. Take your pick."

"None of them were found dead. There were no serious investigations into any of the cases, despite pressure from the embassies of the countries concerned. That sounds like corruption to me."

"Hush money, you mean."

"Yes." Christer nodded. "Especially as all these cases –

and remember, I filtered for those who entered with doctorates – entered via Jakarta. The place from which the exploration teams departed. The place where the alleged miracle took place. I have done loads of research in the last few days, and there have been no similar incidents anywhere in the world. When I see two unusual patterns in the same place, it's not a coincidence, it's a ..."

" ... pattern," Wayan finished. "Why are you only now revealing to me that you've been doing significantly more than I have all this time?"

"Because now I need your help," he admitted frankly.

"What do you need?"

Christer scrutinized her closely to see if she was still angry with him and was preparing himself to hear a resounding 'no' when he asked. But her expression remained controlled and her gaze unreadable.

"I need to know whether there have been any criminal proceedings for corruption against any of the mining or energy companies during this period. I have no access to the Ministry of Justice," he replied. "If we can draw that connection, in terms of time and place – the court in Java should have had jurisdiction – then we may end up with a company name, and I want to bet that those people know more than we do."

"I'll see what I can do." She pointed to her three monitors. "You've condemned me to being a secretary until now. Not anymore, do we understand each other?"

"Loud and clear." Christer cleared his throat and nodded.

14

RACHEL

She was settled in the cockpit of the rocket when the launch countdown reached two hours. This meant that she was sitting in one of the four rear seats behind Adam, their commander and pilot, and Madeleine, the copilot. 'Sitting' was only sort of true because the seats had them lying on their backs as they faced the windows that in turn faced the sky.

The Starship – their actual spaceship – was planted on the Super Heavy, towering a total of 120 meters high on the mighty tower with the gripper arms that were currently still holding the ship and booster in place.

Rachel didn't cry. She had already done so before her trip from the Starbase to the launch area when she had said goodbye to Beth and Masha. The hundreds of journalists from all over the world who had gathered to take photos of her and her colleagues had made her realize for the first time, and with full force, just how big this mission was, and how many eyes were on them.

And what a responsibility we have, she thought. Unbidden, the television images of the space shuttle Challenger and how it had exploded after take-off came into her mind. Its crew had been so cheerful and had waved just as she and her crewmates had done. They hadn't known that those would be their last minutes.

"Structural inspection completed, all values nominal," the control center announced by radio.

"Understood, everything on our side is also on Go," Adam replied curtly.

"Hey, this is Mission Control," came the familiar voice of the former personnel manager, who had been promoted to head of mission two months ago.

"Lucille, what can we do for you?"

"Wouldn't now be a good time to tell us the name you've chosen to give the ship?"

Adam turned his head, which wasn't easy in the white and gray pressure suits, and smiled. "Does everyone still agree?" he asked.

"Oh, yes," said Raphael.

"Sure," said Liu, and the others also gave him the thumbs up.

"Starbase, we've prepared something. Lenny from communications knows about it," Adam announced.

There was silence in the cockpit for a long time, then Lucille answered.

"This is Mission Control. A livestream survey. Interesting." Her voice was neutral, leaving no indication as to whether she approved or disapproved of the decision.

"This is not our mission, but a mission of humanity, and we thought that our name should reflect that."

Rachel looked at Liu, who was sitting to her right and looked tense. If she had needed another reason to trust him, she had it now. Democratizing the naming could well be seen as an affront to China – if they wanted to see it that way. And Liu had to realize that there could be consequences for him.

Not necessarily, but there could be. Despite this, he had agreed to the idea.

"At least you'll have peace for the next two years," she murmured, and he managed a smile.

"Yeah."

"Hey, that almost sounded Texan," Adam said happily.

"Don't you dare shout Hooyah when it lifts off," Raphael admonished him.

"Count on it, buddy."

"Fueling initiated," reported the control center. The tanks were now being filled with liquid oxygen and liquid methane, and the rocket hull froze from the bottom to the top. Ice formed, which traveled upward as a white layer matching the filling level of the tanks. "Fueling is nominal. All signs still point to go."

"It's really happening, guys," said Raphael, clapping his hands. His gloves, however, swallowed almost all of the sound. "We're going to fucking Mars!"

"For now, we just sit here – or lie on our backs – and sense the blood rush to the back of our heads," grumbled Madeleine.

"Engine checks positive. All thirty-three Raptor units on Go," came the next announcement 15 minutes later.

"Starting final avionics check," Adam announced, tapping through the touch menu in front of his helmet visor, which gave him access to electronic sensors and software heuristics. "Everything looks good. Navigation, controls, internal monitoring."

"Confirm, Ambassador," Lucille replied again.

"Ambassador?" Madeleine paused for a moment. "Ambassador. How apt."

"The livestream has decided. A good choice."

"Ambassador is ready to go," Adam said solemnly, knowing full well that they were surrounded by a dozen cameras in the cockpit, broadcasting everything live on the internet. After months of total isolation, it was a strange feeling for Rachel to know that three billion people were watching her as she 'sat' here in a large cockpit waiting to be launched into space with 72 million tons of thrust.

With 30 minutes left, the final system checks were carried out.

"All valves look good, telemetry data nominal. The launch area is being cleared. We are now entering the final countdown," announced Mission Control. "Weather also looks good, Ambassador."

"Good to hear, Mission Control." Adam stretched his right hand out to the side. Madeleine placed her left on his and Liu, Rachel, Yuki, and Raphael followed one after the other until all were touching in the center. "We can do this. I couldn't think of better colleagues and friends to pull this off. We have humanity with us and probably the most important discovery in history in our sights."

Rachel smiled, although a single tear ran down her cheek. Fortunately, no one paid any attention to her as they all seemed to be preoccupied with their own thoughts. She was glad it was Adam making the final radio announcements and she was just a passenger. She was terrified.

When the countdown reached ten seconds, she closed her eyes and thought of Masha.

At the moment of ignition, Rachel felt her heart accelerate. Ambassador's cockpit vibrated around her, and the Raptor engines of the Super Heavy stage unleashed their tremendous power. With 72,000,000 tons of thrust, the spaceship slowly lifted off from the spaceport in Boca Chica. Violent vibrations shook her body.

Rachel felt the force of gravity pressing her into her seat as the spaceship picked up speed. She couldn't help but be impressed by the sheer power of the engines carrying her into the sky. At the same time, the thought of the unimaginable forces almost drove her crazy. As the booster continued to accelerate, they finally reached a speed of more than 1,000 kilometers per hour, and shortly afterward broke the sound barrier.

As they penetrated the denser layers of the atmosphere, the moment of first stage separation arrived. With a powerful jolt, the Super Heavy separated from the Starship's second stage. The engines of the second stage ignited to propel the Ambassador further on its journey into orbit. Rachel couldn't help but feel a moment of awe as she gazed at the fading Earth below them, which she could see on one of the monitors providing camera data.

They reached Mach 3 in the flight's second stage, and Rachel felt the extreme G-forces acting on her body. She concentrated on breathing calmly and releasing the tension in her body as she adapted to the unfamiliar sensations. She was fascinated by the precision with which the engines worked to bring the spaceship into the correct orbit.

After passing through the mesosphere, the Starship finally reached the exosphere, where the atmosphere is extremely thin and the transition to space occurs. Here the separation of the payload fairing that had protected the Starship during the ascent took place. With a soft click, the fairing separated and Rachel could see the vast expanse of space before her.

As they approached the planned orbit, Rachel felt gravity begin to ease up, and her body began to shed its weight. The second stage thrusters were shut down, and the Starship was now in a stable orbit around Earth, ready for the prepared new booster that would provide their thrust to Mars. Rachel was amazed at the beauty of Earth passing beneath her and suddenly felt tiny, like a drop floating above the ocean.

While the Ambassador maintained its orbit and Adam

and Madeleine prepared for the docking maneuver with the booster, Rachel slowly began to breathe consciously.

They had made it into orbit.

"Ambassador, this is Mission Control." It was Lucille. But they were supposed to be talking to the Head of Flight Control. Rachel tensed reflexively. Something was wrong.

"Ambassador here, we're listening."

"We have a problem."

15

CHRISTER

"Are you awake?" he heard the voice from the speaker on his phone.

"Yes, I am, now," Christer grumbled, trying to fully dispel the dream that was only slowly slipping away from him. He had been swimming with a dolphin and had tried to bake bread, only to find that he had no salt with him – apparently it had dissolved in the sea, which was why he'd had to bake with just water and flour. The dolphin had been upset with the 'baking result' and then swam off to explain to disabled children in Japan why he normally avoids their shores.

"Mr. Johannsen?" Wayan asked, obviously not for the first time.

He cleared his throat. "Okay, I'm awake."

He swung his legs out of bed. The air conditioning hummed incessantly in the background. The anachronistic-looking alarm clock on his bedside table showed him in red digital format that it was 6:33 in the morning. "Has a nuclear war broken out?"

"No."

"Then why are you calling me?"

"I expected you to still be working," the agent replied.

"I was working ... on reducing my sleep deficit. What is it?"

"I found out what you wanted to know."

"That fast?" he asked, puzzled.

"Yes. I work for the domestic intelligence service. My information channels are usually quite direct," she replied. "Don't you want to hear what I have?"

"Yes, I do." He set the smartphone to one side after putting it on speaker and tried to rub the sleep out of his eyes. "Go ahead."

"There were proceedings on suspicion of corruption in the award procedure for the mining concessions. The Mount Gede Pangrango National Park was inaugurated in 1980, but was only protected by legislative action in 1983. The three years in between were a gray area. Nevertheless, the allocation was highly controversial."

"Who was accused?"

"A senior civil servant in the Ministry of Construction and the serving Minister of Energy."

"What company?"

"Megah Adara Tbk was accused of having bribed the aforementioned decision-makers. The case was eventually dropped. Megah Adara won the bidding contest because they not only had the financial strength to make the exploration a success, but also the experience. It is the merger of two energy companies from the 1970s: Adara Energy and Tambangrayu Megah. The former specialized in early photovoltaics and wind turbines, the latter in coal mining and power generation."

"So they had the necessary know-how for drilling and presumably wanted to get into the nuclear sector, should there be a decision in favor of uranium mining and corresponding nuclear technology for power generation. I see."

Christer nodded, even though she couldn't see him, and looked out through the window next to his bed at the lights of Jakarta. They formed a sea of fireflies below him, stretching from horizon to horizon, beautiful but also restless. "What were the results?"

"What results?" asked Wayan. "The exploration permits were revoked a year later. No shafts were created."

"They were certainly digging and taking measurements before the first drill was set to work." He snorted. "No company foolishly throws money away at a concession auction without having minimized the risk beforehand."

"Nothing is known about this."

"Not officially."

"No," contradicted the agent. "Not even unofficially."

"How sure are you about your source?" he asked.

"Very sure. My informant sits at the relevant levers in the Ministry of Justice and has put his own assistant on the research. Megah Adara has surrendered the concession as requested and withdrawn from the exploration area."

"Monitored by the state, I presume?"

"No, but the sites submitted by the company for drilling at the time were visited and inspected after the deadline. Everything was properly sealed and abandoned," she explained.

"Mm-hmm," Christer said. His mind was already working again.

"You don't believe it."

"Of course not. Who checks things like that?"

"An employee of the Ministry of Energy or the Environment, usually together with a ranger, as it was already a nature reserve," the agent replied and paused. "You think they were bribed?"

"If Megah Adara was already suspected, there's a good chance of it. How hard would it have been for them to financially secure a few lowly officials and a ranger back then?" he asked. "Especially in a nature reserve that's half the size of my home country, and where no one is likely to look too closely afterward because it's all deserted. There are no roads there, I assume?"

"Right. What's your theory?"

"Megah Adara only applied for the concessions back then because they had already discovered uranium deposits. So, there was illegal pre-exploration. One hundred percent. Then they won, jumped on it, and paid a lot of bribes. If I understood you correctly, they didn't even sue the government for breach of contract."

"That is correct."

"So they seized an opportunity, made a few more bribes, and kept digging – with the help of foreign specialists they kidnapped because they couldn't have recruited them officially," he continued. "Corporations are easy to see through. Everyone is accountable to the board, and the board is not accountable to anyone if they do things right. Only to their shareholders, but everything is pre-filtered for them. The main thing is that the figures are right, because then nobody asks questions."

"They didn't officially recruit anyone, because then the government authorities could have made a connection. Maybe we should take a look at that area ourselves," Wayan suggested – although it sounded more like a decisive statement.

"You can obviously read minds through the phone." Christer smiled, although the idea of having to descend into the green hell made him feel queasy.

"Meet me in the lobby in half an hour."

"From now?"

"Yes."

"Shouldn't we get a few people together first?" he asked, and the last bit of his sleepiness was blown away.

"No, the two of us can do it," Wayan said.

"Is that a good idea? I mean, the jungle isn't exactly safe."

"Are you afraid?"

"Yes."

The agent snorted – or perhaps it was a sound of amusement. "You're being honest. That's good."

"It's about politics, am I right?"

"My job is always about politics. If we make a big fuss out of the investigation, Megah Adara will make sure that heads roll. Our heads. It is the largest energy supplier in the country and has a virtual monopoly in Jakarta. Its influence is correspondingly great."

"Only if we don't find anything," he said.

"Yes."

"So you think we won't find anything?"

"I'm not secure enough to put my job on the line for this, and it could take my superiors with me."

"All right, then. See you shortly."

Christer hung up and ran his hands over his face. He couldn't shake the feeling that he was going to curse his unerring instinct – because it not only told him that he had discovered a pattern, as had often been the case, but he knew that the mission's danger level had just increased with their decision.

16

Deep beneath the icy surface of the Arctic Ocean, the Russian nuclear submarine glided like a shadow through the endless darkness. On board the steel colossus, an atmosphere of tense calm prevailed as the crew went about their daily tasks. They were specialists in their fields, handpicked and trained to operate in the most hostile environments on Earth. Yet despite their professionalism, there was an undeniable tension in the air as they knew they could be ordered to unleash their deadly cargo at any moment.

Lieutenant Commander Grigori Morozov was experienced enough and, as commander, was able to recognize and control the tension among his crew. He spent his time going from station to station, talking to his subordinates and encouraging them to be alert and ready to act at all times. His presence created a sense of security and trust among the men, who knew they were in the hands of a capable leader.

In the narrow corridors of the ship, technicians and engineers monitored the countless systems and machines that kept the submarine running. They made sure the nuclear reactors were stable, the batteries were charged, and the air supply and life support systems were working properly. It was a never-ending routine, but one they carried out with cool discipline.

Meanwhile, in the darkness of their cabin, the sonar technicians worked to keep the submarine hidden from enemy ears. NATO had been on heightened alert for days, now that the launch of the Mars mission was approaching. They listened carefully to the sounds of the ocean and analyzed the echoes to ensure they remained undetected. Their work was crucial, as they knew their survival depended on their ability to move silently through the depths of the sea.

Inside the submarine, in a specially secured room, was the reason for the tense atmosphere on board: a state-of-the-art ballistic missile capable of hitting any target with deadly precision. The weapon was the result of years of research and development, and it embodied the pinnacle of Russian missile technology. It was designed to be fired in complete silence and without warning, making it an invisible and deadly threat to anyone within its range. At its last test, Morozov had not yet been a commander, but had been confirmed in his desire to lead his own submarine command.

In this atmosphere of vigilance and tension, the long-awaited and much-feared order suddenly came, although no one dared to verbalize it. A coded signal reached the bridge, its message unequivocal: take aim at the target and prepare for the launch.

LtCdr. Morozov passed on the order and everyone hurried to carry out their tasks. The tense silence on board turned into a hectic buzz as the crew made every effort to bring the submarine into the correct position and prepare the missile for launch. To do this, they altered course slightly to aim for an ice-free spot in the North Sea that was even closer than the one previously mapped 20 miles ahead.

The navigation officer monitored the instruments and

calculated the submarine's exact location, while the depth rudder and helm crews worked together to bring the ship into a stable firing alignment. The sonar technicians increased their vigilance, making sure their sub still remained unde-tected as they approached their unseen launch site.

In the missile chamber, the weapons officers and missile specialists monitored the missile's systems and prepared it for launch. They programmed the target into the on-board computer and carried out final checks on the propulsion systems and warheads. From his command center, LtCdr. Morozov monitored every step of the process and coordi-nated the efforts of his crew to ensure that everything went smoothly. They had practiced this often enough, but knowing it was serious this time raised the proceedings to a whole new level.

The tension on board reached its peak as the submarine approached its target position a few meters below the surface and the missile was ready for launch. The missile hatch opened – just a blip on a monitor. The crew held their breath as they waited for the decisive signal from the high command in the Kremlin that could herald the beginning of a new and uncertain future.

LtCdr. Morozov looked at the faces of his crew and sensed the threatening atmosphere that filled the room. He knew that some of them were toying with mutiny because they feared the consequences, but he was also aware that no one would dare to speak their thoughts aloud or break out of the chain of command.

The submarine fell silent as the crew awaited the final order. Every man on board knew that if they took this step, there would be no turning back. They would change history in a way that could never be undone.

"Do you really think the order will come?" asked his executive officer, who was standing next to him with his arms folded and his forehead sweaty.

"If it had just been a threat, we would have been ordered to surface."

"It could still be a threat."

"Quite possibly," Morozov admitted, without believing it.

Then, in a moment that made the tension almost unbearable, a new signal came in.

Launch!

17

RACHEL

"The Russians have what?" Adam asked grimly.

"They have informed us that they are going to destroy a satellite for testing purposes, and they are going to do it now," Lucille radioed from the control center.

"Now?"

"Yes. We have just received the relevant information. Our Ministry of Foreign Affairs and the Ministry of Defense are not sure whether this is just a threat, or whether they will really go through with it."

"How long until we know?" asked Madeleine.

"They told us the target. An old communications satellite from Soviet times. It's currently over Asia in LEO, a little higher than you are at the moment. According to Space Force Command, it only takes a few minutes from launch to impact."

"Damn those Russians," cursed Raphael.

"Tensions with Moscow have risen in recent months, probably because they are not part of the project," Lucille explained, sounding almost apologetic. "But we never expected them to go this far. Maybe it's just a threat."

"What does this mean now – for us?"

"What this means for us down here remains to be seen, but for you there are two options. Either you initiate the abort sequence immediately, so as not to take any risks, or you go through to the rendezvous point with the booster earlier than planned. We can't say with certainty how the debris cloud will behave if they do proceed, but it will definitely affect the LEO, and the longer you wait, the greater the danger. The planned four hours to docking would be too great a risk."

"Understood, Mission Control. Get back to me as soon as you know anything. We'll discuss it here," Adam said. He unbuckled his seatbelt, nimbly spun around in zero gravity, and looked back at them. Rachel, still sitting in one of the four seats, had started to sweat.

"What does this mean?" she asked. "Are they planning to shoot at us and make it look like an accident because they supposedly wanted to hit a satellite?"

"No, that would trigger a war with all the nations involved. They'll have to make sure it looks like an accident."

"If they really hit a satellite, it's a disaster," Yuki said. "You have to think of the debris cloud as a funnel-shaped cloud of junk hurtling around the Earth at orbital speed, with the potential to hit many other objects in orbit – other satellites, for example. At these speeds, a fragment such as a screw has the energy of a small bomb and can shred anything in its path."

Rachel shuddered.

"Such tests are outlawed for a reason," added Raphael. "They significantly increase the risks for space travelers and can spark the Kessler syndrome."

"Kessler syndrome?"

"A chain reaction. The initial debris hits other satellites, creating yet more debris. The amount of ultra-fast space debris increases exponentially, and carries with it the risk of further collisions, until the Earth is enveloped in a sphere of different sized projectiles that makes any space travel – including new satellites – impossible. And traps humanity on our planet forever. We, on the other hand, would be locked out."

"We have no choice."

Now all eyes turned to Rachel. For a few breaths it was silent except for the buzzing of the electronics around her, which had become a constant background noise in the cockpit.

"If we turn back now ..." Liu began.

But Rachel shook her head and took a deep breath. "No. That's not what I meant. We have no choice because we can't go back."

Madeleine frowned. "There's always a choice. We should at least talk it through."

"No, she's right," Raphael said slowly and grimaced. "If we break off now, our mission will have failed. And the Russians will be blamed."

"Rightly so," Adam said grimly.

"Justly blamed or not, you know what that means. If war breaks out because of us, there may be nothing to go back to."

"It wouldn't break out because of us! Russia launched this missile."

"Being in the right doesn't prevent wars," she explained, "but if you have the opportunity to prevent a war – which would probably be Earth's last one – you have to take it. This gives everyone involved the chance to avoid escalation and to consider less definitive responses."

"She's right," Raphael agreed. The quantum physicist pointed toward the cockpit windows, in front of which the stars twinkled on the right and Earth glowed on the left.

"We're doing this in the hope of bringing a divided world together, and our families are waiting down there. We can't put them in danger just because we're worried about getting caught."

Adam nodded and looked around. One by one, they all nodded. Only now did Rachel remember that they were being overheard and watched the whole time, by billions of people. She had forgotten in the midst of the excitement.

"Raphi, Madeleine, you calculate the fastest route to the booster with the lowest possible fuel consumption. Coordinate closely with Houston. We still need enough juice in the Ambassador to land on Mars. Liu, get on the radio and adjust the planned thrust pattern for the Mars injection accordingly. That's going to mean lots of recalculations with the new mass ratios." Adam returned to his seat. "Y'all better all buckle up, because we're going to have to do some maneuvering shortly. Mission Control, do you read us?"

"All the time, Ambassador. We have heard everything, and our teams around the world are already working to support you with the appropriate calculations," replied Fred Kowalski, Head of Flight Control.

Rachel wondered if Lucille was already off to an emergency meeting or something similar, or if the missile had long since been fired. It felt awful to be forced to the sidelines, unable to do anything. She wasn't a good mathematician, nor did she understand the complex orbital mechanics that meant that no flight from point A to point B was easy. Speeds and trajectories had to be carefully planned because they were not flying in lines, but rather, between different orbits where objects were in different places at different times.

Everything was in motion like handfuls of marbles circling in a wide and shallow funnel. Added to this was the almost 30,000 kilometers per hour at which everything was racing around the Earth in low Earth orbits. Under these conditions, precise communication and navigation were essential, especially as their orbital path was not as empty as most people thought. There were countless satellites that must not be hit. Even the smallest collision could mean the end.

Ironically, their sudden change of plan increased the risk of this, even though they were only doing it to avoid a possible debris cloud. There was a reason why weeks of meticulous planning had determined their trajectory.

"Ambassador, this is Mission Control. The Pentagon has just confirmed that there has been a missile launch from the Arctic Ocean."

18

The Nudol ASAT unleashed its tremendous power as 2,500 kilonewtons of thrust catapulted it out of the rocket hatch. In a fraction of a second, the projectile broke through the surface of the water and hurtled into the sky. The rocket engine of the first stage, which contained a mixture of dinitrogen tetroxide and an asymmetric dimethylhydrazine, ignited and set off a chemical reaction that released an almost unimaginable amount of energy.

As the rocket passed through the troposphere, huge amounts of water and air swirled around its hull. The air, heated by the rocket's blistering heat, began to ionize, creating a trail of light that was visible for miles and made the ice of the Arctic Ocean shimmer. Despite the enormous speed of several kilometers per second that the rocket had now reached, it was still affected by terrestrial gravity.

When it arrived in the stratosphere, the conditions changed dramatically. The first stage separated and plummeted back toward the surface. The air became thinner and resistance decreased, allowing the second stage to ascend even faster. Temperatures dropped to minus 60 degrees Celsius, and the rocket had to use its internal systems to protect the sensitive electronics from the cold.

After passing through the stratosphere, the rocket reached the mesosphere, where temperatures dropped even further. Here it unfolded its aerodynamic fins and used the remaining traces of the atmosphere to precisely correct its course. The speed increased further and catapulted the weapon toward the thermosphere.

Due to the absorption of high-energy solar radiation in the ultraviolet and X-ray range, all the particles in the thermosphere were highly excited and caused the temperature to rise to almost 2,500 degrees, which had hardly any effect on the rocket body due to the low particle density. The second stage was separated and seemed to drift weightlessly away into the darkness for a moment. The rocket now ignited its final stage to take the last step into orbit. At a speed of 7.9 kilometers per second, it now sped around the planet, only about 200 kilometers away from its assigned destination.

Invisible to the human eye, but closely tracked by the highly sensitive sensors on and in the warhead, an old Soviet communications satellite floated alone through space. Its metallic surfaces reflected the sunlight and radiated the heat into the cold vacuum of space.

The missile approached its target like a predator sneaking from the shadows. The on-board computers calculated the final trajectory to hit the satellite with deadly precision. In the final seconds of the approach, when the missile was already less than a kilometer away from the satellite, its nozzles fired one last time to fine tune the impact angle and speed.

The impact was tremendous. The missile shattered the satellite and turned it into myriads of debris that were hurled in all directions at a speed of more than 28,000 kilometers per hour. Every single particle, no matter how small, turned into a dangerous projectile that began to race around the Earth at breathtaking speed.

The energy of the impact was so powerful that some of the satellite parts were thrown down into the upper layers of the atmosphere and burned up there like fireflies. Other parts were hurled into higher orbits as a deadly shrapnel funnel.

19

RACHEL

"Strategic Command is sending us real-time data on the debris cloud, which is currently spreading in LEO," Fred stated from the control center in a calm voice. "It is not yet clear how much damage it will cause to other satellites, but it will reach your position in about twenty minutes. We're comparing the data with that of our partners at ESOC in Darmstadt and CNSA Beijing. It does not look good."

"We're just getting that data now." Adam pointed to one of the large displays further forward for the crew. It showed an almost incomprehensible mass of dots and lines of different colors. Some stood out because they were dark red and moved in a funnel shape. They looked slow in the image, but the curvature of the Earth at the bottom made it clear what distances were involved. Various dashed paths emanated from the lines and blinked intrusively where they approached green and yellow dots.

"The risk of a chain reaction is extremely high, although we can't determine it yet. You must leave your orbit immediately and move at least one hundred and fifty kilometers away from your current orbit," continued Fred from Mission Control.

"I'll initiate the thrust in thirty seconds," explained Adam.

"We haven't finished the calculations yet," Madeleine warned next to him.

"Then you can continue calculating on the way. Send Mission Control what we have. Fred, warn us if we're in danger of hitting a satellite or space debris."

"Understood. Good luck, Ambassador."

"Is everyone strapped in?" Adam waited for their confirmations and then tapped carefully on his touch displays until he had made all the entries. After a brief check, Madeleine confirmed herself as copilot, then he put a hand around the control stick on his right armrest, but didn't move it. The on-board computer took over, and manual input would only be necessary in an emergency.

In preparation for the decisive maneuver, the Ambassador activated its Raptor engines, which were based on the principle of closed-cycle combustion. The outer three at the stern roared to life, sending a sonorous roar all the way to the cockpit, 50 meters ahead. Methane and liquid oxygen mixed in the engines' combustion chambers, where they would release a tremendous amount of energy under extreme pressure and heat. The laws of physics dictated a relentless battle between the unleashed forces and the silent resistance of the void around them.

The moment the last control valve was opened, the Raptor engines unleashed their full power, a tremendous explosion of energy and thrust, precisely calculated and controlled to catapult the Starship higher, out of its current orbit. The acceleration increased steadily, pushing Rachel gently into her seat, making her feel almost like she was back on Earth.

With each passing second, the Raptor engines pushed the Starship further into the atmosphere, through the invisible layers of Earth's orbit and toward the waiting booster that had been parked in orbit weeks ago. The forces acting on the Starship's structure reached their peak when the engines unleashed a thrust of several thousand kilonewtons. Despite these unimaginable loads, the Ambassador remained stable and on course.

"It looks good," Adam exclaimed.

"Ambassador, Mission Control here," Fred reported frantically. "Abort! Correct trajectory to ..."

The radio transmission broke off abruptly as they were interrupted by a loud clonk! followed by a hiss and several red warning lights on the displays. An alarm blared.

"What's going on?" Rachel shouted.

"Madeleine?" asked Adam, typing frantically on the display in front of his head.

"We were hit," she replied with an enviable calm. "No loss of pressure so far."

"Check your helmets anyway!"

Rachel fumbled for her visor and the seal mechanism at her chin and realized that her hands were shaking and her ears were ringing. What she had initially thought was adrenaline was white noise coming from the speakers in her helmet.

"What's going on?" she asked again, but no one answered her. Adam and Madeleine were talking to each other, tense but with such professional calm that Rachel would have liked to shout at them and shake them. But instead she remained rooted to her seat.

They were obviously accelerating again, because the direction of gravity was constantly changing. Sometimes she was pushed to the left, then to the right. Yellow lights began to flicker and beg for attention. Adam used the flight stick with his right hand, so Rachel knew there was an emergency. Her head jerked back and forth, then the trajectory stabilized as weightlessness set in again.

"Trajectory stable, speed adjusted," Adam announced and took a deep breath. "Madeleine, do you see the booster?"

"On the radar, yes. Five kilometers away."

"Good, Raptors are switched off, DRACO maneuvering jets on standby."

"We lost one."

"We can cope with that. How does it look otherwise?"

"Communication is offline," Madeleine replied.

No communication? Rachel thought in horror. No contact with Earth?

"No." Only now did she realize that she had spoken that one word.

"It seems that one of the pieces of debris hit our main antenna and the control units of the redundancy systems," the copilot said.

"There's bad luck, and then there's this," grumbled Raphael next to her.

"We're still alive," Rachel commented, breathing heavily. "I wouldn't call that worse than bad luck."

She was thinking about Masha, though, and the prospect of no longer being able to speak to her. But she forced herself to calm down, hoping that there would be a solution later.

Don't panic, Rachel.

"That's right. The booster is within range, and we just have to perform the docking maneuver without the help of Mission Control. Then we'll know if we'll make it to Mars," the pilot agreed.

"What if the debris cloud has already become uncontrollable?" asked Yuki.

"At this point it's irrelevant for us. We'll concentrate on what lies ahead," Adam decided. "That's all we can do for now. First we have to make sure that the most important systems are working. Life support, for example. Fuel lines. Engines. Landing nozzles. Heat shield. Avionics and control systems."

"Everything is green for me, except for communications. The replacement antenna seems to be physically intact, but the control unit has been hit," Madeleine replied. Indeed, some of the red lights were starting to go out.

"What about the solar sails?"

"Didn't get any damage either."

"Without communication, we have no weather forecast for Mars, no updates on the landing site, no help with the calculations if something changes in the landing pattern," Raphael objected. "We'll have to improvise."

"We could reconfigure one of the CubeSats to use it as a relay station," Liu suggested.

"Good idea," said Adam. "But only after we've started our journey. The window is small and short. Madeleine, check the atmosphere in here for any chemical residue that might indicate a leak of some kind. Then we'll start the docking maneuver."

Adam ran his eyes over the controls and instruments that filled his display in full digital form. Every digit, every indicator bore witness to the incredible precision required for the upcoming docking maneuver. Rachel watched him as if hypnotized.

The first step was to adjust Ambassador's speed and trajectory to that of the Super Heavy booster, a 70-meter-long tube that lay in the darkness. Through the window, it could be seen as a shimmering line illuminated by the sun's rays.

Adam used the spaceship's reaction thrusters to make fine adjustments to the trajectory. At the same time, he carefully monitored the telemetry data collected by the spacecraft's sensors and LIDAR systems. This information gave him valuable insights into the relative position and speed of the two spacecraft. Madeleine confirmed each of these on her own screen and gave him appropriate feedback.

With a watchful eye, Adam observed the rate of approach, which steadily decreased as the distance between the two spacecraft diminished. Time passed in slow motion as they drew closer and closer. Finally, the Ambassador was close enough to the booster to use the rendezvous radar and docking camera. These instruments provided a precise picture of the orientation and position of the docking devices.

Adam activated the Starship's docking clamps and switched to manual control mode. He now had to take control and execute the last few meters of the maneuver with precision. Every movement had to be accurate. A misstep could have catastrophic consequences and destroy the booster, and potentially them as well.

With gentle movements, he steered the Ambassador into the correct position while he checked the visual displays and telemetry data.

"Very gently," Madeleine said earnestly. "That's looking good."

The distance continued to shrink, centimeter by centimeter, until only one meter separated their stern from the booster's bow. Rachel watched the black-and-white image, artificially brightened by the on-board computer, seeing a huge ring as the camera approached. The contact nozzle seemed to circle slightly and was aimed right in the middle of the Super Heavy's funnel-shaped frame.

"Contact," Adam reported, exhaling a long breath. Madeleine pressed her display and the clamps closed around the docking device with a soft but audible click that seemed to spread through the hull of their spaceship.

The docking maneuver had been successfully completed.

Immediately and automatically, the on-board systems of the two spacecraft began synchronizing data and checking the connection. The Ambassador and the booster were now merged into a single spacecraft, 120 meters long – the same as at launch – and ready to continue their mission.

The relief in the cockpit was palpable. They all exhaled and shook hands. Adam gave the go-ahead for them to take off their helmets and unbuckle their seatbelts.

"All right, that's that. We're now several hours ahead of schedule. I suggest we look for solutions to our communication problem and get as accurate a picture as possible of the Ambassador's condition before we light this candle," Adam said.

As it turned out in the hour that followed, they learned four pieces of debris had penetrated the hull below the habitat areas beneath them, which was extremely lucky. None of the many thousands of heat tiles were damaged, as only the top had been hit. The leaks in the steel weren't emitting any gases, so they weren't losing anything.

Nevertheless, Madeleine seemed concerned that they would have to do a spacewalk on the way so that when they entered the Martian atmosphere there would be no problem that could no longer be controlled. It didn't matter for their journey through the vacuum unless more serious damage was yet to be discovered.

However, the communication system and its redundant replacement systems could not be repaired because they simply did not have access to them, which seemed extremely improbable, but it was their new reality.

"We could try sending optical signals through the window," Raphael suggested as they hovered next to the seats and discussed how to proceed. "Flashes of light. We can be sure they have directed everything they can at us."

"They are already receiving data from the booster and know that we have successfully docked," Madeleine said.

"Nevertheless, we have to try to inform them," said Adam. "We could try to drop a signal in the VHF or UHF range. The ISS hasn't disappeared around the bend yet and could pick it up."

"The range is really marginal. They would probably only pick up scraps."

"Then those scraps should be meaningful. The fact is that they're eavesdropping as best they can right now, so we should take advantage of that," Adam replied.

"First of all, we have to improvise such an antenna. And then it would be inside here, where we are well shielded because of the cosmic radiation," Liu pointed out.

"We have the materials for the CubeSats. They have UHF antennas," Madeleine suggested.

Adam nodded. "Let's get to work. Then we'll let them know we're moving on and heading for Mars."

20

CHRISTER

They drove away from his hotel in a car that Wayan had rented with an obviously fake identity.

Christer spent most of the journey with his nose pressed against the window. He looked at the houses that lined the streets like pearls on a string. The façades were scarred by the tropical humidity and looked disorderly with the many 220-volt power lines that snaked in bundles from house to house. Nevertheless, they exuded an unmistakable charm. A multitude of colorful signs advertised stores and restaurants – a vibrant world that revealed the pulse of the city. The first rays of sunshine were still hiding behind the horizon, but it was already getting warm. Rather, even warmer.

The streets filled with the swelling murmur of traffic, and the metropolis seemed more and more to adopt a common rhythm. Cars and motorcycles wound their way through the maze of alleys and streets, while pedestrians moved along narrow sidewalks through the urban bustle as if following invisible lines on the asphalt. Occasionally Christer caught a glimpse of the Ciliwung as it flowed through the city like a silent witness, its waters mysterious and unapproachable. It carried the filth of human civilization out to sea, stinking, and exposing the human inability to really think about tomorrow.

The journey took them out of the center of Jakarta and into the suburbs, where the houses became smaller and marked by poverty. They gave way to corrugated iron huts and improvised tents here and there, until finally nature took their place. Vast rice fields stretched to the horizon, interspersed with palm and baobab trees that bore witness to the fact that this land had once been claimed from the jungle. From time to time, Christer discovered small villages that rested like pearls in a green oasis, their huts made of bamboo and wood surrounded by tropical gardens.

The road Wayan took next grew worse and worse, winding through the hilly tropical landscape like the remnants of a lost civilization. The few other cars they encountered had to keep braking to avoid potholes in which entire motorcycles could seemingly disappear.

The mighty Pangrango had been visible in front of them for some time. Its lofty volcanic cone rose out of the mountain range of West Java, densely overgrown like a green giant. The rugged contours stood out against the sapphire sky and seemed to grow larger and more impressive with every kilometer. The volcano towered over the landscape like an ancient guardian, its flanks covered in dense forests – a beautiful sight.

The thought that corrupt politicians could have sold off something so beautiful to money-grabbing mining companies depressed him.

As they approached the first foothills of the Pangrango, the roads became even narrower and bumpier. Brittle asphalt was replaced by gravel and hard clay, which probably turned into impassable mud during the rainy season. They passed small plantations where coffee, tea, and spices were grown – the fragrant treasures of Java, exported all over the world.

With every kilometer they covered, they seemed to travel deeper into the past. Sparsely populated and cultivated by poor farmers, nothing here reminded him that one of the world's largest metropolises lay just a few dozen kilometers away – apart from the smog dome that could be seen in the rear-view mirror sitting over the landscape like an unnatural cloud.

Finally, they reached a secluded clearing at the end of a mountain path, where they parked the car. The sun had fully risen by now. It had taken them almost two and a half hours to cover 60 kilometers. In the last half hour, he had seen no evidence of human civilization.

"Are you sure your contact will be here?" Christer asked doubtfully as he surveyed the small gravel parking area. A weathered wooden sign informed them that they were now in a national park. A board next to it had probably once served as a list of rules of conduct, but it was so old and weathered by the omnipresent damp that none of it was legible.

"I don't know. I booked him on the internet," explained the agent. She had not worn her usual trouser suit today, but instead the clothes of a tourist – lightweight shirt, hiking pants with zipper pockets, and a wide-brimmed hat. She had taken her disguise so seriously that she even had a selfie stick with her.

"On the internet?"

"I told you we were doing this undercover."

"You think I'm chasing a mirage," he speculated.

"Yes. But you're the UN's expert, so I'll do my best to see the mirage too. That's only possible if we don't attract attention."

Christer opened the car door and took a deep breath of fresh mountain air. It was his first free breath in weeks and it felt good. The humidity was still formidable, but no longer so oppressive. A narrow path stretched out in front of him, winding through the dense green of the jungle and leading into the unfathomable depths of the volcano.

And from this path, a local man in a green T-shirt came toward them. "Hi," he said with a broad grin. "I'm Suparman."

"Superman?"

"Suparman is an Indonesian first name, Darling," Wayan purred. She looked changed, a little affected and excited. She ran to Suparman's side with her smartphone and took a selfie with him before he had fully collected himself. But the hiking guide smiled politely. They were clearly not his first tourists.

"It's not often that customers ask me to start a hike from behind the southern tea plantations," Suparman explained cheerfully, pointing to her car. "Have you got drinks and stuff with you? It's going to be a long walk."

"Yes. Mats and snacks, too," Christer assured him.

"Most foreigners drive to one of the parking lots halfway up to the summit. From here we'll probably need two days."

"We don't mind, do we, Darling?" Christer asked, turning his face in Wayan's direction.

She shrugged her shoulders and adjusted her hiking pants. "Oh, how bad can it get?"

Suparman looked irritated for a moment, but quickly regained his professional smile. "Good, good, let's go then."

"Don't you have anything more than your backpack and bedroll?" Christer asked in surprise, pointing to the light pack on the back of the man, who was much smaller than himself.

"Oh, I don't need much." Suparman grinned broadly and pointed to the seemingly impenetrable greenery in front of them. "Just the jungle."

"Have you seen Congo?" Christer asked as they trudged after their hiking guide along a tiny trail.

"No, what's that?"

"A film adaptation of Michael Crichton's novel of the same name. Gorillas guarding a secret, and greedy humans who want to uncover it. Most of them die."

Wayan laughed. It was the fake laugh of her new persona. "There are no gorillas here, Darling."

Only now did he realize that he had just been addressed by his supposed 'wife.'

"But snakes," she continued. "And poisonous frogs. And leeches."

"I don't like the jungle very much," he grumbled. "Everything wants to kill me."

"Most of it just wants a piece of you."

"Oh, well, that makes me feel much better," he replied sarcastically.

They silently followed their guide into the impenetrable jungle, which enveloped them like an overgrown relic of civilization. The vegetation was dense – wild and uncontrollable – a labyrinth of intertwined branches and lianas, which relentlessly confronted them. As they carefully made their way along the barely existing paths, the damp, stuffy air enveloped their bodies and seemed to whisper ominous warnings to him. Everything here was living and dying at the same time. It smelled both of must and fresh leaves, flowers and excrement in equal measure. Intense and ominous.

The jungle seemed to be an entity unto itself, jealously guarding its secrets and concealing them behind a confusing veil. The sounds made by the exotic animal residents worked their way deep into Christer's ears, a strange concert that simultaneously captivated and disturbed him. The shadows of the huge leaves danced around him in the pale light filtering through the dense canopy, transforming the ground into a bizarre mobile patchwork of shifting light and dark.

The air tasted of secrets, and Christer increasingly felt that not only had his instincts let him down, but as oftentimes before, they had once again put him in danger. The unknown lurked everywhere, and the dangers were at least as numerous as his fears about what they might find at the end of their trek. He felt like an intruder in a strange world, at the mercy of unseen eyes lurking in the shadows.

As they moved deeper into the heart of the wilderness, Christer noticed how the jungle around them changed, as if it were a living creature that sensed their presence and slowly turned against them. First were the leeches, which numbed his skin with their initial bites, so that he barely felt anything until they became so heavy the weight tugged at his skin. Then came the mosquitoes, attracted by his sweat. They landed on every space not covered by his clothes. Although Suparman was showing them the way, Christer could not shake the unsettling feeling that they were in a world that wasn't meant for them – a world that would devour them if they weren't careful.

They walked until the last hours of the evening before setting up camp, and although he was surrounded by dense, fecund vegetation, he felt like he was on a platter. Before the first light of day, he would know that all of today's fears had been proven wrong – because things were about to get much worse.

21

RACHEL

For the first two weeks after they left Earth orbit to make their way to Mars – or rather, toward the place in Mars' orbit where the Red Planet would be in three months' time – Rachel cried every night. She missed Masha and worried constantly – ironically – that her daughter might be worrying about her. But these concerns were relegated to the nights when she floated strapped into her sleeping bag, struggling to sleep. Thoughts from the night were not meant for the day, and so she distracted herself with work during the waking hours, which they had set for 16-hour days by using the daylight lamps on board.

After they had sent a signal to the ISS – or at least they thought they had – Adam had fired the booster's Raptor engines and initiated the trans-Mars injection to shoot them out of their stable Earth orbit and into the pre-planned 'Hohmann transfer orbit' to Mars. The thrusters had fired for eight minutes, giving them a final taste of gravity before they slid into the endless drift phase at maximum speed and it had become frighteningly quiet.

While the first few hours had been exciting, as they had

hung from the windows to admire the increasingly impressive starry background, the depth of space, it had quickly become clear why it was so important to stick to daily schedules. Her colleagues had enough to do – with experiments and simulations, as well as preparations for their time on Mars – to fill several years. Many of the tasks for which there had been no time on Earth had simply been shifted to the travel phase.

They certainly had plenty of material, because the Starship was designed for a payload of 100 tons, and with the help of the booster, the planning teams had been able to make full use of this enormous capacity.

The spaceship consisted of the cockpit at the very top, and a viewing deck at the very front that offered the best view and plenty of room to enjoy the weightlessness – a gimmick that had been argued over until the last possible moment. In the end, however, the opinion prevailed that they would need enough space for a bit of fun along the way.

One floor down was the work module, eight meters in diameter, containing various workbenches for zero-G and Martian gravity, laboratory equipment, and chemical and biological materials behind well-secured flaps. Below this was the exercise module with all kinds of exercise equipment so that they wouldn't suffer from muscle atrophy on the way, and one more level below was their living module with a communal dining area, storage compartments, and their bunks.

Even deeper were the storage rooms in which the endless number of transport crates were magnetically or physically lashed down.

Thanks to her efforts during the first two weeks, Rachel knew exactly where everything was. After her two hours of exercise each day, she had gone through one list after another and, as needed, asked her colleagues what this or that meant.

She did not want to be a burden to them and intended to make herself as useful as possible as quickly as possible.

On one of the days after she had slept particularly poorly, she found Liu in the lab after completing her exercise session and a quick 'shower.' He was assembling something complex-looking on one of the workbenches. He had secured his feet under the loops on the floor and was using his hands to assemble the various components, which were attached individually to one of the magnetic rails on the side.

"What are you doing?" Rachel asked curiously, glad to have a little distraction.

Liu looked up at her and smiled kindly. The Chinese man was wearing his white CNSA overalls with the Chinese flag on one shoulder and the blue Earth on a red background on the other, just like hers. "I'm experimenting a bit with possible setups for after we arrive on Mars."

"I thought people like you only hung out over telescope data," she replied.

"People like me?" He raised an eyebrow and laughed. "I studied physics and did a PhD in optics and photonics because it's not so theoretical right now. There are lots of experimental applications in my field."

"I must confess that I always thought that photons were particles of light," she said apologetically.

"Basically, they are, except that unlike other particles, they also have wave properties. Photons are the elementary quanta of electromagnetic radiation and the basic building blocks of light. They belong to the family of bosons, particles that are responsible for mediating fundamental forces in nature, in this case the electromagnetic force. They are massless at rest, but they have energy and momentum that is closely linked to their frequency or wavelength. Their energy can be calculated using Planck's famous formula $E = h\nu$, where E is the energy, h is Planck's quantum of action, and ν is the frequency of the photon."

Rachel cleared her throat, but Liu didn't seem to notice in his enthusiasm.

"Photons exhibit both wave and particle characteristics, a phenomenon known as wave-particle duality. In their wave nature we encounter phenomena such as interference and diffraction, while their particle properties can be expressed in other phenomena such as the Compton effect or the photo-electric effect.

"One of the most fascinating phenomena in photonics is quantum entanglement, which you've probably heard of, where pairs of photons are created in a state where the prop-erties of the two photons are instantaneously correlated, even over large distances. Entanglement has led to groundbreaking developments such as quantum communication and quantum cryptography.

"Photons therefore play a crucial role in our under-standing of the universe and the technologies that shape our everyday lives – from optical communication to energy gener-ation from sunlight. If those aren't concrete applications of my field, I don't know what is."

"Do you think such entanglement effects have anything to do with the signal on Mars?" asked Rachel.

"In my opinion, that would be a first clue, yes. Most of the experiments we have carried out on Earth on quantum entanglement are based on experiments with photons. We can entangle them with each other at will. In doing so, it is possible to correlate their polarization or energy properties."

"As with Bell's principle of inequality."

"Exactly." Liu nodded. "Photons are sent to two detec-tors that are far apart to see if the measurements of one photon immediately affect the measurements of the other. And they do. Einstein lightheartedly called this 'spooky action at a distance,' and it is indeed mysterious. We still have no explanation. We only know that it happens – but, only at the time of the measurement."

"Does that mean that if we reach Mars and find the photon beacon there again, we could measure one of the lightbulbs there and in Jakarta at the same time to find out whether the phenomenon there is related to the one on Mars?" asked Rachel, intrigued. "Then we could theoretically see if the two are entangled."

"Theoretically, yes. But there are several problems. The measurement causes the entanglement state to collapse. The connection, if you want to call it that, is destroyed. In addition, we would have to determine the time very precisely so that we can draw the appropriate conclusions."

Liu thought more deeply and paused his construction project.

"There is another problem that is even more serious. Such experiments were carried out with generated photons, not with existing ones. They would both be measured immediately after their creation, if they were also photon sources in Jakarta."

"You don't sound like you believe that."

"Photons are not created just like that – at least not as luminous emitters. They are created in the form of thermal radiation when the temperature is above absolute zero – in other words, almost everywhere. The sun or a hot stove top. There is also chemo- and electroluminescence, such as fireflies or light-emitting diodes. Fluorescence and phosphorescence. Radioactive decay - gamma radiation - is also a natural source."

"None of these is an option for Mars or Jakarta, am I right?"

"No." Liu shook his head. "I should say yes, you are right. That's the big mystery. Photons are only produced locally in filaments when an electric current flows through them. And on the surface of Mars? Completely out of the question."

"I don't understand that," Rachel objected. "You said that photons are created by heat. Temperatures above absolute zero are everywhere where atoms are moving, so in fact they're pretty much everywhere. So, there are photons everywhere."

"Correct. Photons are emitted and absorbed incessantly, almost everywhere. Even out here there is cosmic background radiation in the form of microwave radiation. It still comes from the hot expanding universe after the Big Bang. But this is not comparable to an emitter source that gives birth to photons so locally and densely," Liu said. "There is simply no explanation for this."

He put a few more parts together and then seemed satisfied.

"What's that?" She eyed the device. "It looks like a slightly misshapen mailbox from Montana."

"This is a microwave radiometer. We can use it to measure the cosmic background radiation and ..."

"Try to keep it simpler this time," she requested.

"It consists of a sensitive antenna that receives microwaves from different directions and a receiver that converts the received signals into electrical signals. The electrical signals are then amplified and analyzed to determine the intensity of the microwave radiation in the observed direction. In this way, a microwave radiometer can provide information about the temperature, humidity, and other environmental factors associated with microwave radiation."

Liu tapped the small device. "One of these was supposed to be installed from the beginning, and there is one in the bow, but not inside here."

"The one in the bow is out of action, isn't it?"

"Yes, probably hit by one of the pieces of debris." Liu sighed. "I hope Earth still exists when we get back."

"Me, too," Rachel murmured, raising her eyebrows as he pressed a cable into her hand.

"Go ahead and plug it in. I'll get the tablet and we can take an initial test measurement. How does that sound?"

"Okay, sure."

Liu pulled his feet out of the loops and flew over to one of the cabinets to grab a tablet. He attached it to his forearm with the hand strap so as not to lose it in the weightlessness and returned to her just as she'd inserted the plug.

"Tada," she said, performing an awkward bow. "I have made electricity."

"A born engineer," he joked, and began tapping relevant areas on the tablet's display to establish the Bluetooth connection to the microwave radiometer. "There we have it. And here's the first data."

He waved her over and turned his arm so she could see what he was receiving. The program looked boring and tidy, just as she had expected.

"On the left are the numerical values, on the right are color-coded charts, the big one down there is the graphical representation, diagrams in this case," Liu explained, pointing to a line at the very top of the coordinate system that had tiny downward indentations.

"Is it good that it's so high up?"

"The X and Y axes are still loading the reference values, which sometimes takes a while. The whole thing probably drops when the data is sorted accordingly, that happens more often."

The numbers finally loaded and gave the diagram proportions. At the bottom was the measurement period, and on the left, the spectral intensity.

"There must be an instrument error," Liu muttered.

"What do you mean?"

"The values are almost off the top of the scale. Normally the cosmic background radiation is the same everywhere. It has an almost perfect black body spectrum. But this …"

"Liu? Why do you sound so worried?" Rachel asked tensely.

"This is either a misreading or we're dealing with a solar event," he replied, leaning forward to check some connections. "I hope it's the former. Otherwise we have a serious problem because we won't survive the flight to Mars."

"What?" she gasped.

"Please do me a favor and tell the others to meet me in the cockpit."

Rachel wanted to ask if it was really that serious, but the strain in Liu's voice was answer enough. She floated over to the nearest switch for the ship's intercom and announced that they should meet in the cockpit immediately. Liu, meanwhile, typed on his tablet, and the furrows on his brow deepened.

"Are you coming, Liu?" she asked when she reached the circular opening at the top. She had to say his name again before he flinched and nodded.

22

CHRISTER

The first signs that the former exploration area was not as deserted as publicly assumed came in the middle of the night. He was jarred from sleep by a distant roar, perhaps also by the accompanying slight tremor that made it feel like he was lying on a vibrating table.

They slept on thin camping mats in the middle of the jungle between a stream and a small hill. Suparman had laid out a plastic sheet on the ground to protect them from the smaller jungle creatures.

When Christer had awakened it was pitch black except where the moonbeams penetrated the canopy, and the many-voiced bird concerts had been silent for at least two hours. Apart from the occasional calls of monkeys or other animals he didn't know, it was silent.

Christer looked at Wayan next to him, lying peacefully curled up on her mat, her clothes as sweaty as his own. Suparman on the other side lay on his back, hands clasped behind his head, snoring softly.

Apparently neither of them had heard it. Just as he was wondering whether he had imagined it, he heard it again: a distant roar, followed by a low-threshold, mechanical beeping, like the warning systems that construction vehicles use when they shift into reverse.

The fact that he had heard it at all was probably due to his shallow sleep after Suparman had instructed him to be careful when peeing during the night because of the snakes, which preferred to hunt frogs after dark. Without a protective tent around him, Christer felt like he was on the receiving end of all sorts of dangerous animals. He knew there were also wild boars and tigers in the Indonesian jungle.

His body begged for rest after barely sleeping the previous night and wandering through this green hell all day, but his head wasn't going to let him rest. The noises somehow resembled those of a city, yet the nearest town was many dozens of kilometers away.

The quake – perhaps he had just imagined it – had not been particularly strong, and statistically it trembled more or less strongly every day on Java. But he had noticed the strange noises twice now.

He looked over at Wayan and again at Suparman but rejected the idea of waking them. Instead, he crawled to the end of his damp sleeping mat and sat up. Since they were in a tiny clearing and the moon was at its zenith, he could make out a surprising amount of his surroundings: the various trees all around, the outlines of vines and creeping plants clinging between and to the tree trunks. He could discern the stones, moss lichens, and mushrooms.

The rocky hill, which was open and rough on this side as though half the slope had just broken off, was crowned by a banyan tree, its drooping branches developing roots that penetrated the Earth again and became more trunks. The upper branches fanned out for 30 or 40 meters, forming whimsical shadows in the pale light of the moon.

Christer let his gaze wander over the damp rainforest

undergrowth and tried to imagine how many snakes might be lying in wait between himself and the banyan tree. He was just toying with the idea of going back to lie down again and waiting until it got light when the noises started up again.

"All right," he whispered, and got to his feet with a groan. "Dear snakes, there are no frogs here."

He took his forehead flashlight, which Wayan had bought at a hikers' outfitter, and made his way to the small hill. He took the time to check everywhere for snakes, but as expected, he didn't find any. During the day, Suparman had repeatedly pointed out various wild and small animals around them, most of which had only become recognizable when their guide had come close enough with a stick that he had almost touched them. To the untrained urban eye, there was hardly any life here, except that which nipped at them or clung to their bodies and sucked their blood.

Having reached the top of the hill and one of the main trunks of the banyan tree, he surveyed his possible routes upward.

"This is a stupid idea, Christer," he said quietly, changing his voice as he answered himself, "Yes, you're absolutely right. But we should do it anyway and break our necks. Oh, how wonderful. That sounds really smart."

He sighed and began to climb. The bark was damp like everything else in the jungle, so he had to keep pausing to rub his hands dry one after the other before reaching up to each new branch. Due to the relatively dense tangle of branches, it was not particularly difficult for an inexperienced climber like himself to reach the treetop. It just took a long time because he had to continually take care not to slip.

Christer's height helped him to stick his head through the canopy like a meerkat. In doing so, he startled a flock of small birds that had obviously been sleeping there, startling himself so thoroughly he almost fell. Only when his heartbeat had slowed down a little did he take a deep breath and look around.

The hill on which this tree was located appeared to be part of a long ridge stretching east and west. In the silvery moonlight augmented by the many stars twinkling above, the landscape around him looked like a soft gray carpet. The cone-shaped Pangrango looked close enough to touch, although it was still several kilometers away, and only its sheer size was responsible for the optical illusion. The only thing separating them from its first slopes was a valley that lay between the mountain and the hill he was currently on.

He almost wouldn't have noticed the strange lights if they hadn't appeared at the right moment among the vegetation. Apparently there was a larger cleared area a few kilometers away on the edge of the Pangrango. Christer's eyes had begun accommodating to the darkness again soon after he had switched off his headlamp, and he was able to see more now. Although the clearing was not illuminated like a night construction site, it gave off a faint glow that could not be of natural origin. Contrary to what he had first thought, the lights that seemed to be flashing did not disappear behind the foliage, they were rotating. They were warning lights.

They're building there, he thought, and as if to underline his thought, he heard the distant backup beeping again. They're building inside a national park and nature reserve.

Christer would have liked to be wrong, but his instincts were apparently still more than intact. He carefully took his smartphone out of his trouser pocket and took a few photos before opening the compass app and determining the exact direction they would have to take.

When he headed back to rejoin the others, Wayan was waiting for him at the foot of the hill with her arms folded across her chest.

"I thought you were asleep," he said quietly.

"I can't sleep in the jungle," she replied. "Besides, I had to see what you were up to, wandering around at night."

He showed her the photos, the quality of which was far from ideal due to the distance and the lighting conditions.

She frowned. "You can't see much, but it looks like a night-time construction site."

"Yes." Christer nodded. "How many construction sites with heavy equipment are there in national parks like this?"

"None, because there are no access roads. Only the parking lots and a few eating areas are being built," the agent explained.

"Construction site?" asked Suparman, who was stretching on his sleeping mat and stood up yawning. "What kind of construction site?"

Christer wanted to reflexively say, "Nothing, it's fine," but in his experience, that was guaranteed to make someone even more suspicious. So he took a different approach. "I saw a building site inside the national park."

"Hmm, that's funny." The hiking guide scratched his head and stifled another yawn. "But not impossible, either. We're not here to look at building sites, are we?"

"Construction is allowed in the national park?"

"Sure, the Forestry Commission builds things from time to time."

"But along the hiking trails and such?" asked Christer.

"Yes. Mostly yes. Or it's about construction projects that serve civil protection, such as measures against flooding and things like that. There are also some measuring stations for earthquakes, seismic sensors and associated huts for the scientists who keep coming back for maintenance work," Suparman explained with a shrug. "But it's nicer further east where a whitewater river runs out of the mountains and we'll have a good chance to see hornbills."

Christer did not respond to Suparman's alternative suggestions. "And who issues building permits?"

"I have no idea." The Indonesian raised his hands helplessly, but didn't seem particularly interested in the subject either, and began to rummage through his provisions. Over the rustling, he whispered good-humoredly, "I'm not a politician or anything."

Christer looked at Wayan. "Could it be the Forestry Commission?"

"That's a good guess. The Ministry of Environment and Forestry has its own sub-authorities that are responsible for this and, for the most part, independently managing the national parks. So whoever spots a construction site in the jungle would think that the Forest Department is active."

"Yes."

"The relevant people there should be easy to bribe."

"Corruption is a serious problem in our country," Wayan explained. "But not everyone is corrupt."

"I didn't mean to say ..."

"What I'm saying is that Megah Adara wouldn't even bother paying anyone there. Those who roam the park as forest rangers and game wardens are poorly paid and have learned not to give their superiors a headache. They are probably the only ones who would stumble across a construction site in the jungle and the last ones to open their mouths. For them, it's just another project they haven't been informed about and they are better off keeping quiet if they want to keep their jobs."

"Then we should take a closer look," he suggested and she nodded, even though he saw something cloud her face. He couldn't say exactly what it was, but she suddenly looked depressed.

23

RACHEL

"How long before we sustain permanent damage at these levels?" asked Adam calmly, arms folded. They were now all in the cockpit, secured to foot straps or handholds, and the atmosphere was appropriately tense.

"That depends," Yuki replied a bit breathlessly. "If these levels ... have been there for hours ... then we've probably ... already suffered serious DNA damage." The ship's doctor had arrived in her workout clothes, her choppy speech underscored by the dark, perspiration patches under her arms and on her torso.

"We are shielded against radiation. All our water supplies are in the walls," Madeleine said, making a sweeping gesture.

"Perhaps it's another CME," Liu suggested. "Solar flares often occur in clusters, and a large ejection is often followed by smaller coronal mass ejections."

"And without contact between us and Mission Control, no one could warn us that we were flying straight into it."

"What bad luck." The Chinese man shook his head. "The space between us and our target point is gigantic, and the plasma cloud hits us directly?" he asked.

"It seems so." Adam held on to the fittings of his seat with one hand and pointed at the Japanese woman with the other. "Yuki, can you tell how bad the damage is?"

"Yes, but I would wait a few more days to make a clinical assessment. Please report any symptoms such as nausea, vomiting, weakness, dizziness, reddening of the skin, or bleeding. Since no one shows signs of burns, and no one's hair is falling out, the dose was obviously not high enough to cause acute radiation syndrome. Therefore, the duration of exposure will be crucial."

"I'll take a measurement every ten minutes," Liu decided.

Adam nodded.

"I want all of you to put on your dosimeters, even though they were only meant for Mars," Yuki said. "They're fitted with an alarm, as you know. If it goes off at any time, we'll make sure we get you into the radiation cocoon."

Adam nodded again. "Do we have enough resources on board to examine us?"

"Yes. I have everything here for tests on white and red blood cells and platelets as well as cytogenetic analyses," Yuki assured him.

"We're not taking any risks," Adam decided. "Everyone into the radiation bunker immediately. I'll go out every ten minutes to take the measurements."

Liu looked as if he wanted to object, but bowed his head.

They shimmied nimbly down through the round openings into the work area where the mailbox-like microwave radiometer was set up, and from there through the open hatch of the radiation bunker in the 'floor.'

It was a tiny room with six seats where their knees touched. It was shielded by the water from the reprocessing plant rushing around the walls as well as a layer of high molecular weight polyethylene.

They sat there for a while, during which time seemed to stretch out endlessly.

Rachel kept catching herself pulling her hair and trying to make it look like a casual scratch. In reality, she was trying to see if any tufts of hair were coming loose. In addition, she began to itch all over and imagined that these were areas of skin that were slowly opening up and starting to bleed.

What an irony it would be if they died of radiation sickness now, before they even reached Mars.

Nobody said anything until Adam opened the hatch upward after exactly ten minutes, which felt like an hour, and held out the tablet that Liu had given to him. He waited for the Bluetooth connection and then withdrew it.

"Still high, but a lot less," he said after pulling his arm back and closing the hatch.

"If the tablet still works, it can't have been too terribly bad, can it?" asked Rachel hopefully.

"Not necessarily. The fact that the electronics are still working could at least mean that the level of radiation isn't exorbitant, although everything on board here is specially built with radiation-hardened electronics and advanced shielding." Adam waved his tablet. "That's why this thing is so thick. I'm more worried about the duration of the radiation exposure. Who knows how long it's lasted?"

"That's exactly what contact with Earth is so important for," Raphael said with a sigh. "But what use is it now? At least we're finally together again, aren't we?"

"Oh, yes, I've really missed you," Madeleine replied laconically.

After the next ten minutes, during which they began to talk tentatively about their current experiments and tests, Adam took another measurement. The radiation levels had halved in the meantime and normalized after the next ten minutes.

When they slipped back into the lab, they stayed there together for a while.

"We should make a few changes," Liu suggested. "Even without the help of Earth, we must be able to warn ourselves somehow."

"I could modify one of our dosimeters and attach it to the hull. If I can establish a physical connection to us, it could give us an acoustic signal when radiation peaks are measured on the hull," Adam suggested.

"I can place it – I have a PMT experiment planned for next week, for which I have to keep the device out of the airlock. That would be a good idea."

"What's PMT?" asked Rachel.

"Photomultiplier tubes. The experiment has been planned for a long time. I want to find out if I can capture the photons from Elysium Mons out here. In six days and a few hours, we'll be in a position with a direct line to the volcanic peak," Liu explained. "If anything changes in the expected photon density, at least we'll have one more answer."

"That's how we'll do it, then," Adam said. "Yuki, please prepare the tests. I want to know as early as possible whether we should take medication."

The Japanese woman nodded and they split up again into their designated activities as if nothing had happened. Once again, Rachel felt like an outsider among her five comrades. They weren't just luminaries in their scientific fields, they were astronauts – real astronauts with enviable nerves of steel and almost unshakeable stoicism. Sometimes she wondered if she was trapped with a group of robots who weren't capable of the same emotional, irrational reactions as herself – or other humans. They seemed programmed only to their work and the goals of the mission. They never complained or whined, were always collegial and friendly, and focused with an enviable focus on what was in front of them.

And Rachel found she did envy them.

The medical examinations went quite quickly – temperature measurements, cardiovascular functions, and blood sampling. Yuki prepared the samples by labeling them and placing them in the appropriate lab equipment, where they were centrifuged to separate fat and plasma.

After a few days, during which there were no more radiation alarms, they had the results. Each of them had suffered radiation damage, which increased their risk of cancer significantly more than the long journey had already done. But there were no acute consequences, as far as the doctor could tell.

Strangely enough, this fact hardly seemed to worry anyone else in the team. It was simply accepted, nodded off, and they carried on. Without knowing how, Rachel did the same, perhaps because no one would have listened to her whining.

The EVA to attach the modified dosimeter a week later was in principle a minor matter, as Liu didn't even have to leave the airlock. The improvised device, which was the size of a very thick wristwatch, simply had to be glued to the hull. Then there was the PMT experiment, for which he had to hold a large photomultiplier tube outside for a few minutes like a fisherman with a landing net. It fell to Rachel to accompany Liu and hold his safety line, which they used to make sure he didn't accidentally lose contact with the spaceship.

Of course, she realized that she wasn't entirely needed, as the line – which was more of a cable – was naturally attached to hooks provided for this purpose. Adam probably wanted her to gain as much experience as possible, especially in terms of scary things like being confronted with the infinity of space directly from a spacesuit. In addition, the others had lots to do, and each EVA took hours to complete the complex suiting and testing procedures before they could even open the airlock's outer hatch.

When everything was ready, Liu hovered next to her in the airlock between the white walls that resembled a padded cell. With a smile, he began to speak to her, radio to radio. "Rachel, will you please open the storage box for the PMT?"

"Sure," she replied, squinting at the small light above the still closed outer hatch. It was glowing red. He seemed to notice her gaze and smiled again through his large visor. She nodded silently and opened the box, which was attached to her belt with a small clip. The device inside looked like a cross between a spark plug and a light bulb, only much larger.

"The PMT is an incredibly sensitive instrument that detects even the weakest light signals. It's really quite fascinating. Inside it is a photocathode that reacts to the detection of photons and releases electrons. These electrons are amplified by several dynodes and ultimately generate a measurable electrical signal." Liu pointed with one of his chunky gloved fingers at what looked like a flat light bulb on the front.

Rachel knew he was trying to distract her and was grateful for it. Training in a pool of water was different from being on the verge of opening a door to nowhere. From her position, there was nothing far and wide – and on a scale that didn't even exist on Earth.

Liu paused, then continued, "We want to find out whether photons are traveling from Elysium Mons on Mars toward Earth. The Ambassador is currently exactly in line between the two points. If we keep the PMT out of the airlock and point it at Elysium Mons, we should be able to detect the photons' journey and gain valuable information about the light emission from the Martian volcano."

Rachel just nodded and continued to stare at the light. It began to flash, and she pointed at it. Liu nodded and turned to the control panel for the outer hatch. A short time later, it opened in complete silence, as the airlock had long since evacuated its atmosphere.

She didn't know what she had expected, but the effect it had on her was virtually non-existent. Whether she would feel grandeur or fear, or the absolute insignificance of her existence before the magnitude of the universe – she didn't know. What did happen was that a round piece of steel moved to the side and she saw a small section of the twinkling network of stars, mostly obscured by her colleague.

It was spectacularly unspectacular when she thought about the general conditions: they were speeding away into the darkness at 100,000 kilometers per hour through a vacuum. But there was only silence, and outside the many points of light looked like motionless holes in black jewelry. Ironically, a fast car journey at home on a country road would have felt more dangerous.

Liu attached the tube to a flexible arm they had prepared so that it could protrude out of the airlock and be pointed in the direction of Elysium Mons. This took almost half an hour, during which the taikonaut tapped away on his tablet with his bulky fingertips. His movements looked like those of an arthritic senior citizen due to the stiff fabrics. When he was satisfied, he pulled back a little and hovered next to her.

"So, the alignment seems to be good. Adam, can you confirm that from the bridge?" asked Liu.

"Confirm. The first data is already coming in."

"The photons that are being emitted from the surface of Mars – if they are – hit the tube and generate electrons that are amplified by the dynodes, as I've already explained. The resulting electrical signals are sent back to the bridge via these cables and analyzed by the computer."

They watched the screen of his tablet intently as the data came in, which was also evaluated by automatic programs in the cockpit. A line diagram displayed the intensity of the detected photons in real time.

"The photon count is surprisingly high," Liu murmured, obviously fascinated by the lines, which meant absolutely nothing to her. "Normally, you would expect the light emission from the surface of Mars to be fairly uniform and dominated by solar radiation."

"But there's nothing normal about the phenomenon there, I suppose," she replied.

"No. Obviously not."

"We already knew that, though, didn't we?"

"While there are some ways a volcano on Mars could produce increased photon counts, the number of photons we're seeing here far exceeds those natural processes," he continued, as if she hadn't said anything. He swiped a graph with his index finger. Then he looked at her. "We have no explanation as to why there are so many photons buzzing around out here, but at least we know one thing now: The phenomenon above Elysium Mons is still there, and it's spewing out photons galore."

"Not in the spectrum visible to us, I presume?"

"No. In various longer and shorter wavelengths," Liu said. "We should measure again tomorrow to find out whether it's a kind of photon beam in the direction of Earth, or whether they're scattered everywhere."

"Then at least we'd know if it's a directed signal to us humans and our planet, or just a beacon that has no specific target," she thought aloud.

The Chinese man nodded in his huge helmet before he set about attaching the modified dosimeter to the hull.

24

CHRISTER

"Does this look like a Forestry Commission project to you?" he whispered. The morning was only a few hours old when they hid in the undergrowth at the edge of the clearing he had spotted during the night. It was smaller than he'd expected, barely more than 50 meters in diameter. There was a large hole in the middle with a small house next to it.

The construction vehicles he had seen and heard were tractors with special attachments. They had come along a forest path leading from the west. With their powerful wheels, they had probably simply cut the path by forcing their way through everything in front of them. Contrary to expectations, however, they were not building anything, they were planting new trees around the strange hole. Workers in camouflage clothing and olive-green safety helmets walked between the three heavy machines and gave hand signals to move the seedlings into the right places.

"They are not following any recognizable pattern," he noted.

"They want to make it look like natural rainforest growth, I suppose," Wayan replied quietly.

"Uhh, shouldn't we keep going? It's still several hours to the summit and ..."

"Shh," Christer cautioned.

Suparman behind them raised his hands defensively. He was clearly uncomfortable as a former ranger who had been taught during his career not to see anyone with more power and influence than himself out here.

Christer couldn't blame him. "What's this supposed to be? It looks like an excavation site."

"It looks like a mining tunnel to me, only without any buildings," Wayan disagreed. "There's probably been construction work of some kind in the last few weeks and months and now they're covering their tracks. That's how illegal palm oil plantations are run in nature reserves in Sumatra. One group harvests what has been illegally cultivated and another covers their tracks. There are whole mafia-like structures that have formed."

"Obviously a remnant of the concessions back then."

"Back then," Wayan echoed quietly. "That's what I don't understand. If it took place in the eighties, that's one thing. But now?"

"Megah Adara is still around, isn't it?" he asked.

"Yes."

"So it would make sense for them to operate an illegal mine – especially with regards to uranium. The value of the element has risen exorbitantly since the energy crisis following the war in Ukraine."

"But uranium smuggling is a completely different matter compared to corruption and normal illegal mining," she pointed out.

"In capitalism, everything is just a question of price." He shook his head. "I'm willing to bet that's exactly what it is: an illicit uranium mine."

"Then where are the transport vehicles? The raw materials would have to be transported away," she replied, not sounding convinced. "There must be some form of infrastructure to get the uranium ore to a port where the employees are well paid and look away at the right time or tick the correct boxes on their forms. All I see here is a hole in the jungle that is being reforested around. No real paths."

"You won't find them, either," Suparman said behind them, and something in his voice sounded different. It was no longer as breezily friendly as before, lacking the unconcerned ease he usually portrayed. Christer frowned and turned onto his side so that he could look at the local.

Instead, he stared into the muzzle of a gun aimed directly at his forehead.

"What are you doing?" Christer asked, feeling incredibly stupid. It wasn't particularly difficult to put two and two together in this case. "You work for them."

"Every hiking guide and park ranger here works for them," Suparman amended with a hint of guilt in his voice. His expression looked a little pained as he motioned for him and Wayan not to move. Christer was certain that the agent was armed, but equally certain that she had no chance of getting to her weapon faster than their newly revealed adversary could pull the trigger. The look she gave him from the side seemed to be telling him exactly that.

"Why are you telling us this?"

"Because you'll never get away from here anyway," Suparman said with a sad sigh. "Why did you have to insist on coming here? I did my best to talk you out of it."

"Sometimes we have no choice." Christer did his best to suppress the feeling of defeat that spread through his gut like a monster and tried to grab hold of his thoughts. He breathed calmly and deeply, and carefully turned onto his back. He kept his hands outstretched so as not to appear threatening.

"I don't like doing this," continued their hiking guide, and Christer believed him.

"Let's just go, then ..."

"He won't let us go," Wayan interrupted him.

"How do you know that?"

"He doesn't have a choice." She stood up and patted her hands on her hiking pants to remove the dirt from the jungle floor.

"Tuan-tuan sedang apa? Anda harus tetap berbaring! Hei, saya bicara dengan Anda! Berhenti sekarang juga, atau saya akan menembak!" Suparman started talking excitedly to her in a torrent of Indonesian and waving his gun around.

"Saya adalah bagian dari tim Anda, tenangkan diri," Wayan returned impassively. "Anda telah memberikan pertunjukan yang baik, tetapi sekarang saya yang akan mengambil alih."

"Could someone tell me what's going on here?" Christer asked helplessly. He thought about getting up too, but Suparman looked extremely upset, and it wouldn't have surprised him if the man simply pulled the trigger out of sheer nervousness.

"That's what these gentlemen will do," Wayan replied, as at the same moment two armed men came out of the undergrowth toward them. They wore ghillie suits with green and brown strips hanging down from them, rendering them almost invisible against the backdrop of the dense jungle. Only their faces were visible, although not clearly. In their hands they also held camouflaged assault rifles with short barrels.

"On your knees," ordered one of them, an American by accent. Through the dark make-up on his face, Christer could only make out the whites of his eyes. However, one look was enough to make him realize that the man would not say it twice. So he pulled himself up onto his knees and linked his hands behind his head.

"That's not necessary," Wayan said impassively. She was so calm and composed that he envied her. But only until she continued. "I delivered him as ordered."

"What are you talking about? Get down on your knees," said the other mercenary. His English wasn't perfect and had a French accent.

Mercenaries for sure, he thought, and only now did Wayan's words penetrate the adrenaline rushing in his ears. Excuse me?

"You can tell your tale to the boss. On your knees now, or blood will start dripping from your forehead," the man snapped at her, and the agent shrugged her shoulders and complied. She remained a picture of self-assurance and composure, while Christer almost wet his pants. He was a research specialist, not Rambo.

After Suparman had followed a curt order to put cable ties around their wrists and tighten them, he lifted him and Wayan to their feet. The mercenaries stayed a few meters apart and pointed to the left.

"Let's go, zack, zack!"

They were led around the clearing along a barely recognizable path. Christer was sweating from every pore. Heat and humidity were one reason, but he didn't think they were mainly responsible for the fact that he felt like he was melting. He had been in situations where criminal groups had sent thugs or even armed guards to intimidate him or, in one case, beat him up.

But these mercenaries were a different caliber. He had once spent several days with special commandos from the Germans and Israelis when assigned to find a group of kidnapped diplomats in Yemen. These two mercenaries in their ghillies reminded him of the tough guys from back then.

Someone was paying a lot of money for them, and that meant he was in deep shit and it was more far-reaching than he had suspected.

After a few minutes they were herded into the clearing, between the tractors, and toward the hole. The olive-green clothed workers supporting the reforestation efforts ignored them as if they were invisible. The fact that weapons were being handled around them didn't seem to unnerve them in the slightest – which unnerved Christer all the more.

At first he feared that the men would drive them into the hole, but then Suparman halted them with a whistle when only one step separated them from the edge. The opening measured at least ten meters in diameter and was so perfectly round that a natural cause was impossible. For the first few meters down, the walls were still visible, where soil and rock had been milled away in the same manner. Below that, it was pitch black, a yawning hole that seemed to lead into infinity.

It was creepy, especially as cold rose up from it, along with the putrid smell of rot and wet rock.

One of the mercenaries walked past them. Christer didn't dare turn his body, but watched him out of the corner of his eye. He seemed to be looking for something and then knelt down on the exposed forest floor, brushing aside undergrowth and dead leaves. Then he shouldered his rifle, did something with his hand, and pulled open a heavy metal hatch.

"Cut their cable ties," the man with the French accent ordered in Suparman's direction. Shortly afterward, Christer's hands were free and he was able to rub the red welts on his wrists. "Get down there."

Christer turned to the mercenary, who looked like a piece of forest come to life, and who pointed his weapon at the new, much smaller hole in the ground. His comrade was standing a few meters away by one of the tractors, aiming at them.

"If you'd let me in on your plan now," Christer whispered in Wayan's direction, "I'd feel a lot better."

"Shut up," the agent barked at him. "You're the loser. Get over it."

She went first and climbed down into the hole. Christer wasted no time following her despite his queasy stomach, and shortly afterward found himself on a ladder which, after about ten meters, led to a room with two elevator doors.

"Elevators?" he asked incredulously. "Out here?"

"I told you to shut up!"

"You've been in cahoots with them all this time, am I right?" He sighed. "I guess I'm not as good at my job as I told myself I was."

"Clearly not. In any case, you obviously didn't learn much about my country before you came here."

"Treason is not exclusive to certain countries. It occurs in the best of nations." He snorted laconically in a touch of gallows humor. "At least I was right."

One of the elevator doors opened. There was no floor indicator. A cold voice, English with an Indonesian accent, sounded from a loudspeaker: "Get in the elevator."

Christer looked around, but apart from the ladder behind him and the bare rock walls all around, there was no one who could force them to do anything at gunpoint. At the same time, he realized that the only way out was up, and that the two mercenaries would be waiting there to put a bullet in his head if he reappeared. So, he followed Wayan, who hadn't even hesitated, and stepped into the large cabin. There was an old-fashioned control panel with buttons that seemed to date back to the 80s, although the wall covering looked relatively new.

Without them pressing anything, the elevator started moving and descended into the unknown.

"Was I assigned to you, or did you make sure it happened this way?" he asked without looking at the agent next to him.

"Does it matter?"

"Everything plays a part."

"For someone who is trained to recognize patterns, perhaps," she replied coolly. "But I'm not doing you that favor."

"Did your friends at Megah Adara see to that, or did you set the appropriate levers in motion so that you could intercept me before things got dangerous?"

"Just accept it – you've lost."

Wayan remained silent for the rest of the journey and gave the impression that she wouldn't say another word.

After what felt like forever, the elevator cabin came to a halt and the doors slid to the sides. They stepped out into the middle of a large cavern, which led into a long tunnel that disappeared horizontally into the mountain. Far above them, a circular section of sky could be seen.

The borehole.

"So, here you are," said a man in a white chemical protection suit. His skin was too light and his eyes too narrow for an Indonesian. Christer guessed that he was Japanese, not least because of his accent. Behind him were two guards with submachine guns, locals who didn't seem to be in particularly friendly moods. To their right was a small passenger trolley on narrow-gauge rails.

"How dare you unleash your dogs on me, Saruko?" Wayan barked at the man. Christer only now noticed that the Japanese man was wearing a nametag.

"Excuse me?" Saruko sounded angry.

"I brought Johannsen here, so you should be thanking

me on your knees. I even called Suparman so it couldn't be more obvious."

Saruko's anger seemed to recede. "Nothing of the sort has been brought to my attention."

"Because you don't notice anything down here. The board needs Johannsen, so I brought him here."

"We don't need anyone," the Japanese man contradicted, piqued.

"I hope you're sure, because the board definitely does not think that way," Wayan replied sharply. "Wait. You don't know who this is, do you?"

Saruko didn't answer, but his eyes narrowed even more as a hint of uncertainty mingled with his gaze.

"He's a UN expert in information technology and pattern identification. You're going to use him. Is that clear?"

"You have no authority to command me," the man barked.

"No, but if you're clever, and I've read you that way so far when I've looked at the reports, then you'll use the resources brought to you before you're replaced. You know what happens in that case, don't you?"

25

RACHEL

She floated in the observation deck, curled up like a fetus, her gaze focused beyond her drawn-up knees and out through the large, armored windows. The stars seemed like glittering jewels stretching across the immeasurable black sheet of the universe. Countless light years apart, they formed a web of light and dark that stretched into infinity.

The loneliness of the flight still overwhelmed her, and yet it offered her an unexpected opportunity for self-reflection. Out here, where there was nothing but silence and space, time spent on thoughts about past and future seemed wasted. The isolation and distance from everything that was familiar and dear to her allowed her to think about life and her place in the cosmos. The stars became companions to her thoughts, silent witnesses to her inner dialog, which was dominated by hopes and fears that gradually degenerated into an echo.

She still thought about Masha most of the time, but no longer in a way that made her cry, but rather from a kind of bird's eye view of life. Who could ever know if this experience was good for her daughter? How presumptuous was it to believe that the plan of the cosmos could be fathomed? Why spend time anguishing over it when she could know nothing in the face of the immensity out there in front of this oxygen-filled metal can hurtling through the void?

The farther Rachel was from Earth, the more she realized how fragile and precious life was. Every star that shone outside in the darkness reminded her of the countless things the universe had to offer, and of the many lives she had left behind on Earth. In these moments of deep contemplation, she understood that solitude and silence could hold a strange beauty. They were like a mirror that reflected the soul and revealed the essence of human existence: consciousness, the reflected experience of what was. Sometimes she thought she understood everything and yet could not grasp it. Was she merely consciousness, embedded in a general consciousness that was becoming aware of itself? Might that be the perfect definition of beauty beyond all things?

Even when these brief, precious moments of realization left her, Rachel was finding a new perspective on her life and her role in the universe. She realized that she was part of an unimaginably large and complex system made up of countless galaxies, stars, and planets. Each of them had its own history, its own secrets, and its own wonders.

As she listened to the stars on her lonely journey through the darkness of space, she felt her thoughts and feelings traveling to the farthest corners of the universe.

Here and now, in the silence of the infinite expanse, she found a deep inner peace that filled her with new strength and clarity. It simply came over her, like a welcome guest. She understood that life was a journey made up of many different moments and experiences – solitary and communal, destructive and uplifting, sad and happy. Each of these moments was an indispensable part of her existence, a step on the path to self-discovery and self-realization. And yet they were not really moments, not ephemeral things, but snippets of something that had been there all along. She could not verbalize her realization, but she felt it with a depth that could not be denied.

As Rachel continued to glide through weightlessness, surrounded by the silence and gentle whisper of the stars, she felt strangely fulfilled and grateful for the opportunity to make this unique journey. Despite the isolation – and the seeming endlessness of space – she had found something she couldn't have found anywhere else.

And then the apparition occurred. If she had been in any other mental state than her deeply felt realization of timeless wholeness, she might have been frightened. But as it was, she calmly observed the complex play of light that unfolded around her.

At first, she noticed barely perceptible and delicate shimmers moving like twinkling stars in the darkness of the observation deck. The lights pulsed gently, gradually evolving into more complex patterns that spread around Rachel in a mesmerizing dance.

The light filled the room and seemed to vibrate in harmony with her own breathing and heart rate. At that moment, she felt wholly connected to the universe, as if she was floating in a warm embrace of cosmic energy. There were colors, constantly changing from soft blues and greens to pleasant yellows and oranges, sparking a deep, soothing warmth inside her, as if they were awakening something that had been there but invisible all along.

The light patterns became more complex and mesmerizing, seeming to dance in intertwining spirals and mandala-like formations. Rachel's senses were captivated by this visual symphony and she forgot everything around her, even her name and the meaning of the word 'I.' She felt like she was immersed in a state of pure presence and awareness, where space and time were irrelevant because they were mere concepts that lacked substance.

Rachel felt a profound calm and serenity that dissolved her previous fears and worries into laughter, a laughter that came from a place beyond her personality. It was the laughter of a Buddha that needed no reason or intention to pay homage to her existence. She felt imbued with an indescribable lightness and fulfillment that the play of light seemed to reflect back to her.

In this moment of complete surrender and immersion, she discovered the true beauty and wonder of the universe that surrounded her. She really recognized it, not just in brief glimpses as before, not merely as a result of contemplation, but as a consequence of a realization beyond all transience.

The play of light finally reached its climax and enveloped Rachel in a radiant glow that enclosed her like a cocoon. She felt her spirit expand and merge with the infinite expanse of the cosmos. In this moment of perfect unity, she felt touched deep inside.

Then it ended as abruptly as it had appeared, and darkness swaddled her. Not terrifying darkness, just the absence of photons.

She smiled quietly.

"Rachel?"

It took a few moments before time returned and she realized that she should answer.

"Yes?" She grabbed one of the handholds and turned around.

Liu floated in the hatch to the forward cargo module, surrounded by a ring of light that penetrated the observation deck from below. "I'm sorry about the light," he said contritely.

"What do you mean?"

"There was a power spike in the dorsal superconductor

cables that caused some malfunctions. I meant to disconnect the power to the lights in here so you wouldn't be disturbed, but then I forgot." Liu bowed his head. "I'm sorry if I startled you."

Rachel frowned and looked at the lights, which were embedded as small strips in the struts between the window elements and merged with the surface.

"That was the light?"

The astronaut looked at her in confusion. "What do you mean?"

"The light was on?"

"Uhh, yes. I'm really sorry," he repeated. "I didn't mean to disturb you. I know our private time in here is precious, I should have remembered."

"Mm-hmm."

Liu waited a moment. Then he floated into the observation deck with her and closed the hatch. "Is everything all right?"

"I don't know," Rachel admitted. "I thought ..." She shook her head. "No, it's all right."

"What were you thinking?"

"You'd just call me crazy."

"It's just as crazy to keep things to yourself that could be relevant. We are flying to Mars because a light has been burning there for whose existence there is no scientific explanation known to us. How can anything be crazier than that?" he asked, smiling encouragingly.

"I saw ... lights," she explained reluctantly. "They were beautiful, all around me. I felt so good. No, good is the wrong word. Totally. Timeless. It was somehow right."

"Don't be upset with me for asking you this question, but are you overly worried? Do you feel lonely?"

"Of course." Rachel shook her head. "And no, I'm not angry with you for asking. I know what you're getting at. You have good reasons, and I would ask you the same thing. Yes, I feel lonely, and of course I'm worried, too. I still think that I don't belong here – unlike the rest of you. You've dedicated your lives to space. I'm just a linguistics professor."

"You know," Liu said, hovering next to her to look out at the twinkling stars with her, "the idea that we could talk to an alien intelligence on Mars seems more and more unrealistic and downright ridiculous the longer we travel. It's as if we've been taken in by a dream that can't be real if we look at it rationally. Maybe it's the lack of contact with Earth, I don't know. But it has somehow become ... surreal."

"Hmm ... I don't feel any more useful now than I did before hearing that," she replied dryly.

"On the contrary, Rachel, we need you more than ever. We astronauts work, day in and day out, on the assigned experiments and preparations. It's easy to forget the fact that humanity did not come together because of a pipe dream. Humanity did not overcome unimaginable financial hurdles because of a dream. They did it because they were afraid. If we're honest, that's exactly what it is. If there is an alien beacon on Mars, then it begs important questions: Where are the aliens? Are we being watched? Are we in danger?" Liu shook his head. "The best proof that we really are here because of aliens is the very fact that we are here, if you understand what I mean."

"I do understand."

"So, what did you see?"

"Light. All around me." Rachel sighed as he looked at her. "I know that sounds stupid, because obviously the lights were on, but it was different."

"Strange?"

She tried to determine whether he was taking her seriously or just asking out of politeness while he was mentally shaking his head. But the taikonaut looked at her thoughtfully and attentively, free of judgment – at least she couldn't see any in his eyes.

"No. Not 'strange.' Different. And beautiful, yes, but not really strange. I felt like time stood still and everything was perfect the way it was." Rachel looked at him when he didn't respond, and she let out a long sigh. "I know how that sounds. I'm feeling lonely and a little lost, and then the light comes and I'm feeling wonderful."

"I'm no linguist, but what sounds like something doesn't have to correspond to what it is, does it?" asked Liu.

"That's the one sentence I've been trying to convey to my students for years – in many different ways."

"I've been meditating for twenty minutes a day since I was in my early twenties. Do you know why?" Liu suddenly changed the subject.

"No. I've never tried it before."

"There are moments in meditation when the sense of self dissolves and with it, time and all judgment. Zen Buddhists call such moments of realization satori. I had such an experience as a child during a car accident in which my mother died."

"I'm very sorry about that."

"Thanks. It's all right now. Anyway, in that moment of shock, everything was suddenly okay – a satori, I found out years later. Such experiences are precious and rare, and are even being studied by brain researchers because there is no explainable connection so far. But I really wanted to know what it was and sought the answers in meditation later, after I was convinced that I hadn't lost my mind."

"So?" she asked, "Did you have one of those moments again?"

"Yes, but there are pitfalls. Sometimes people confuse stirrings of the spirit with real satori. Only you can know which it was."

"Maybe we can watch the video recordings?" Rachel listened to herself. What she knew she should say next didn't feel true, but maybe believable, and although she felt the heaviness of even thinking it, she said it anyway. "It could be that the sudden light caused a neural reaction that felt like what I tried to describe?"

"Are you sure?"

"Yes."

"Then let's take a look."

They floated from the observation deck into the cockpit and sat down in Adam and Madeleine's chairs. Liu let her take charge so that she could scroll through the camera footage herself. He looked at his watch and gave her the approximate time.

It was strange to see herself in the picture, floating, a dark silhouette in front of the windows, curled up with her arms wrapped around her knees. She seemed so motionless, even though so much had been going on in her head, sorting and settling. She kept speeding up the playback speed until the light came on in the video. Suddenly and abruptly, the whole room was flooded, brighter than expected.

"That must be the energy peak. Too much power going to the lamps. Actually, the supply should have been automat ..."

"Look," she interrupted him, and pointed to the display in front of them. She saw herself reaching out a finger as if to touch something that wasn't there. "I look like a crazy person."

"Don't worry, you're not crazy," he assured her. "What do you say we do it again tomorrow? If it happens again, maybe we can make a connection."

"Okay," Rachel said. She felt dazed. Had she suffered some kind of short-term psychosis? Cold fear crept into her bones, even though – or perhaps because – the sensations and the light had felt so right. As if she had discovered some kind of long-forgotten home within herself.

"The light on Mars upsets us all a little, you know," Liu said sympathetically. "I dream about it every night. I guess it's the nature of our journey and the obsessive thoughts we all have about what we might be up against."

"Thank you." She unbuckled her seatbelt and paused. "What did the second PMT experiment reveal?"

"The amount of photons is constant, no matter where we are, and it is increasing, which was to be expected. Minimal increases in the measurements, but recognizable."

"It's increasing?" Rachel asked. "So it's a non-directional beacon on Mars – if that's what it is. It's not directed at Earth and it's increasing in intensity, as you'd expect when you get close to the source of something radiating from a center."

"That's exactly what worries us."

"You're worried? Why?"

"Do you know the dark forest theory?" asked Liu.

"Yes. A possible solution to the Fermi paradox by our colleague Cixin Liu: We have not yet encountered any signs of extraterrestrials, although the universe is full of potentially habitable worlds, because they are all silent and hiding."

"Exactly. According to the theory, each civilization intentionally remains silent so as not to attract the attention of other, possibly hostile, civilizations. The premise is that, due to the limited resources in the universe and uncertainty about the intentions of other civilizations, there is an inherent risk in making oneself known. If a civilization reveals its existence, there is a risk that a technologically superior – and possibly aggressive – civilization will perceive it as a threat and destroy it before it can pose a threat itself."

"Yes, due to the unbreakable chain of doubt that arises when two foreign peoples make contact with each other. That's been a big problem in communication between different language groups here on Earth," said Rachel. "And it could be infinitely worse with aliens. Even if both civilizations try to communicate honestly and openly, misunderstandings and cultural differences can lead to misinterpretations that further increase mutual mistrust. And such misunderstandings have always existed in our own history, even though we have the same DNA."

"The chain of doubt arises when one civilization tries to fathom the intentions of others through communication or observation, but they cannot draw definitive conclusions because the information they receive can be interpreted in different ways. This leads to a vicious spiral of mistrust and uncertainty that intensifies as more information is exchanged or picked up from observation. Eliminating the others is the only way to break the chain of doubt – in the truest sense of the word. Those who are dead cannot be a danger to me."

Liu called up one of the satellite images of the light phenomenon over Elysium Mons on Mars and pointed his finger at it. "That is the exact opposite. A large beacon that tells the universe at the speed of light: Here I am."

"Not quite," she contradicted. "It was only visible when the coronal mass ejection took place – through an interaction with plasma."

"In our optical spectrum," Liu objected. "For all we know, it could always have been there."

"In that case, we're on the safe side because no one has knocked on our door yet," she replied with a smile.

A little optimism never did any harm, and it might even dispel some of her gloom.

26

CHRISTER

His eyes followed Wayan as she walked with one of the security guards to a phone attached to a panel on the rock face. The cables ran up toward the borehole on the surface.

Saruko pointed to the trolley. "Get in."

"Let me guess. If I say no, then the rest of the day won't be very pleasant for me?"

"If you say no, I'll shoot you," the Japanese man replied emotionlessly enough to leave Christer little doubt as to how serious he was. But he saw what might have been a micro smile – or even just the twitch of a corner of his mouth. Neither of which contributed to his sense of inner well-being.

"What if Agent Suryani set you up?"

"That's for the board to deal with. I'm here to keep our operations running down here. They are there to make sure that no one on the surface is hindering me and my team."

They took a seat in the cramped compartment. It was musty smelling but at least it felt pleasantly cool. Although there seemed to be no operator, the trolley started moving as if by magic and rumbled along the narrow-gauge rails into the shaft in front of them.

Christer felt the reflex to turn to Wayan, hoping that it had all been just a feint on her part, but he let it go. She had made her decision, he had seen that in her eyes. She had fooled him while he was absorbed in something that shouldn't really exist.

The shaft in front of them was rather sparsely illuminated. After about 100 meters, the walls were no longer rocky, but lined with concrete. Numbers and letters marked regular points, and here and there were yellow-painted doors. They followed a fork to the right and descended deeper.

"Rise and shine, Mr. Freeman," Christer murmured. "Rise and shine."

"What are you talking about?" Saruko asked disapprovingly.

"Half-life. This must be Black Mesa." A cold shiver ran down his spine as he thought of what had been waiting for him as a computer gamer in the fictional Black Mesa. "I don't know whether to feel honored that they picked me specifically, or insulted that Agent Suryani isn't doing this herself."

"We're all just doing our job here."

Christer scrutinized the Japanese man and his chalky white skin. "You don't get to the surface often, do you?"

Saruko's hard gaze intensified and he didn't answer.

"That's what I thought. They're keeping some kind of secret here, and Megah Adara couldn't have kept it secret since the eighties if they gave their local staff free rein." Christer exhaled a long, drawn-out breath. "You were once like me, am I right? Kidnapped and forced to work here."

The Japanese man's silence was answer enough for him. Not only to his question, but also to many of the other speculations in his head. If this man hadn't found a way out of here, there wasn't one. The fact that he knew the board probably meant that he had come to terms with his fate out of necessity and made the best of it. A variant of Stockholm syndrome, perhaps. At a certain point, switching to the perpetrator's side is perceived as less painful than remaining a victim.

"We must be useful or we are deemed expendable," Saruko said after a while, as they arrived in a vertical shaft. A crane grabbed their cart with a magnet and swung them over a deep hole. A hydraulic system vented somewhere in the wall. Then the hum of a winch sounded and they were lowered down.

Christer made the mistake of looking down through the window and jerked back with a sudden attack of vertigo. It was so far down that he couldn't see the bottom.

"What is this?" he asked breathlessly.

"Your future. Or your grave. Down here, there are only two fates."

At first Christer thought the Japanese man's humorless smile was sadistic, but then he realized that there was nothing malicious behind the gleam in his eyes, only a deeply felt conviction.

"I was mistaken. You're not a prisoner," Christer said. "You used to be, but you really believe in whatever it is you're doing down here."

"Of course I do!" Saruko snorted. "We're changing the world. It's an honor to be a part of it. If it comes at the price of no more vacations and never seeing my family again, I'll pay it willingly."

They continued their descent in silence. It grew increasingly colder, so much so that Christer began to shiver as the sweat on his skin evaporated. After what felt like an eternity they reached the bottom, where the surroundings changed abruptly. If the area above could have been mistaken for an abandoned mine shaft that had only been preserved in a rudimentary state to allow maintenance crews and structural engineers access, it looked completely different here. The walls were concreted and labeled with signs in English and Indonesian. He read 'Infirmary,' 'Laboratories A1-10, B1-5, C10-20,' and 'Quarters for maintenance crews.'

The rail system ended after a short time and they got out. The cavern they were in seemed to be a kind of roundabout. Several steel cables hung down from above, from where they had come. Markings on the floor were directional indicators for small electric carts that went one way or the other, with drivers who didn't seem to notice them. Workers in yellow hardhats with a figure eight on each one were riding inside along with men and women in white coats with nametags. He saw workers squatted in foursomes on the loading plat-forms, chatting animatedly and pointing at the displays of tablets before disappearing into one of the six outgoing tunnels.

One of these tunnels was sloping and its edges were painted red. A warning sign for radiation danger was attached to both sides, and a heavy gate blocked the way. In front of it stood two guards in dark uniforms, each holding a subma-chine gun.

"My God," he said. "How many people work here?"

"Three hundred," Saruko replied, pointing to one of the electric carts. "Three hundred and one now."

"What happens to those who don't want to work here?"

"There are no such persons. At least not for long." Some-thing in the Japanese man seemed to relax a little. Did he feel uncomfortable being up near the surface because he had been down here for too long?

Only then did Christer notice that everyone in each group was dressed the same. Scientists wore white coats and gray pants, workers yellow coveralls with yellow safety helmets. The security guards were in black with black helmets but the two at the mysterious gate were the only ones he had spotted so far. The other two had stayed in the trolley that had brought them here. Each piece of clothing was adorned with the figure eight.

"Let the work of persuasion begin," he said with a touch of fatalistic humor. He wasn't exactly keen to get to know the torture repertoire for the abductees, who had obviously been brainwashed.

"Good," Saruko said, as if Christer had actually made a good suggestion.

His concern grew.

They drove the electric cart through one of the shafts and then to the right into a much smaller corridor, where they parked in a larger room and Saruko pushed him toward one of the doors. Along the way, he had noticed, there were cameras everywhere, filming every corner.

The door he was heading for was labeled 'Admissions.'

"That sounds like a hospital." When Christer stepped through the door, he was not surprised. He found himself in a doctor's exam room: a treatment table, medicine cabinet, desk, chest of drawers, and another door. The door he'd entered slammed shut behind him.

Now he found himself alone with a doctor who turned to face him. "Have a seat. I am Doctor Melnikov," said the man with a Slavic accent and pointed to the table, which was equipped with a roll of paper.

Christer obeyed the command and searched the room for instruments of torture. He couldn't find any, instead just the backdrop of what could have been a medical practice from the 1990s. "Rabbit hole, for sure," he mumbled. It was all so bizarre that he couldn't believe it was real. He felt like he was in a game that everyone understood but himself.

"Excuse me?"

"I'm Alice and this must be Wonderland."

"No. No Wonderland." Doctor Melnikov drew up a syringe and rolled over in his chair. "I only had half an hour to prepare, so I'm going to give you the full cocktail of vaccines."

"What?" Christer stared at the approaching syringe like it was a snake.

"We can't have any epidemics down here. We've been through that before and it set us back years." Melnikov looked annoyed. "So expose your upper arm so we can get this over with."

Christer considered simply attacking the man, but immediately rejected the idea. The fact that Saruko had left him here alone could only mean that he saw no danger in him, and even if he escaped from this room – what then? He wouldn't even be able to get his bearings, and the cameras would be watching his every move – until he was shot.

"Listen, tall guy," Melnikov rumbled, and his accent became even more rolling. "I can make sure you don't get sick and infect anyone, or you can try to kill me. But you'd better make up your mind, I've still got more work to do."

Christer blinked in irritation. The next moment he felt a needle in his arm.

"Ouch!"

"That's it already. Do you want an Indian plaster?" the doctor asked ironically.

"If you have one. Or else I'll take a Star Wars one."

Melnikov snorted and pushed a thumb-sized piece of gauze into his hand, and Christer pressed it onto the puncture site. Next, the man locked an ankle cuff on him with frighteningly practiced hand movements.

"It finds you day and night. But not only that, it also warns you of anomalies and accidents. Then it lights up in a certain color. Red means you stay put. Flashing red means that you should go to the nearest shelter – simply follow the flashing, colored-light strips on the floor. Green – all good. Yellow – battery soon empty, then you come and see me."

"Anomalies? Accidents?"

"You'll live to see both." Melnikov waved him off. "We all have."

"Where are you from?" asked Christer.

"From Voronezh, in Russia. Why do you ask?"

"I don't know, I ..."

"You want a story about whoever is working with your kidnappers. Give the cruel torturer a human touch." The doctor laughed boomingly. "I know because I was like that myself twenty years ago. It goes away."

"I don't think so."

"That's what everyone thinks until they see it."

"See what?"

Melnikov sighed. "You'll only get to see it once, but that will be enough to make you never want to leave again."

"What makes you think that? I have a life at home. I ..."

"You're a scientist, aren't you?"

"A data analyst."

"Then you'll have forgotten your old life in no time."

While Christer was still thinking about what the doctor might mean by this, the door through which he had come opened and Saruko entered.

"Is he ready?" asked the Japanese man.

"Yes, Director. All done. He may have a fever and a headache, but he should be fit for work in a few days."

"Good." Saruko gave Christer a wave to follow him. They went back to the electric cart and drove back to the central cavern, where they turned into another tunnel.

"You're the director? The facility manager?"

"Yes."

"Where are you taking me?"

"I'll show you what you're looking for. That's why you're here, isn't it?"

Christer didn't know how to answer.

"It won't take long," Saruko continued. "Your quarters are still being prepared. I've had a collection of your favorite books brought here. A deceased colleague apparently had similar tastes to yours."

"My favorite books?" He felt stupid because he was stammering the whole time like a primary school pupil, but he didn't understand a thing.

"I got the memo when you were with the doctor," the director explained, steering their cart around a group of scientists. "You thought you were looking for samples in the basement of the Ministry of Energy, but in fact we found out everything about you. We analyzed you."

"How many others have been in this dungeon?"

"A few. There are many similar facilities around the world, Mr. Johannsen. They work. The system works, that's all that matters. It took a little longer for you, as you can see from the report."

"You don't know anything about me."

"We know that your given name is Christian, but that you had your name changed because of your violent father of the same name. We know that you are homosexual but are single after a failed marriage and you still mourn your ex. We know that Hyperion is your favorite novel, and that you detest coarse toilet paper. You're a night owl and have tried to kill yourself before, but found new optimism after successful therapy," Saruko enumerated as if he were reading off a list.

Then he stopped the cart in front of a small door in the side wall, above which was written 'Observation' and 'Access for authorized personnel only.'

"How ...?"

"How is not important," the Japanese man interrupted him. "What is important. And what is hidden behind this door."

Saruko held his eyes in front of a retina scanner that had

been placed right next to an old-fashioned key card control panel that had obviously been around for several decades. The doors opened to reveal an old elevator car. His companion pointed inside. In a daze, Christer complied with the gesture, only to realize that the Japanese man had no intention of accompanying him.

"Take all the time you need, Christian Johannsen. You have now reached the end of your research. I'll be waiting for you up here and you'll have lots of questions, but you'll never want to leave this place again. I promise you that."

The elevator doors closed and the cabin jolted into motion. Once again he felt himself dropping into the depths.

27

RACHEL

"So, Rachel," Yuki began softly, "you saw lights while you were on the observation deck, and that you even felt like you could interact with them. Let's go through a few possible explanations together."

Rachel nodded in agreement, while the doctor apparently collected her thoughts before continuing. "One possibility is that you have experienced a temporary disturbance in your visual perception, known as an aura. Such an aura can occur in connection with migraines. Have you ever had a migraine in the past, Rachel?"

"As a child. But not since I started taking a lot of magnesium." Rachel shook her head. "I didn't have a headache at the time, either."

"Mm-hmm." Yuki nodded and continued. "There are also visual migraines, which are often painless and are characterized by a so-called scintillating scotoma. It looks like a jagged, sometimes flashing rainbow in the field of vision."

Rachel shook her head.

"Another possibility would be a hallucination caused by

stress or fatigue. You work in a demanding environment, and the stress can sometimes trigger such phenomena. However, the fact that you stretched out your hand as if you could interact with the lights speaks against a simple hallucination."

Yuki paused for a moment to consider Rachel's reaction. "Simple hallucinations appear briefly and then disappear. What you described was long-lasting."

"It must have had something to do with the light. I mean, you can see on the video that I only do this stuff with my hand for as long as it's on. Right?"

"Yes, and that leads to my next guess: a neurological disorder, such as a temporary dysfunction of the brain. This could lead to disturbances in visual perception that manifest themselves in the form of light phenomena. Such a disturbance could, for example, have been triggered by the sudden flash of light in combination with the energy peak in the superconductors."

"You mean like an epileptic seizure?" Rachel asked.

"Not a seizure, no. Your muscle tone was obviously within the normal range. There are various neurological disorders that can be caused by abrupt light induction." Yuki bowed her head apologetically. "But remember, I'm not a neurologist."

"Is it dangerous? Should I be worried?"

The Japanese woman smiled reassuringly. "It's not usually dangerous, but we should carry out further tests to make sure there are no signs of an underlying illness. I think that is highly unlikely because we were examined from head to toe before the mission began, but we'd rather play it safe. In the meantime, I recommend you pay attention to your stress levels and sleep habits to minimize potential triggers. I can give you something to help with that."

Rachel shook her head. "No, I'm fine without it. To be

honest, I've felt a lot more relaxed since this happened. That might sound strange, but it's true."

"Maybe it was just a spiritual experience." Yuki shrugged and shifted her weight to her right leg, whose foot was stuck in one of the straps on the floor.

Rachel tilted her head skeptically.

"What? That can't be ruled out."

"Are you making fun of me? Liu has already told me about his meditations. I was pretty much expecting you to call me crazy."

"Spiritual experiences are not something that contradicts current science. It is well researched in medicine, for example, that meditation techniques originating from Indian yoga – a spiritual tradition – statistically work just as well as medication in terms of depression and stress, only without the side effects. Why? Because patients observe their thoughts and learn not to get attached to them. A few decades ago, this was dismissed as esoteric. We also know that after spiritual experiences – even those caused by taking psychotropic substances such as LSD or so-called 'mushrooms' – people are more often satisfied, empathic, and relaxed. Practiced meditators can induce such states through deep contemplation, which is amazing and real if you ask me."

Yuki paused and gave her a warm smile. "Basically, it's like this: you experienced something and you feel better since then, right?"

"Yes."

"Since it's not affecting your well-being, it's not something I need to treat. Whether it was a spiritual experience or a hallucination, the important thing is that you're feeling well. Physiologically, you seem healthy. I could draw some blood, but to be honest, I don't know what we could learn from the values I can test for here."

"Thank you, Yuki," Rachel said. "I just wanted to make sure I hadn't lost my mind."

"You haven't, don't worry."

After leaving the small sickbay, she headed toward her bed, but on the way she came across Madeleine, who was hovering at one of the workstations and staring at the display as if she were hypnotized.

"Are you all right?" Rachel asked.

"What? Oh, yes, everything's fine." The computer scientist with the once mighty mop of hair, now shaved and covered by a cap, winced slightly and rubbed her tired eyes. The rest of the crew had obviously already retired to their beds. "I'm still going through the data."

"What data? Are you still working on your analytics plug-in?" Rachel pulled herself closer to her colleague. Madeleine nodded and rolled her obviously tense shoulders.

"Yes, the images from the HiRISE camera of the Mars Reconnaissance Orbiter have a short exposure time, but a relatively long processing time. We are dealing with large amounts of data from a system that is now twenty years old. Once the MRO was aligned, it was faster because the targeted section above Elysium Mons is quite small. Nevertheless, each shot took minutes."

Madeleine pointed to the image of a bright yellow and white dot against a monotonous brown landscape. "That means we recorded about two hours out of the three during which the phenomenon lasted, with three to four minutes between each snapshot. I wrote a program that uses machine learning, or ML, to process and analyze the data. This includes cleaning up the data, adjusting contrast and brightness, removing noise and all that sort of thing. But I don't want to put you to sleep."

"To be honest, I'd like to know more," Rachel replied.

She wasn't tired yet and could do with something that made her think.

"Well, then." Madeleine seemed to become a little more alert and some of her enthusiasm for the subject found its way into her eyes, their dullness vanishing into thin air. "I warned you."

"Give me the full broadside." Rachel smiled.

"In order to train an ML model, the data must be divided into so-called training sets and test sets. Colleagues already did this before our departure. However, I have spent the last few weeks working on data augmentation."

"On what?"

"I used data enrichment techniques to increase the number of available images, which improves the comprehensiveness of the model," explained Madeleine. "This was followed by feature extraction, which had already been prepared at home. Using pre-trained neural networks, we identified relevant features from the images, such as fluctuations in radiation intensity or fluctuations at the edges of the light sphere. I had to retroactively adjust this a little so that it matched my changes. Yesterday I finished my CNN, which in turn finished analyzing the data a few hours ago."

"I'm sure you don't mean the TV station," Rachel joked.

"Right you are. It stands for 'Convolutional Neural Network,' which is a model to analyze the extracted features for anomalies or patterns. The training data is run through and then there is a validation phase using the test data. Boring stuff, but necessary. A few hours of optimizing hyperparameters and then adjusting the model – et voilá," Madeleine said as she dramatically tapped the 'Enter' key, "accuracy and efficiency have improved by forty percent. That's what I've been doing for the last few weeks."

"I only understood half of it, but ..."

"Aha!" the computer scientist said so suddenly that

Rachel jerked and reflexively pulled her foot back from the strap on the floor. She grabbed one of the handholds next to the workstation and anchored herself again.

"What's wrong?"

"Results, my dear! Results!" Madeleine pulled herself closer to the display and feverishly scanned the complex data curves running across it. Lines of text and numbers automatically sorted themselves on the right. "Take a look at this! Analysis of the MRO data has revealed spectral anomalies within the light patterns that could indicate an unsteady energy source. I don't think these are simple reflections or other natural phenomena. Look at the sudden change in topography near Elysium Mons! These could be radiation events that stir up the dust almost as if raindrops were falling on it – as charged particles are released, there may be interactions. These changes occur cyclically, every six minutes, see?"

"I can't see anything in your data salad," Rachel confessed, but even so, she felt Madeleine's excitement starting to infect her.

"The synchronized movement patterns within the light phenomena suggest a coordinated activity or at least some kind of design."

"So could it be true that it is some kind of signal that we can't decode yet?" asked Rachel. "Like some scientists postulated before we launched?"

"According to this data analysis, quite clearly ... yes. And here's the really interesting part. The light phenomenon gets stronger and weaker at regular intervals, suggesting that it's some kind of cyclical event. The AI analysis also shows that the bandwidths vary in intensity and pattern, suggesting that they pass through different wavelengths. What makes the whole thing even more mysterious is the fact that the light phenomena only occur during a CME. It is as if the increased radiation from the solar flare enables or activates these 'light signals' in the first place. Or else they only occur in higher or lower wavelengths that we cannot detect optically or with infrared technology. We have to try to decipher the meaning of these patterns."

Madeleine turned to her and bit her lower lip. "But one thing we can say for sure: there is definitely no natural phenomenon behind it."

28

CHRISTER

He could detect the smell of oiled metal and imagine the long history that the elevator cabin suggested, judging by the worn floor beneath his feet. When it started to move he heard an ugly grinding sound – as many had done before him.

With every meter Christer descended, the air became cooler and the sounds from above faded until all he could hear was the whirring of the elevator motor and his own breathing. Shadows danced on the steel walls, while the light from the ceiling flickered and threatened to go out.

The elevator finally reached its destination, announcing the fact with a harsh clunk. The doors slid aside, revealing an unadorned room whose simplicity and coolness had an eerie effect. Air conditioning whirred quietly and a stream of icy air brushed against Christer's skin as he entered the room.

He shivered.

The wall on the opposite side of the room was a thick pane of glass that stretched all the way across. He assumed it was bulletproof, because it looked extremely thick and robust. Christer stepped closer and noticed that the glass wall was unusually hot. He touched it carefully and jerked his hand away. He had come close to seriously burning himself.

"Damn!" he cursed, looking at the reddened skin on his fingers.

When he returned his eyes to the glass, he saw an enormous cavern stretching out before him. In the middle, a massive ring, perhaps ten meters in diameter, hovered just above black rock with a central hole from which a reddish glow shone upward onto the ring. The air above the object shimmered as if there was an invisible sphere there, bending and warping the structure of the air. All around it were solar panels – at least that's what he thought they were – spaced 100 or more meters apart, in closely packed concentric circles, like the rings of some mysterious tree.

A circular walkway with railings surrounded the cavern, and as he took in the incredible scene, Christer tried to imagine who would voluntarily walk around it. His gaze was drawn to the deep hole beneath the floating ring, and the reddish glow emanating from it reminding him of the eerie glow of lava.

The whole scene was fascinating – sublime, and at the same time, deeply disturbing – to Christer. He stood there, overwhelmed by the majestic beauty of this hidden world. He was unable to fathom its meaning or purpose no matter how hard he tried. He only saw the floating object that seemed to defy the laws of nature as he stared at the sphere of shimmering air above it. He could have mistaken it for heat shimmers if it hadn't formed that spherical shape a few meters above the center of the ring. It looked ... wrong.

The longer Christer stared out into the cavern, the more details came to him. Here and there in the rock he discerned fine cracks that spread out like spider webs, and he noticed small reflections of light cast by the solar panels onto the walls and dancing there like fleeting ghosts. The walkway's floor seemed to be made of a smooth, dark material that contrasted with the rugged, uneven texture of the cavern. The railings were deformed and looked pitted, likely from the extreme heat.

Christer felt his pulse quicken as his mind plumbed the depths of the mystery before his eyes. His thoughts raced as he tried to make sense of what was unfolding before him. What was the purpose of this facility? Who built it? Was it human, or was it the work of another, unknown intelligence, as some astronomers on the talk shows had suggested? The alien hysteria following the discovery of the light phenomenon on Mars had infected him for a while, he'd had to admit, until a few months later when the realists gained the upper hand. The passage of time had quieted his imagination – until now.

The bulletproof glass raised its own questions that Christer couldn't answer. Was it there to keep something or someone out, or to protect him from something in the chamber? The material's heat indicated that it had been subjected to extreme stress. But how had the ring been used in the first place? And why hadn't the solar panels melted?

His gaze slid back to the air above the ring. He wondered if this invisible sphere was a barrier, or perhaps some kind of portal? The shimmering almost seemed to have a life of its own, forming tiny offshoots, expanding and contracting again in a pattern he recognized but could not name or comprehend. It seemed just beyond the grasp of his mind – too alien, too strange. The floating lights that moved around the edge of the sphere seemed to dance like stars in the night, but passed quickly like fleeting, visual disturbances.

Despite the coolness of the room and the currents of icy air brushing across his skin, Christer felt a growing heat rising inside him, fueled by fascination and an instinctual fear.

He didn't know what the ring was all about, or what the

flickering was, but he had understood one thing the instant he'd laid eyes on it: it was not of this world. The structure of the object was too perfect, the material too smooth and featureless, and the spherical effect in the air, pale and barely recognizable as it was, seemed simply otherworldly.

"A mistake in the Matrix," said someone behind him.

Startled, Christer whipped his head around to see Saruko stepping out of the elevator. "What?"

"I came here just after that movie, and that was the first thought that went through my head at the time. A mistake in the Matrix."

"That might be close," he admitted. "I thought you were going to wait for me upstairs?"

"I always say that, but in the end I take advantage of the privileges of my job." The director stepped up next to him and stared out through the thick bulletproof glass. "It's incredible, isn't it?"

"Yes," Christer breathed. "What is that?"

"We still don't know. This ring is an incredible mystery. We have found out a lot about it over the last thirty years, but there are still many questions we need to answer. We have already stretched the limits of our understanding of physics."

"But you have found out something."

For the first time, Christer was sure he saw the otherwise stern-looking researcher twitch the corners of his mouth – perhaps a kind of precursor to a smile?

"First of all, it probably draws its energy from the lava deep below through an advanced type of geothermal energy. There are no cables or anything like that, but there is a transfer of energy. We have found that there is a deep access to the Pacific Ring of Fire here that is not from us or our collaborators. This area was discovered in the 1980s during exploration work. Back then, more than thirty people died while exploring a natural system of lava caves." Saruko pointed through the glass. "This one."

He paused to give Christer time to think before continuing. "The composition of the ring is remarkable. The shell is extremely dense, down to the nanometer level. There seems to be an effect from the inside that strengthens the molecular bonds between the atoms of the material. This exhibits extremely high strength and thermal stability, in a way that eludes our previous methods of analysis. It may be a metamaterial or a complex crystal structure that requires sophisticated technology."

"A technology that we don't have," Christer summarized.

"Correct."

"Then who did it come from?"

Saruko tilted his head slightly. "We don't know. The assumptions debated most often among the staff are that it is either from a highly evolved extinct predecessor civilization on Earth, or from an alien intelligence that left artifacts behind."

"Could it be something like a power station?" Christer asked, without taking his eyes from the scene on the other side of the bulletproof glass.

"It could be anything. But it does produce energy that we capture with ever more advanced solar panels."

"What about this anomaly?" Christer pointed at the shimmering sphere.

"The whispering?"

"Whispering?"

"That's the alternative name we sometimes give to the shimmer. When you're on the walkway there, you hear incessant whispering. Maybe it comes from the lava in the depths, no one knows, but it sounds eerie. We've never been able to pinpoint its origin or meaning. But it seems to have a kind of hypnotic effect that, at worst, could cause you to approach involuntarily."

"Like some kind of pheromone?"

"Something like that. Don't listen to it. The effect seems to be very weak and will not affect you unless you are overtired or heavily intoxicated."

"What about this shimmering effect?" asked Christer.

Saruko tensed up. "We have determined that it is based on photons in wavelengths below the visible range. The energy they emit is unusually high and seems to come from an invisible source located above the ring. We suspect that this could be an effect of quantum optics, in which elementary particles interact with each other in a special state. These so-called 'entangled' photons could be responsible for the shimmering."

Saruko lowered his voice, drawing Christer's gaze, and looked him straight in the eye. "The truth is, we still know very little about this place and its secrets. But now that you've seen it, perhaps you understand why our previous lives no longer matter to us. What could be more important than solving this mystery?"

"Does this ring have anything to do with the miracle in Jakarta?" asked Christer.

"My team and I feed the energy we generate – everything that exceeds our own requirements, that is – directly into the city grid via our Muara Karang power plant on the outskirts of the city. It's enough to provide Jakarta with a continuous supply of electricity. What we don't understand is why only lightbulbs were glowing. That thing there is probably responsible for the phenomenon, but we have no idea why."

"Have you ever thought that you are doing exactly the wrong thing here?"

Saruko's brow furrowed. "You mean the secrecy?"

"You bet I mean the secrecy. I just don't understand it. If

that object there has so much potential, why don't you show it to the world? The entire scientific community has far more knowledge and potential than a few hundred – admittedly highly qualified – experts."

"That's not for me to decide. I was abducted, too, remember?" Saruko explained calmly. "I used to think like you. However, there are several legitimate reasons for the secrecy. Firstly, we don't yet know what dangers this technology harbors. That's why the board decided it should stay right where it is – and there's no more space here than what we're already using. The risk of uncontrolled usage and proliferation is substantial when we consider that we are dealing with a potentially alien enigma."

"But we could work with other nations to minimize the risks," Christer replied. "The research data could be published so that everyone can contribute. Universities would provide their brightest minds."

"Spoken like a true scientist." Saruko nodded thoughtfully. "That's all true. International cooperation would be helpful. More minds have more ideas, and there would be fewer blind spots. But as long as we don't fully understand the technology, the risk is too great. With many different ideas, there will also be stupid ones. Secondly, international cooperation is complex and carries political risks. There is a danger that some countries could try to use this technology for military purposes, or to strengthen their political power. Not to mention the risk of power struggles, perhaps even wars, breaking out over location and access."

Christer merely grumbled in reply. The counterarguments made sense to him, albeit he admitted it reluctantly.

"There is also the risk of the technology falling into the wrong hands and being used in an uncontrolled way," Saruko continued. "Thirdly, if we make the ring available to the world, we also expose ourselves to the risk of industrial espionage and technology theft. Companies that receive research contracts may be tempted to keep data for themselves, or steal materials to gain an advantage over the competition."

"But all of this already belongs to a private company," Christer said thoughtfully. "It's all about profit anyway."

Saruko snorted. "I thought you were smarter than that. Think about it again."

Christer's mind continued to whirl and it suddenly clicked. He should have seen it all along.

"Do you really think that an Indonesian energy company like Megah Adara is able to pull off so many kidnappings and ensure that there are no deeper investigations? To set up a blind spot in the heart of Java where we can do whatever we want? To set up something as complex as this and keep it secret?"

"This has long since been run by the secret services," Christer whispered.

"Yes. Of course. We down here don't know for sure, but in principle it's obvious to everyone because it's logical. The CIA was probably involved first, but with the funds needed for something like this, there are likely to be at least a handful of financially strong allies on board." Saruko waved a hand dismissively. "It doesn't matter to us down here. Whether there are managers or secret service officials on the board, the project has to keep going, and it has been doing so smoothly for decades."

"It still feels wrong to commit crimes out of political and organizational necessity," Christer insisted.

"If you ask my staff, none of them will want to leave," the director assured him. "How could they after seeing this?"

"At least now I understand Agent Suryani setting me up. She was informed long ago by some other secret service that I was coming and that the project needed me."

"Of course. You're a data scientist, and we have plenty of

data. Since we've been working with the new GPT analysis models, the computers have been spitting out patterns and anomalies galore that we can barely sort out. According to your file, you are better than any AI at assessing and interpreting such patterns."

"Maybe for a few more years." Christer looked around the room. It no longer felt like a prison, but more like he was trapped on the movie set of an X-Files episode. It was fascinating, but he still felt trapped. "But my career plans no longer matter, do they?"

"Think about it carefully," Saruko suggested. "With the knowledge you have now, and the life that's out there waiting for you, would you really want to leave here and carry on as before? Or wouldn't it be more likely that after just a few days you'd be annoyed that you're no longer here to help solve the greatest enigma in human history?"

Christer thought about it and fell silent.

"That's what I thought. You know, we've given a lot of thought down here to the selection process of the abductees. We came up with a few commonalities and one of them was that no one was to be selected who had family or children who depended on them. Whoever is responsible for us being here has taken into account that employees who become depressed, violent, or suicidal would not be of much help here. What do you say I brief you on your future work?"

29

RACHEL

The final weeks leading to their arrival at Mars passed much more quickly. While the journey had seemed endless to Rachel at the beginning, the days were flying by now. Perhaps it was because she'd had most of it ahead of her at first, and then she had begun counting backward from the halfway point as well as growing used to the monotonous but busy daily routine.

Her crewmates Liu and Raphael involved her more often in their experiments and tests because she learned surprisingly quickly and was more than capable at assisting. If she believed Adam, who kept praising her and encouraging her to get more involved, she might even become something of a casual engineer one day. Madeleine had formed something of a bond with her after their joint discovery – even though Rachel had done nothing to help except ask questions. It was as if they shared a secret that bound them together forever.

Raphael spent his days investigating the influence of cosmic rays and plasma on quantum states, his thoughts often lost in the depths of quantum mechanics. He was obviously looking for answers to questions Rachel didn't begin to grasp. Once the German quantum physicist had tried to explain to her after 'work' what quantum mechanics was all about, but she hadn't understood any of it. The few times she thought she was on the verge of understanding something, it had turned out to be completely different from her thoughts. At that point, the ESA astronaut concluded with a joke. "Anyone who claims to have understood quantum mechanics has not understood quantum mechanics." At least he had a good laugh.

Meanwhile, Liu was spending 12 hours a day working on the sophisticated optical systems they were carrying to investigate the phenomenon on Elysium Mons. As these had been developed before launch and had not yet been thoroughly tested, he used the travel time to optimize them. His experiments with light and its interactions were mostly carried out in sealed metal tubes and didn't make much of an impression, but Rachel understood more and more about the 'data salad' that the computers were pulling out of the devices. She was more than fascinated by what could be investigated with modern technology – beyond the visible world in which she moved.

Adam was constantly on the move maintaining and optimizing the countless technical systems. He was always looking for ways to save energy and make the life support systems more efficient. Their mission would last only nine months in total because they were flying to Mars with an extra booster that had long since been used up. Every bit of reaction mass they had on board – and didn't have to tap into – was significant. The solar panels, on the other hand, were not working at maximum efficiency because they were traveling farther and farther from the sun.

Yuki tested their blood regularly and informed them of their values, which didn't look particularly good. The results didn't produce worry lines on their doctor's forehead – so at least she didn't let on if she was worrying. The radiation outbreak had obviously damaged them all, but only time would tell how much it had shortened their life expectancy. The Japanese woman was honest and didn't sugarcoat anything: the first of them could expect malignant tumors to develop in a few years – or perhaps not for decades.

Madeleine didn't seem to worry in the slightest, as she spent most of her time in the world of algorithms and artificial intelligence. Ever since the discovery of the anomalies and patterns in the MRO's recordings in Mars orbit, she had been looking for new ways to find explanations. Sometimes she did this with the others, but so far they had not been able to agree on a theory as to what kind of signal it was. Madeleine didn't seem to be bothered by it and spent the rest of the time training the on-board AI, which hadn't even been activated yet.

The reason was quite simple: Adam didn't trust it. He kept emphasizing that he was old school and wouldn't trust a machine with a treasure like the Ambassador. But he would have to do it soon, because landing on Mars was complicated and it would go much better and be more precisely managed by a highly developed AI.

The model was based on the latest version of GPT, combined with an artificial neural network that fed into all the ship's systems and could act autonomously. It had been trained with all the data that all the countries involved had been able to pull together. Madeleine's aim was to give it a more human touch. After all these weeks, they were close to the day they would find out how the AI would behave.

The days and nights merged to the beat of the ship's clocks. They followed their strict schedules, which left no room for boredom. Meanwhile, Rachel saw the advantage in the monotony and effort of life on board. She had neither the time nor the energy to worry about tomorrow or to dwell on yesterday. The here and now was all she could handle. They did meet regularly in the common room to share their meals and exchange news, but it was mostly about work, a few jokes, and a few inside jokes they had established – for example, about Madeleine's non-existent hair.

And then the last day of their trip came, sooner than expected. Rachel got dressed, brushed her teeth, and started with an exercise session – two hours on the full-body trainer, in which she strapped herself in and moved her arms, legs, and torso against weights at the same time. Afterward, she bathed in the wet room, a now commonplace experience that she had initially found disconcerting because the water seemed to move over her skin of its own accord.

Then work began as it did every day, although she knew that they would all stop at 4 p.m. shipboard time today because they had to discuss the final approach and their landing. She was sure that each of them had long since downloaded the relevant plans from the on-board network and committed them to memory. If there was one thing she had learned by now, it was that plans had to be adhered to. They created a sense of security and confidence.

As the halfway point of the second shift drew close, Rachel finished her work on a small botany module Adam had assembled in his 20 minutes of free time each day, and cleaned her hands. Then she made her way out of the lab to the common area, and from there through the left hatch to the observation deck, where the others were already waiting for her.

"Hey, there she is, our nerd," Raphael called out cheerfully. He hovered with his back to the windows that made up half the bow and waved to her.

Rachel realized to her surprise that she was the last one. Liu and Adam 'sat' on the padded 'floor,' each having one leg hooked under a restraining strap. They smiled at her, their backs to the windows like Raphael. Yuki and Madeleine were hanging below the ceiling and seemed to be engrossed in an excited discussion. They too had turned their backs to the stars.

"I thought we were working until four p.m.," Rachel said, closing the hatch behind her so that the light from the common room wouldn't disturb them. Only now did she realize that she hadn't come back here to look at the stars since her strange experience. In a way, the observation deck was the only 'nice' place on board where she was entitled to 20 minutes of privacy a day. It wasn't as if she had avoided it, she just hadn't thought about it because she had been working so much.

"But not today." Raphael clicked his tongue. "You're sounding more German than me!"

"When it comes to something important, it's the academic quarter that counts," Adam exclaimed gleefully. It was the first time she had seen him so exuberant.

"CT actually means fifteen minutes later," she reminded him with a grin as the burden of her work fell away and the relaxed mood spread to her. She soaked it up like a sponge after weeks of a life that would have been more suited to a robot than a human being.

"Not on the approach to Mars," said Raphael. Only now did she notice that he was holding a small bag in his left hand.

"Can you see it yet?" She pushed off in the direction of the windows to be met by a storm of indignation.

"NO!"

"Hey, what are you doing?"

"Are you crazy?"

"She's screwing it up!"

"What's wrong?" she asked irritably, catching herself on one of the handholds on the ceiling.

"You can't look yet!" they all shouted in one variation or another and promptly signaled to turn around.

"Maybe if you'd let me in on the secret rituals of astronauthood, I wouldn't have brought you superstitious guys to the brink of a communal nervous breakdown," Rachel replied with a grin. "Instead, I'm talking to a wall now."

"I'm glad for the first time that we don't have communication with Earth and they can't watch us do everything," Madeleine said, chuckling from somewhere behind Rachel.

"That's a lie," Raphael remarked dryly. "I remember your diarrhea in the lab."

Silence fell for a moment, then laughter erupted from the others and resounded off the walls like a song of merriment.

"Sure, the world should have seen that," Madeleine objected, piqued. "After all, there's never been anything like it in history."

"And it will never happen again," Liu said firmly. "Not after we sell the recordings to the highest bidder."

Another roar of laughter.

"The brown volcano will go down in history."

"The Martian gyroscope ship," shouted Raphael with a chuckle.

"That's disgusting, Raphi," Yuki reprimanded him with a wrinkled nose. "We'll stick with the brown volcano, because that's exactly what it looked like."

"That was your weird kidney medication," Madeleine complained. "The devilish stuff tasted so disgusting, too."

"But diarrhea is not on the list of side effects." Yuki paused for a moment. "Neither is brown volcano, by the way."

This round of laughter was unstoppable for a few minutes, and Rachel's vision was blurred after a short time because tears of mirth had formed in her eyes. In the weightlessness, they did not run downward and she had to wipe them away several times.

"I'd say we're slowly getting to the heart of the issue," Adam said in a wry voice. "Mars. It's already quite large outside these windows, if we haven't lost our way, and we want to look at it together. That's why I'm suggesting a countdown."

"Moooment!" Raphael interrupted him and pulled out his bag, from which he pulled out six smaller plastic bags that looked like drink packs with their short, resealable straws.

"Forget it, Raphi, I don't toast with water," Madeleine clarified. "It's bad luck."

"Which is also the reason why I brought – drum roll – champagne."

"You brought what?" they all asked at the same time.

"Champagne. It's even carbonated, at least that's what my fence from the ground crew promised me." The quantum physicist scratched his head and shrugged his shoulders.

"When we get home and are celebrated as heroes, you'll have immunity for life. Then you'll have to reveal the secret of how you did it." Coming from Adam's mouth it sounded like a command, but at the same time almost reverent.

"I promised him that ..."

"Nooooo!" Madeleine interrupted him.

"Are you crazy?" shouted Yuki.

Even Liu joined in the storm of protest. "Don't say it!"

"You and your superstitions." Raphael rolled his eyes, but grinned and tossed them a pack each in turn. "You're welcome, by the way!"

"You're the best mad German scientist doing stuff with quanta," Madeleine assured him and blew him a kiss.

"Thank you, Raphi," Adam said seriously as he picked up his champagne. "Fine move. Really fine move."

"Ahh, it's a pleasure. A theorist like me has to be good at

something practical."

"Shall we turn around?" Adam invited them, and there was silence. "Three, two, one."

Rachel skillfully turned around with one hand on the ceiling handgrip. As her body weighed nothing in the weightlessness, it was nothing more than a skilled finger exercise.

She held her breath as the Red Planet appeared before her in all its majestic splendor. It seemed to embrace her with its luminous crimson glow, stretching across half the window and suddenly filling every corner of the room with its presence. For a moment, she was spellbound, unable to take her eyes off the fascinating celestial body.

A flood of emotions awoke in her heart, like a powerful storm that coursed through her mind and swept away all thoughts. She felt awe, curiosity, and a deep-rooted longing that she hadn't even known lay dormant within her. Nothing she had seen of the planet so far, no photograph, however beautiful, had prepared her for being so close to it now, really and physically close. She had traveled further than any other person before her, an unimaginably distant distance – so far away that the destination had seemed surreal at times, like an illusion. But there it was – Mars – an angry jewel shining fiery red in the black void.

It seemed to be waiting for her, as though it were a lost lover who had finally returned after a long separation. Its fascinating reliefs and mysterious scars reminded her of the dreamy epics and heroic stories she had devoured in her youth. She felt like an explorer on the edge of a new world – no, she was an explorer. At least right now.

The countless shades of red and ochre that stretched across the planet seemed to belong to inexpressible poetry, as if painted in the sky by an impressionist master. Every wrinkle and bump on the surface seemed like a verse in an epic poem, just waiting to be deciphered and understood by her.

The shimmering ice fields at the poles reminded her of the precious gems of a forgotten crown, lost in the depths of time. Looking at Earth's little brother, it was easy to imagine what most astrophysicists suspected: that Mars had once looked like their home world, green and blue, with dense bands of cloud around the equator.

As Rachel contemplated her journey's destination in all its grandeur and beauty, she understood that she was part of a greater whole, a cosmic spectacle that spanned eons. At the same time, she inevitably felt small and insignificant, but it was not a sad or humiliated feeling – on the contrary, it came with a deep sense of relief.

"The champagne from the plastic bag tastes really awful, man," said Adam, the first to break the silence. "But it's by far the best I've ever drunk."

"Amen," Madeleine agreed.

"I never thought it would look so beautiful. So red," Rachel said quietly. "I expected a ball of brown dust."

"We'll set foot on its surface at this time tomorrow." Liu pointed through the window. "And I could think of no better friends than you to be with as we take the farthest step mankind has ever taken."

"Best friends," Raphael corrected him.

"We're not going to toast with plastic bags just because we're being melodramatic, are we?" asked Madeleine with a grin.

"Oh yes, we are," Adam decided. "That's the first order from your commander."

They brought their drink bags together in the middle and exchanged a few encouraging pleasantries.

Rachel took another sip and nodded at the Texan. "What's the second order?"

"The second order is ..." He paused and looked at Madeleine with a grin. "No green volcano!"

30

CHRISTER

He spent the next few weeks in an office that had been set up especially for him. He had the latest computers and monitors, and almost infinite computing capacity at his disposal, as well as the latest language model APIs to help him sort and analyze the mountains of data that lay dormant down here. His 'recruitment' to the nameless project deep beneath the Province of Jakarta seemed to fill a gap that Saruko had apparently been complaining about to the board for a while. 'The Board' was the leadership level, so secret that no one knew who belonged to it, where it was located, or even what language it spoke.

Christer spent little time with colleagues except in the canteen, which served surprisingly good food around the clock. There were no fixed times, so the other researchers and workers came in groups or individually whenever they took a break. He had fleeting interactions with a materials researcher from Austria who had been there for five years, a Chilean geophysicist with bright eyes but little need to communicate, and a Canadian called Wikipu, a maintenance engineer who spent most of his time crawling around in tunnels large and small to make sure they all had air to breathe.

No one seemed particularly interested in socializing or friendship, and Christer could understand why. They'd all ended up here involuntarily, losing everything they had built up in their previous lives. The price might be acceptable for them – as it was for him – because the question of the ring's origin and function would not let them go. Nevertheless, a beaten dog still feared the next blow, even though it stayed with its new master.

Only Saruko actively sought contact with him, regularly joining him in the canteen to keep him company and ask him about his progress.

This was the case on a day when Christer had spent half the night in front of materials research data sets, hunting for recurring patterns in the deviations between measurement results and previously established expectations.

"What day of the week is it?" he asked the director, who sat down opposite him with a large plate of pancit and fished a pair of chopsticks out of one of the cups provided.

"To be honest, I don't know." Saruko shrugged his shoulders. "Have you thoroughly familiarized yourself?"

"I'm still trying to get an overview of what we know about the ring so far." Christer took a sip of his coffee, which was surprisingly decent. Maybe the beans had come from Java.

"Do you have your personal data pad with you?"

"Yes, why?"

"Open it." Saruko gave him a wave with the chopsticks, and Christer plucked the slim device from his pocket. "I've sent you a report that our materials scientists sent to the board half a year ago. It should fill in a few gaps."

Christer opened his central intranet app, which brought together all the facility's activities and insights into a single organizational hub. There was a new message in his inbox informing him that he had received approval for a 'Level 3' file. He opened it and found a document on his display.

Date: March 01, 2024

Summary:

This report presents the results of our investigations of the Alpha object, which are intended to serve as a substrate for the last 40 years of research. It is important to note that these results are preliminary and by no means exhaustive. Our analyses focused on the material composition and associated properties that make this extraterrestrial technology so exceptionally resistant and durable.

Material composition:

Object Alpha consists of a still-unknown metamaterial, which we provisionally refer to as 'Meta-X.' Meta-X is characterized by an extremely dense atomic structure, which makes it highly resistant to mechanical, thermal, and radiation stresses. It also appears to be immune to chemical corrosion and erosion. The composition of Meta-X is similar to that of nanomaterials and enables high specific strength and rigidity with a low presumed weight.

Self-repair mechanisms:

Object Alpha has self-repairing systems based on a combination of nanotechnology and a type of programmable matter. The latter assumption is based on the observation of small changes to the ring structure that occur at regular intervals of 6 minutes and 33 seconds. These systems allow the object to detect and repair damage at a microscopic level by moving material from less stressed areas to the damaged ones. This process occurs continuously and gives the object under investigation an impressive regenerative capacity.

Energy storage and conversion:

Object Alpha's energy source is based on a previously unknown form of remote induction that enables high energy density and exceptional efficiency. It has advanced storage systems that can absorb energy from its surroundings and hold it in compact, high-density storage units – although the existence of the latter is based on mathematical calculations and, due to the nature of the ring, not on observations. These energy storage systems, presumably able to couple with the never-ending Pacific Ring of Fire at the base of the ring shaft, are believed capable of providing power for the Earth's primary systems over its lifetime.

Radiation shielding:

Object Alpha is virtually immune to ionizing radiation as it has effective radiation shielding. Meta-X itself exhibits remarkable radiation-absorbing properties and can also serve as an effective barrier against electromagnetic emissions. This protective layer allows the ring to operate undamaged even in extreme radiation environments. It can be assumed that any form of signal transmission along the entire electromagnetic spectrum could not penetrate the object's shell, and therefore nothing would reach the other side.

Magnetic field investigations:

Our investigations show that Object Alpha has a highly developed magnetic field detection system. This system allows the ring to precisely detect and react to changes in the magnetic environment. It is also able to generate and manipulate strong magnetic fields, for example, to influence terrestrial technologies, or to protect itself from external influences. This was noticed when the first workers in the 1980s had functioning two-way radios with them, but they were disturbed by a magnetic field that only became active when they switched on the devices to communicate with each other.

Timing:

Object Alpha is believed to have an extremely precise timing system based on a technology that is not understood. This technology enables the ring to measure time accurately down to atomic time scales, allowing it to precisely synchronize its internal processes and actions. This timing system could also be responsible for the extremely long service life and consistent functionality. This can be seen from the exact occurrence of fluctuations every 6 minutes and 33 seconds, after which a convulsive burst of radiation occurs, which then subsides again.

Conclusion:

Object Alpha continues to be the most significant discovery in materials science. The results of our investigations provide deep insights into the extraordinary properties and capabilities of this extraterrestrial technology. There is a possibility that the exploration of Meta-X and its applications could lead to significant advances in terrestrial science and technology. At the same time, there are still many unanswered questions that require further research to decipher its full potential and origins. Meta-X is not destructible, and with our current technology it is not even possible to take a sample as it cannot be damaged.

Christer summarized what he had read. "In essence, we don't know anything."

"I wouldn't say that," Saruko disagreed.

"Okay, what do we know?"

"Maybe I'll explain it to you using the story of the first exploration parties that discovered this place," the director replied.

"I guess we have time."

"In 1982, a team of geologists and engineers began exploring the natural cave systems beneath Jakarta. They were looking for geothermal energy sources – and uranium, of course – and believed they might find it here. The exploration teams made their way deeper and deeper into the labyrinthine corridors until they finally came across a huge underground cavern – which you have already seen with your own eyes. You can imagine how long those poor devils must have wandered around down here before they made this chance discovery.

"At first it seemed to them that they had simply discovered a remarkable geological formation, but as they ventured further into the cavern, they witnessed an incredible discovery: in the middle of the vast space, the mysterious ring hovered above a vertical shaft that apparently reached down into the lava flows of the Pacific Ring of Fire. The 30-strong team was both fascinated and terrified as they realized they had stumbled upon something far beyond their understanding. Unfortunately, their discovery was not without direct consequences.

"The rudimentary exploration crews had neither the necessary equipment nor the knowledge to cope with the extreme conditions in the cavern. They were only there to map and take samples, drilling a small hole here and there. The heat emanating from the lava source was intense, and the unstable rock surrounding the cavern proved deadly. When the explorers tried to approach the ring, there was a devastating surge of radiation that reportedly caused most of them to burst."

"Burst?" asked Christer, shuddering.

"Yes, we assume that it must have been a gamma radiation surge. This happened again in the 1990s when the tour was created and we were not yet aware of the safety distance."

"So the ring reacted to the presence of the explorers."

"That's possible, yes." Saruko nodded. "Maybe it has some kind of automatic defense system. To make matters worse, part of the cavern collapsed. It took years for a rescue team to clear the entrance. But when they finally reached the cave system, all they found were the remains of the unfortunate exploration crew – at least four of them – plus eight shadows on the wall, similar to those of the atomic bomb victims in Hiroshima and Nagasaki. Since this tragedy, we have done our best to explore the ring and its secrets while heeding the lessons learned from the deaths of these brave men and women."

"Why are you telling me this?" asked Christer.

"To give you an idea of how far we've come. Today we know the safe distance, we know about the object's automatic defense routines, and we can at least speculate about its composition. We can also extract energy from it."

"Why is it called Object Alpha? Are you assuming that there are several more?"

"Yes." Saruko finished his meal and placed the chopsticks neatly beside the plate. "The ring is a simple, replicable structure. I know from the board that they've been looking for more specimens for thirty years."

"So?"

"None have been found so far."

Christer thought about the director's words. "Do you think the light phenomenon on Mars could provide an answer?"

Saruko nodded. "That's what we hope to find out. We're going to run an experiment tonight that we've been preparing for weeks: We'll bombard the ring with plasma, at a particle and energy density equivalent to that of the CME that hit Mars and Earth. If a light comes on, we may know the answer before the crew of the Ambassador."

"Since you're telling me about it, I assume you want me to be part of the experiment?"

"Yes, that's right. I'd like you to go in with the team."

"Inside?" Christer asked, his whole body tensing instinctively. "You mean into the cavern?"

"Yes. You have to experience it to understand it. Of course, you still need a safety briefing ..."

"A few hours beforehand? I think it will take a little more."

"What?" asked Saruko. "What do you need?"

"I need a lot more information. I know next to nothing about the ring."

"Ask me."

Christer looked his director in the eye and searched for signs of a rhetorical feint. But he found none.

"You were talking about gamma radiation."

"Yes. The ring emits a constant but weak radiation. Although it has an unusual composition, it is not ionizing, so presumably not harmful to human bodies," the Japanese man explained patiently. "It seems to be somehow related to the energy flow inside the object. But in what form is still a mystery to us."

"Is there anything that we know about the energy flow?"

"Yes. We once temporarily blocked the shaft down to the Pacific Ring of Fire – which is almost forty kilometers deep, by the way – and the whispering disappeared."

"The shimmer effect?" asked Christer.

"Yes. This suggests that Object Alpha is supplied with geothermal energy."

"Wasn't that already obvious?"

"A hypothesis remains a hypothesis until it has been confirmed through an experiment," Saruko reminded him.

"Thermal energy could never do this much."

"Judging by the state of our technology, you're right. But the ring can do it. The efficiency must be remarkable, especially as it must be a form of induction that doesn't require direct contact. As long as we don't block the shaft – and we don't even have the material technology to do that, because everything melts away in a very short time – Object Alpha has unlimited energy."

"Are there any reasonable assumptions about the age of the ring?"

"No. We can't take samples. Even diamond-coated blades and monofilament can't scratch the ring's shell. Without samples, there is no age determination. But our geologists and geophysicists have determined the age of the cavern, and since Object Alpha gives no indication of being mobile, we assume that it has always been here. The cavern was probably formed four million years ago by a gas bubble, which then looked for a way out."

"And in the process created natural tunnels – the cave system," Christer speculated.

"Yes."

"I've seen that there are physicists specializing in magnetic field technology working here."

"These colleagues have been very busy over the last ten years. They have discovered that Object Alpha generates a strong, localized magnetic field that interacts with the Earth's magnetic field in complex ways. We do not know whether there is a mutual influence, but these scientists were able to prove that they fluctuate locally at the same times. It may be a component of geothermal induction, or stabilization of the ring in its floating state."

Saruko stood up and put his dishes onto his tray. Before he walked away, he paused and spoke once more.

"I want you to be there tonight because I believe in your intuition. I've been assured that you have a brilliant mind, but that it's based on intuitive insight. I'm willing to take a small risk to find out. Perhaps you will see something during the experiment that we and the many sensors will miss."

Christer thought about it and finally nodded. The thought of being back with the alien artifact electrified and, at the same time, terrified him.

31

RACHEL

For the landing phase, which lasted several hours, they all sat in their pressure suits inside the cockpit, their helmet visors closed and the life support cables connected to their neck rings. The flexible SpaceX suits were much more comfortable to wear than the AxEMU units they had on board for emergencies. Still, she felt trapped.

"Carter?" Madeleine requested from the copilot's seat.

"I'm online, Madeleine," replied the on-board AI.

"Why did you call it Carter?" asked Raphael.

"Carter stands for Cognitive Advanced Reasoning and Technological Exploration Resource."

"You made that up?"

"Sure."

"That's not really the reason for the name, guys," Raphael assured them.

"Yes, it is, really," Madeleine replied, sounding offended.

Rachel grinned inside her helmet. The friendly banter dispelled the tension a little and was more than welcome. They had now entered an even riskier phase.

"Maddy." Yuki sighed. "No one believes that's where the name came from."

"I'd like to weigh in," Liu spoke up. "Carter stands for Nick Carter."

"That can't be it," Madeleine objected, tapping a button on her screen. The on-board speakers blared out I Want It That Way by the Backstreet Boys, and a storm of indignation followed. But no one asked her to turn the song off.

Instead, they automatically started singing along.

"How could you all forget Maddy's dark secret?" Liu sighed, but it was clear from his voice that he was grinning. "I certainly can't."

"Anyone who was a teenager in the nineties heard the Backstreet Boys. The girls screamed and shouted and the boys were bashful and secretive. Ten years later, it was cult. I bet you all know the song by heart."

When the chorus came, they all sang loudly. It was a moment of absolute release, a simple, shared joy that filled the entire cockpit and made them forget their worries and fears for a moment.

"Tell me why ..."

"We're doomed," Adam sounded serious, shaking his head. "It's a good thing the communications aren't up yet."

The small CubeSat that Adam had modified over the last few months so that it could serve as a relay station had been launched several hours ago, along with two others intended for Mars observation and as redundancies for the first mini satellite. The modified one had already been powered up but was still on the other side of the Red Planet. In order to maintain communication with Earth, they had decided against programming it with a geostationary orbit, even though this meant that they would not always be in contact. With a bit of luck, they could use the other two CubeSats as a detour, so to speak.

"I'm getting the first weather data from the MRO in here," Adam announced, and Madeleine turned the music down so low it disappeared into the background. "There are widespread dust storms to the east of the landing zone that will take a few more days to reach Elysium Mons."

They had been told time and again during mission preparations that dust storms would be the main threat during their landing. These storms could cover the entire planet and envelop it in a mantle of statically charged dust. In addition to the expected interference, reduced visibility played a major role, which was less relevant for the launch into orbit. But some Mars storms lasted several months, and even if they were not particularly impressive due to the low density of the Martian atmosphere, which was less than one percent of that of the Earth, they could disable solar cells.

A storm with wind speeds of 100 kilometers per hour would be no more than a gentle breeze for them and yet a reason for ground operations to be suspended – visibility was another problem here. In effect, they only had a few days before having to wait, potentially for weeks, in the spaceship while knowing they only had three months total time for the mission.

Nobody said what they were all thinking: the mood was too professional and – thanks to Madeleine – even a little relaxed.

"Cube One reports a connection!" Madeleine shouted excitedly.

Rachel tensed immediately. A connection meant there was a response. She inhaled to ask Adam to hurry up, but then saw he was already reacting.

Shortly afterward, a radio message sounded through the speakers.

"Ambassador, this is Mission Control. We have received

your life sign. Thank God!" The voice belonged to Lucille Pendergast and she sounded immensely relieved.

"We've been following your journey, but we feared that something must have happened to you. It was the right decision to leave the CubeSat in Mars orbit. Thank you for sending us your status and the logs from the past three months. We are now working through everything. Your trajectory looks very good from here. God be with you. You still have an hour before you start the orbital insertion. We thought you could use a few greetings after such a long period of radio silence. The bandwidth isn't great, but it should be enough."

On the main screen, two-minute videos of the families of Rachel's friends appeared one after the other, some of them waving at the camera with tears of joy in their eyes and sending their greetings to Raphael in German, Yuki in Japanese, Liu in Chinese, and Adam and Madeleine in English. Rachel only understood the latter but soon had wet eyes from the raw emotions reflected on the faces of people who loved and surely missed the hell out of her friends and comrades.

Then it was her turn. When she saw Beth and Masha sitting on the sofa of her house in Stanford, she began to cry uncontrollably. Beth pointed at the camera, and Masha waved excitedly. "Mom, you're going to be a Mars astronaut," she exclaimed with a broad grin, although her eyes were very red.

Her daughter bent down and picked up a young chocolate-brown Labrador that could only be a few months old. "Beth gave me a dog. I haven't got a name for her yet. We'll pick it out together when you get back. That was Beth's idea. I miss you very much, but everyone at school says you're a hero, which I think is great. You do what you have to do and I want to tell you that I love you and I understand."

Rachel stretched out her right hand, but couldn't reach

the display with her daughter on it. The fact that Masha sounded so grown-up at such a young age gave her a twinge of guilt.

"We're doing fine here, sis," Beth assured her. "We follow you every day on the news and special broadcasts. The hype around your mission continues unabated, and I still can't believe you're a part of it. I'm proud of you. Don't worry about us. Masha even got an A in math because she wants to be an astronaut now, too. We're waiting for you here."

Beth blew her a kiss. Then the picture changed and showed a black woman saying something in Kiswahili and smiling heart-warmingly at the camera. She was followed by a man, perhaps from Mongolia, who also said something in his native language and waved. His picture remained next to the woman's, then a white woman, possibly from Scandinavia, followed and shouted something encouraging.

More and more images, presumably from webcams, joined the first ones. They apparently came from all over the world and included short words of encouragement and praise. Soon the image was full of hundreds of increasingly smaller clips that made them at least vaguely aware that their entire species was united behind them and eagerly awaiting the goal of their mission.

"If we needed another reminder of what we're doing this for, we've got it now," Yuki said devoutly, taking a deep breath. "I don't know about you, but I'm ready."

"Hell, yeah." Adam pressed a few buttons. "Mission Control, we're about to initiate orbital insertion. We'll report back as soon as we've landed safely."

Due to the distance from Mars to Earth, this message would take at least three minutes to reach Houston. By that time, they would already be on their approach vector.

"Time to initiate orbital insertion," Adam said after a while, and pressed the corresponding button. His right hand moved to the control stick at the end of his armrest. Maddy placed her hand on his and turned toward him.

"It's time now," she stated calmly.

"All right." He gave a low growl and pressed another button. "Carter, you're in control."

"Thank you, Adam," the AI replied over their shared radio channel in its pleasant baritone voice.

Under the control of the on-board AI, the Raptor engines at the stern initiated the Mars orbital insertion and gently pushed them into their seats. Slowly, Carter accelerated them until they reached four kilometers per second so they could enter a stable orbit. The precision of the maneuver had to be perfect and required constant monitoring of navigation and engine data – something the specialized AI was more capable of than any astronaut.

After the successful orbital insertion, the next phase followed: orbit tuning, in which the Ambassador's orbit was repeatedly adjusted with small nudges from the maneuvering thrusters in order to reach the best position for its planned landing approach. Over a total of 11 orbital maneuvers, they lowered their orbit and adjusted their inclination. Rachel found herself gripping Raphael and Yuki's hands while she stared at the flight computer data as an idle passenger and interpreted the various vectors and telemetry data. During this phase, they flew faster and faster, almost tripling their speed.

"Fuel consumption nominal," Carter said. "Maneuverability at one hundred percent. No failures in the DRACOs. Initiating deorbit burn phase."

Rachel's memories of hours of lectures and all-night reading sessions ran through every phase. The 'deorbit burn' slowed them down after a quick turnaround maneuver, causing the Ambassador to shake slightly, as if they were in an off-road vehicle driving over a gravel road. The vibrations were caused by the main engines, which were now acting as brakes by providing well- measured thrust in the direction opposite their flight, slowing them down.

"Ten seconds to angle of entry into Martian atmosphere," said the AI with a calmness that only a machine could display in this situation. "Engines faultless, contact with the CubeSat."

Then came the atmospheric entry. Their instructor in Houston had called Mars an 'incontinent' planet. This was an appropriate term, as the Red Planet, with a bit more than a tenth of the Earth's mass, is not massive enough to hold a denser atmosphere. As a result, lighter gases such as hydrogen escaped into space. In addition, it has no protective magnetic field and is defenseless against solar winds and ionizing radiation, which repeatedly erode what little atmosphere remains before anything significant can form.

Nevertheless, entering the atmosphere was not child's play. The Ambassador raced toward the surface at seven and a half kilometers per second in a stretched, downward trajectory. Despite its low density, the atmosphere still formed an obstacle, which soon made itself noticeable as friction and heat. At first there was a gentle wobble, which quickly turned into a violent jolt and vibration before the first flames licked at the heat-resistant windows, reaching beyond the ceramic tiles. They heated up to 1,600 degrees Celsius – a raging firestorm, as if the planet was defending itself against these alien invaders.

"Flight path stable," came Carter's sober declaration. "All flight data nominal, hull integrity at one hundred percent."

"Yee-Haw!" Adam yelled. Rachel smiled, but she didn't dare try to speak.

Now came the aerodynamic braking. During atmospheric entry, the Ambassador used its shape and size to increase drag and further reduce speed. The Starship's fins made precise positional adjustments so that the ship plunged toward the surface in a stable prone position like a steel parachutist. Rachel could watch on the screens as the AI adjusted their trajectory with uncanny accuracy, making split-second micro-decisions to prevent any structural damage from occurring, or their speed from being even slightly too high.

When this phase had also passed according to plan, the supersonic descent began. Unlike on Earth, they did not emit brutal sonic booms that thundered like the wrath of a Viking god, but rather something that would be perceived by someone on the ground as a kind of distant cough. The aerodynamic control surfaces folded in and out, bringing them into a gentle left-hand rotation before the flight attitude stabilized again. The trajectory adjustments continued, but so quickly that Rachel lost her orientation on the monitor. She wondered whether Adam was also glad that Carter had taken over.

"Terminal descent," the AI told them when they were still about three and a half kilometers up. This was the final descent maneuver. The three central Raptor engines ignited, turned sideways, and spun the Ambassador once around its transverse axis so that its tail was now pointing downward. This was the most critical maneuver, as they switched to vertical trajectory, because time and fuel were the limiting factors. Even a correctable mistake could mean they would end up descending too fast or using too much fuel to have enough to return to orbit.

But Carter mastered that part of the maneuver, too, with Rachel pressed firmly into her seat as the massive spaceship braced itself against the 38 percent Earth gravity.

Finally, the hovering phase followed at an altitude of about 20 meters. The Raptor engines used their gimbals to precisely adjust the trajectory so that they hovered straight as a die above the dusty Martian soil, and descended slowly and gracefully, even though the huge plasma flames outside ignited a hell of heat and pressure. Sensors and cameras in the lower part of the Starship analyzed the landing zone through the swirling dust that floated outward for miles. They showed no obstacles in the targeted landing zone.

The thrust continued to decrease until the extended landing props touched down and the engines simultaneously switched off. Suddenly it was eerily quiet.

Instead of bursting into cheers, they all remained silent.

"System check," Adam said, running his index finger through the menus on his pilot's screen. "Fuel levels in the expected green range, no damage reports on the Ambassador's structure, all instruments and sensors operational. Ladies and gentlemen: Welcome to Mars."

Now they cheered, long and loud.

32

CHRISTER

With trembling steps, he entered the cavern where the mysterious ring lay hidden. The sheer size of the cavern made him hold his breath in amazement. It had impressed him as much smaller, more compact, through the bulletproof glass of the observation room.

Christer was following a large team of technicians and researchers carrying white suitcases. They all wore special heat and radiation protection suits, reminiscent of futuristic diving suits, and made of a silvery, flexible material that was designed to keep out both heat and radiation. The helmets were spherical and fitted with a type of polarized glass that allowed them to look at the ring without endangering their eyes.

He was, of course, outfitted the same and wondering if his suit was malfunctioning, because he was uncomfortably warm and already sweating, even though he had only walked here from the electric cart in the parking cavern. The helmet weighed heavily on his shoulders and made him feel like one of the first deep-sea divers who had been lowered from their ships with a bell on a rope.

As they got closer to the ring, he could see the shimmer in the air above the massive object, as if the surrounding gas molecules were gathering in an invisible epicenter and collapsing. The fascination that this sight aroused in him was only trumped by the palpable trepidation that gripped him when he heard the sound, like a distant whisper carried on the wind, murmuring up and down.

The technicians began to set up their equipment: measuring devices to record temperature, pressure and radiation; cameras and sensors to observe the ring from different angles and distances; and finally, analyzers to study the composition of the atmosphere.

While the equipment was being set up, Christer's gaze wandered through the cavern, the photovoltaic systems that seemed so anachronistic and barbaric in contrast to the ring. Seeing it up close and through his visor – a much thinner layer of glass – revealed some features that he hadn't noticed before.

For one thing, there was the color, which he had initially interpreted as black. But if he hadn't known that it had a solid shell, he would have thought the object was a black hole. The material seemed to absorb all surrounding light and make it disappear, it appeared structureless and infinitely deep.

Then there were the tiny streaks from its underside that disappeared into the deep shaft down to the underground lava flows in the Earth's mantle. The reddish glow from them bathed the cavern in an eerie light that radiated danger, as if a silent alarm siren had been switched on somewhere.

He was so captivated by the ring that he only noticed after a while that someone had been tapping him on the shoulder and demanding that he make way. It was the chief engineer – Resnikov, if he remembered correctly – looking like a spaceman from Space Patrol Orion in his bulky suit. He stopped next to Christer and waited for the heavy equipment to be driven through.

"Is that the plasma machine?" asked Christer over their helmet radios. There was a noticeable crackling and popping in the connection.

"Yes, a laser-based plasma generator. It's quite tricky to set one up down here," the engineer replied with a heavy Russian accent. He was Ukrainian, unless Christer's memory deceived him. "What looks like a huge cannon is the high-energy laser, and these thick snakes are its cables. We had to work on them for a long time so that they could withstand the environment here. Not exactly laboratory conditions, if you know what I mean."

"I get it."

"That thing that looks like an artillery shell is a gas nozzle. We use it to shoot helium in the direction of the shimmer. This gives us a gas jet as thick as an arm, which serves as a medium for the laser-plasma interaction," Resnikov continued. "The high-powered laser shoots at the gas jet, whose molecules ionize and are accelerated and heated by the laser's electromagnetic fields. Then we have our speedy electrons, which drag charged ions behind them – et voilà, the plasma stream: the simulated coronal mass ejection."

"What are those devices? The ones directly in front of and above it?" Christer pointed to the devices, which looked like oversized brake shoes.

"Magnetic guides. We use them to stabilize the plasma flow. It's about to get pretty bright in here in about half an hour."

"Is it dangerous?" Christer asked,

This earned mocking laughter from the engineer, who couldn't seem to catch his breath for a minute. "My boy, everything down here is life-threatening. What do you think?"

"I think, if I'm listening to you talk about this, it's because I'm in the wrong place," Christer replied ironically.

"Maybe Saruko wants to get rid of you," the Ukrainian joked with a chuckle and patted him on the shoulder like a shiny, silvery Martian. "But if it makes you feel any better, I can assure you that I would not want to be anywhere else. It's where the action is, down here, and if we can get the plasma flow as good as it is over in the lab, we'll have a fancy little fireworks display here and you'll have one of the best seats."

"Again, isn't that rather dangerous? What kind of fireworks are we expecting?"

"Bright light, of course, like on Mars. Then we could at least prove that the two are connected. There may even be an Object Beta on Mars. Who knows?" Resnikov might have shrugged his shoulders, but perhaps his slightly baggy suit had just been caught by the wind.

"But it could also happen that there'll be a radiation spike, and we're going to be cooked in these things like lobsters in aluminum foil." The engineer laughed as if he had made a good joke and trudged toward his technicians to give them final instructions.

"At least I'm not dying of boredom," Christer muttered, and sighed.

33

RACHEL

She stood on tiptoe in the cockpit so she could see through one of the windows. The landing zone, which had been researched for months in the run-up to the Ambassador's launch, was three kilometers from the summit of Elysium Mons, which would have been far on Earth, probably distant enough to see the entirety of a volcano.

But Elysium Mons was no ordinary mountain. Its huge structure towered more than 12 kilometers above the Martian landscape, filling her with awe and admiration. It was one of the largest volcanoes on the Red Planet, but instead of having a stratovolcano's characteristic crater, it had a flattened dome, as if ancient magma had formed a lid. For that reason, it has been classified as a shield volcano.

The gently curving flanks of Elysium Mons stretched for several hundred kilometers in all directions, marked by the traces of past lava flows and a history of volcanic activity that stretched back millions of years. The surface was covered in a fine layer of reddish dust that seemed like a fleeting breath from another time. Here and there, Rachel also saw larger pieces of rock and the residue of former lava flows that had cooled to basalt.

Rachel noticed the numerous craters and depressions scattered across the summit and the slopes. These volcanic traces bore witness to an active past which, according to current research, had been silent for a long time. The craters looked like scars, evidence of past chaos and destruction.

The colors of Elysium Mons varied from dark brown to an intense, almost hypnotic red that gave the planet its unmistakable character. Rachel could sense the sun's soft light bathing the landscape in a warm, golden glow. She had always imagined Mars to be duller, paler. The shadows of the craters and hills drew a fascinating pattern of roughness and beauty at the same time.

"Really nice, isn't it?" asked Maddy, who had climbed in from below.

"Yes, I'm really surprised."

"I think it looks like Morocco."

Rachel returned to standing flat on her feet. Holding herself up on her toes hadn't been difficult in one-third Earth gravity, even for several minutes.

"That doesn't sound very exciting," she said.

"Morocco is very beautiful," disagreed the computer scientist. "But I guess you automatically compare everything you see, even if it's so far removed from anything you've ever seen before. And I have to say that Morocco looks similar. A bit nicer."

"More beautiful than this?"

"I once traveled on the Trans-Siberian Railway from Moscow to Ulan Ude. The journey took one hundred hours," Maddy explained and sat down in the pilot's seat. She began making entries on the central display, probably system checks. "That was a long-cherished dream. Just doing nothing and riding through the beautiful landscape of the

Urals and later Siberia. Endless forests in the colorful splendor of autumn."

"Sounds romantic."

"And it was. But after an hour, my boyfriend at the time and I started watching downloaded Netflix movies and reading books."

"On the Trans-Siberian Railway?" Rachel frowned.

"Yes. Everything gets boring after a short time. Our brains always need something new. It will be the same here. That's why Adam has decided that we'll go out in two groups for an hour at a time. Just as tourists."

"Do we have time for this? Shouldn't we go straight to the summit?"

"First of all, we have to get reaccustomed to the feel of gravity. We were in zero gravity for three months," Maddy explained, shaking her head. "Even with our exercise regimen, it's a big challenge. You probably notice the slight dizziness and the weakness in your arms and legs, right? Your whole sense of balance has to build up again, even with the easier conditions of the low gravity here."

"Okay, that makes sense."

"We don't want to rush things, even with the approaching storm. When we are acclimatized, we will also be more attentive. It's better if we trudge through wonderland like awestruck tourists now, and marvel at everything around us," the astronaut continued. "Otherwise we'll just make mistakes later because we might not be paying attention."

"Am I in the first group?" Rachel asked hopefully.

Maddy grinned. "That's why I came here. Adam put Liu, Raphi, and you in the first group."

Rachel gasped her thanks and wasted no time running to the hatch, where she slid down the ladder. Even with several meters of depth, it felt more like she was gliding down.

The port airlock was optimized for Mars operations with

a horizontal outer hatch that became a balcony-like platform with a fold-up railing. The airlock itself was used to remove the extremely small, sharp Martian sand, which drastically shortened the service life of all suits and equipment that came into contact with it. It was therefore important they carry as little of it as possible into the Ambassador, as the same problem applied to biological systems such as their lungs. If inhaled, the sand had the potential to injure and permanently damage their airways.

Adam was waiting for her outside the inner door, through the porthole of which she could see that Liu and Raphael were already struggling into the white and red exploration suits.

"Aha, there you are!" Adam greeted her. "I just want you to walk around, look around, and enjoy your time. Nothing more, nothing less."

"Thank you," she said.

"For what?"

"I know how much it means to you astronauts to be the first to do something. Whoever is the first to set foot on Mars will go down in history, whether they like it or not," she replied, placing a hand on his arm. "I understand that."

Adam smiled a subtle smile. "We're so easy to figure out, aren't we?"

"I would rather say that after a year of living and working together under tough conditions, you are easy for me to understand."

"Then you will surely understand the reason for the decision, which was made collectively, by the way."

"What decision?"

"That you'll be the first to step down, of course," said Adam.

Rachel stiffened. "Me?"

"Of course. You're the one who is a real astronaut but

never wanted to be one. You didn't even think about wanting to be the first. Am I right?"

"Well, I did want to get out there as quickly as possible and feel the Martian sand under my boots," she replied a little contritely.

"But not because you wanted to be the first, and to go down in history."

"No, I honestly thought one of you would do that. It makes me rather nervous. What am I supposed to say?"

"Whatever comes to mind at the moment." Adam waved her nervousness off. "Each of us has probably written a thousand notes with ideas, but can they really be as valuable as the first thought that comes into your head? Unfiltered, unprepared? You are the one who is the least ego-laden among us, and the only one who didn't want to be here in the first place. We all agree that you are the best choice for the first human on Mars."

"And that was really the unanimous decision of the crew?" Rachel asked hesitantly.

"No. It was a unanimous decision by your friends."

Without further ado, she wrapped him in her arms and nodded. "All right."

"It's time to go, then. Those two are already waiting."

Not needing to be asked twice, she opened the inner airlock door and joined Liu and Raphael in the room, which resembled a padded cell thanks to its white honeycomb walls.

"There you are. We thought we'd have to do the walk without you," Raphael said with a grin. He was already dressed in his exploration suit, which was reinforced at the chest and joints, and decorated with flags of the mission, Germany, the EU, and the ESA. 'Brandt' was written on his chest. Liu's suit, on the other hand, was embellished with those of the mission, China, and the CNSA. Both men held their helmets under their arms and set them aside to help her.

Rachel took off her jumpsuit and stowed it in the locker bearing her name, which consisted of a rectangular door in the wall with a small compartment behind it. Then she checked the fit of her functional underlayer and took her own exploration suit out of the locker. The pants were extremely stiff, like a motorcyclist's leathers, but she could still manage on her own. Once she had slipped into the boots and joined and sealed them to the pantlegs, the more difficult part came: the top of the suit, which was still hanging down her back.

Her colleagues helped her work her arms and torso into it and then close all of the press studs and seals. The entire suit weighed around 15 kilos on Earth, but only a bit over five now. When she was fully clothed and the head-up display in her visor showed her that all systems were 'green' and working properly, they checked their radios and gave each other the thumbs up.

"This is Maddy, you're coming in loud and clear. Good luck out there. Don't tread all over Mars at once, will you?"

"All right," Liu replied, and opened the outer airlock door. In her suit, Rachel didn't notice any change in temperature or airflow. When they stepped out onto the 'balcony,' which was about 30 meters above the ground, they stopped and looked around.

Rachel leaned her head back and looked up at the strange sky. It shimmered reddish-brown like the flesh of a butternut squash. Clouds of carbon dioxide ice drifted eastward high above her, some as white as sheep's wool, others steel gray to bluish. The air seemed hazy, like a damp day on Earth.

"The sky looks so different," she remarked reverently. "So strange."

"That's from the fine dust particles in the air," Liu explained. "They scatter the sunlight in a way that highlights the reddish and yellow wavelengths, giving the sky its characteristic color."

"You natural scientists know how to destroy any romance," she said not unkindly. "The sun looks reddish. And small," she said with a sigh.

"We are one and a half times as far away from it as we are on Earth, so it is only about two thirds the size it is at home," Liu explained. "The apparently reddish color and the significantly lower luminosity are also due to the refraction of light by the many dust particles in the thin atmosphere." He nodded toward the sky, and then raised his hands defensively when he noticed her gaze. "Okay, I get it, I'll stop now."

"No one has ever been here before. Eyes have never before seen what our eyes are seeing," she replied, fascinated. The feeling was magical. She was one of the first three consciousnesses to perceive this place. The idea that something like Mars could exist without ever having been seen and experienced by a conscious being – this silent, wondrous structure of rock in the fabric of time – was beyond conception.

Raphael was the first to detach himself from the sight of the rocky wasteland around them and began to fiddle with the fasteners of the winches holding the platform in place.

Rachel let her gaze continue to wander over the landscape around her. The Ambassador stood like a skyscraper on a wide field of flat rock with a few small boulders. There was hardly any sand here, probably because the exhaust flares from the Raptor engines had either melted it or blown it away during their landing. With a little imagination, she could see that the landscape rose to the west, toward the summit. It was hard to comprehend that they were 12 kilometers above base level, so gently did the slopes of Elysium Mons rise.

She realized that Madeleine had been right. Her surroundings did indeed look like an earthly rocky desert. What she found drastically different from Earth were the ideas that her mind automatically superimposed on the surroundings, that everything was new, as if it was only generated the moment she looked at it, like a computer game. How real could a place be that had never been seen before?

"Are you ready?" Madeleine asked over the radio.

"All the fasteners look good," Raphael reported, and Liu nodded from his side of the anchorage.

"Then I'll take you down now. Hold on tight."

Rachel grabbed the railing to her right and shortly afterward her colleague began to operate the winch mechanism that lowered the platform on which they were standing, taking them toward the surface. With every meter they descended at an agonizingly slow pace, their excitement grew, as did their understanding of how significant this moment was, and how lucky they had been to have no major problems up to this point. Apart from the communication failure, of course.

When their external elevator finally stopped – and she imagined she heard a soft chirp from the threads – there it was, directly in front of her: the rust-brown Martian surface. She looked at Liu, and he nodded at her with a somber expression. Then she looked at Raphael on her other side and he nodded encouragingly.

Rachel almost expected one of them to jump ahead and be the first to put his boots in the sand, but they stood still to let her go first. Part of her wanted to pull back, feeling it was unfair that she of all people should have the honor. But perhaps it truly was the fairest solution for everyone.

Am I not being petty for thinking about something so trivial when it comes to real human history? she thought, taking a deep breath. She knew she was being filmed from above. The camera equipment had taken up at least as much space in the preparation as everything else, and since Adam's CubeSat was working as a communications relay, they were also sending audio and video signals again. That meant that in three minutes the whole world would see and hear what she was doing and, more importantly, saying.

Rachel lifted one foot and stepped onto Mars. She brought her other foot down, feeling her boots sink a little. Apparently she had stepped into a small hollow from which not all the sand had been blown away by the boosters.

For a few breaths, she just stood there looking down at her boots, then stepped backwards, onto the platform again, so that she – and her helmet camera – were aimed directly at the two prints.

"My footprints," she said, emphasizing every syllable. "But an achievement of all mankind."

As she looked down at the grooves left by her boots, she felt strangely familiar with this place, as if she had been here before. Perhaps it reminded her of her vacation in Oman last summer? She turned to Raphael and Liu in turn, who smiled and nodded.

"Hwang Liu," she addressed her Chinese friend, pronouncing his name as she had practiced it in Mandarin. Then she said to Raphael: "Raphael Brandt. I'm following you two."

At first they seemed a little confused, but then they obviously understood, nodded to her after a long look, and stepped onto Elysium Mons.

The vast plateau of the landing zone, which stretched out below the summit of the majestic shield volcano, seemed almost endless from there. But compared to the almost 600-kilometer diameter of the mountain, it had looked like a tiny speck from orbit. It was part of the flattened peak, in fact, although they were three kilometers away from its center and the location of the light phenomenon.

The wind whistled softly around her helmet, and the thin dust that permeated the atmosphere like suspended particles in an ocean swirled up in small, ghostly eddies.

The landscape had a sublime, almost eerie beauty, characterized by rolling hills lost in the distance, and deep, mesmerizing shadows cast by the slanting sun. The terrain was littered with boulders and debris that looked like the remains of a shattered, ancient golem. Rachel could make out the fine layers of sedimentary rock that had piled up over millions of years, sculpted by the tectonic forces that had created this massive volcano.

The mighty shadow of the Ambassador stood out sharply on the red ground. It was hard to imagine that this was a place where humans had never set foot before, and Rachel felt both exalted and humbled as she took her first steps on this strange world. Everything looked so strangely normal, so much like Earth when she thought of the rocky deserts of Utah, New Mexico, and Arizona.

Although she was isolated from her surroundings by the protective suit, she could literally feel Mars – the cold that prevailed despite the weak rays of sunlight at her altitude, and the unrelenting silence that was only interrupted by the occasional crunch of her footsteps, which she heard through her suit. The atmosphere was so thin that even the wind barely made a sound, leaving her to focus only on her breathing and her thoughts.

She took another moment to absorb the scenery and take in the endless expanse of the Red Planet. It was a world so different from Earth in terms of evolutionary history, and yet it felt profoundly familiar – as if she had landed in the primeval past of her own home planet.

Finally, she turned her gaze back to her colleagues, who were also standing still. Liu was the first to speak.

"Ambassador, starting reconnaissance now," he said, and began to walk off.

The gravity of Mars was astonishingly low at 38 percent that of Earth's. During her countless parabolic flights in training, she had spent several hours in the equivalent of Martian gravity. Back then, she had been surprised at how light it felt, and how much her steps resembled jumps. This was how she had imagined movement on the moon, which had significantly less gravity still. This time they weren't in an airplane and weren't limited to 30-second parabolas – and they took advantage of this fact to start running, or rather jumping.

With ease, they made leaps of several meters and she couldn't help but laugh. Liu and Raphael might be too professional for that, but she let herself be carried away by the moment of relief and joy, running around a boulder sticking like a tooth out of the smoothly polished ground.

"Ambient temperature at minus thirty degrees," Liu announced over the radio. "Radiation levels within the expected normal range."

"The ground is very hard, probably compacted basalt," Raphael added. "Further west, outside the landing zone, there seems to be more regolith."

Rachel let the men deliver their robotic verbal reports and confined herself to not being an astronaut. She touched one of the man-sized stones lying some distance from their spaceship, feeling it with her gloved hand. Then she knelt down and let the first regolith she found – a mixture of rock and minerals eroded into sand and dust – trickle through her fingers. She held her gloved hand up to the pale sun and watched as the falling grains began to sparkle beautifully like tiny diamonds.

She took this time, which was all about being present and giving people back home a sense of what it was like to enter an alien world, knowing the serious part of her mission would soon begin.

She had a feeling that the nature of her exploration would change abruptly.

34

CHRISTER

He stepped onto the ceramic walkway leading to the circuit that went around the cavern at the base of the many photo-voltaic systems, which, due to their shape, resembled a crater with a drain in the lower half. Except, this glowing red drain looked like the mouth of Hell, malevolent and blazing.

Christer waited there for quite a while, during which time the technicians in their bulky suits set up measuring instruments, shielded cameras, and a whole host of other things he couldn't identify. Most of their equipment was hidden under protective films, but he didn't think he would have been any more successful under any other circum-stances. This wasn't his area of expertise, if an artifact like this could be anyone's area of expertise.

The people here are probably the closest to that level, he thought, and leaned against the rock face behind him. He avoided looking into the lava chasm and kept his eyes fixed straight ahead on the ring. It was scary too, but nothing like the abyss. Not that he could see all the way down – the hole was far too deep for that. Just knowing that it went dozens of kilometers down was enough to make his hair stand on end.

He watched tensely as one of the technicians – possibly Resnikov – made the final adjustments to the plasma generator. The device resembled a futuristic weapon, consisting of an elongated, cylindrical construction supported by a sturdy bracket. At one end was a transparent dome in which a complex system of mirrors and lenses was arranged to precisely focus the laser beam.

After a while, Christer was sweating so heavily the beads of perspiration ran down into his boots and collected there. Another hour and he would be boiling in his own bodily fluids. Just as he thought there had been a mistake and was about to radio to ask if they should leave, there was an announcement.

"This is Saruko speaking. Everything looks good on our side. Start the trial as soon as you're ready."

The technicians in their silver suits looked intently at the ring and, in turn, at the complex device, while one of the scientists made the final preparations.

The plasma generator came to life with a quiet whirring, effortlessly drowning out the eerie whispering and the hissing of the capacitors. To begin with, they fed helium gas into a special chamber inside the plasma generator. The high-power laser beam was then directed at the gas through the transparent dome and the system of mirrors and lenses. The laser beam's high-energy photons ionized the helium gas and excited the electrons of the atoms, causing the gas to enter the plasma state.

The beam of ultra-hot plasma shot forward, penetrating the shimmer and interacting with the photons that caused the phenomenon. The result was a luminous sphere that shone with a dazzling, iridescent light. The sphere's colors changed constantly, as if it wanted to display all spectral colors at the same time, until a bright, breathtakingly beautiful and disturbingly powerful sun shone in the heart of the cavern.

Even with the mirrored visor of his bulky helmet, Christer had to raise his arms to protect his eyes.

The cavern was transformed by the sphere's luminosity into a glowing nothingness that overwrote all contours and reliefs. Instead of structures, there were only reflections. The scientists and technicians around him paused for a moment in awe-struck amazement, marginalized by the light into narrow silhouettes in the storm of photons. When the plasma jet dried up, it was suddenly over and everything looked as it had before.

Christer realized he'd been holding his breath and found himself gasping for fresh air. But inside his suit the air smelled stale and sweaty.

Only gradually did the bystanders turn back to their measuring devices and records to analyze the new phenomenon.

There had been something hypnotic about the scene, and he sensed that the sphere was still there: the little star they had awakened.

No, we didn't awaken it. It is there all the time, we just don't see it, he thought, trying to imagine how utterly blind they were if this alien machine was really producing photons all the time that they just couldn't see. The spectrum visible to the human eye is so small that their blindness was not surprising. But they had made it visible, which didn't change the fact that it had been there all the time with this all-encompassing power and force.

All of a sudden he felt out of place, like an intruder in something that was too big for them. Did any of them have the right to be here? Or were they like ants that had strayed into a house? Could they ever hope to fathom a mystery like this, which was obviously centuries, if not millennia, ahead of them technologically?

He had his doubts.

"It's definitely a permanent effect," Saruko said louder than the radio interference. It took Christer a few seconds to understand that he was using a private channel.

What does this man see in me? he asked himself, not for the first time. The Japanese man seemed to be taking him by the hand and guiding him very closely, being downright over-friendly. But why? What does he hope to gain from this? Christer saw no reason why he should be worth more than the many better-paid scientists in the facility, especially as they had much more experience with Object Alpha. What is this man up to?

"Obviously," he replied, sniffing against the boiling sweat in his suit. "The question is, what can we do with this information?"

"Come back and freshen up. Then I want to show you something," Saruko said somewhat vaguely before he cut the connection.

35

RACHEL

She waved to Adam, Liu, and Raphael one last time before she used the control panel in front of the inner airlock door to close the outer door, leaving the three astronauts on the platform.

During several hours of preparation, they had unloaded their two rovers and equipped them so that their friends could set off for their actual destination: the Mars Anomaly.

She would stay behind with the other two women on the crew and keep in touch with them, constantly informed via video and audio feeds. The decision that Adam would be the engineer and commander had already been made during the planning phase, especially as he'd had the most training with the rover. The same applied to Liu and Raphael: the Chinese photonics expert was indispensable for the first investigation, and Raphael, as a quantum physicist, was also predestined for the first contact with the signal source.

Madeleine, as a computer scientist, was most valuable here, and Rachel's specialty wouldn't be needed unless there was some form of communication. And they hadn't seen anything of E.T. yet. Yuki also stayed behind as their doctor, to be ready in case of an emergency with one of the men. So far, they had nothing else to do but sit together in the common room and stare at the monitors they had pivoted out from the slots in the large table, which could thus be transformed into a modular workstation.

They watched via the outside cameras as the three men took seats in the front rover, which was not enclosed and therefore offered no protection from radiation. This decision had been made by the mission planners because the crew would only be in the northern hemisphere of Mars, where the radiation intensity was significantly lower than in the southern hemisphere. Carter autonomously controlled the cargo rover that was packed with crates like an overloaded river barge. The AI would have no problems in the relatively easy-to-handle terrain and had proven itself reliable by delivering excellent results in tests on Earth.

The two vehicles, which looked like wheeled tanks cut in half horizontally, had batteries that lasted for about 1,000 kilometers at 60 percent engine power. Once again, they had benefited from the Starship's extreme payload, because at least they didn't have to worry about their friends running short of battery power.

"That's where our boys are going." Madeleine sighed. On the image from the outside camera, a plume of dust formed behind the vehicles as they drove leisurely up the minimal incline to the west. Another monitor showed live helmet-cam footage from the three of them, automatically labeled with the appropriate name.

"Envious?" asked Yuki.

"You bet your life!" Madeleine exclaimed.

"I don't think it's so bad in here."

"What do you mean?" Madeleine looked at her questioningly from the side. "Have you really enjoyed our tin can that much in the last three months?"

"To be honest, yes," the Japanese woman replied with a nod.

Rachel looked for signs of sarcasm in her expression but couldn't find any.

"In my culture, we like minimalist environments and designs. In here, everything is white with a few green elements. We even have a few plants – albeit plastic ones, which make nice visual accents and when I want to relax, I put on one of the VR goggles and I'm in the forest. But out there," she pointed behind her toward the wall, "it's barren, hostile, and desolate. Don't get me wrong, the walk was impressive, but mainly because everything on Mars is new and untouched. But it's much friendlier in here. Besides, I think I'd be extremely nervous right now if I were in the men's shoes."

"I know what you mean," Rachel replied. "Just the idea of standing almost fourteen kilometers out in front of something that I can't see with my own eyes, but which is a hundred and fifty meters in diameter and floods the entire area with photons, makes me shudder."

"You have too much imagination," Madeleine remarked gruffly, but her smile was friendly.

"That's why they chose me."

"That's true, but those three don't have that. Otherwise they wouldn't be able to work with such precision and concentration in situations like this."

Three months in a relatively confined space and nine months of close cooperation in preparation had ensured that they knew each other better as a team than many married couples would ever know each other. That was why she understood what the computer scientist's statement meant.

"You're quite right. That's why I'm so grateful to be in here with you."

"Adam, what's the status?" Madeleine radioed, pressing a button on the keyboard in front of her.

"Everything looks good. We're sticking with fifty percent engine power. The driving experience takes some serious getting used to with the low gravity. I wish we could have simulated it better at home. But it works. It's a bit like driving a snowmobile."

The women followed their colleagues and friends as they drove through the barren landscape, looking through the men's helmet cameras as though through their eyes. The volcano's shield, which stretched for many kilometers, appeared to have been sanded smooth by the millions of years of Martian storms, however gentle they might be. There were few obstacles for Adam to avoid, so the journey proceeded uneventfully. The AI-controlled rover always kept to the exact programmed distance and it went around every boulder that Adam drove around.

After about 15 minutes, they reached the summit of the inactive volcano and slowed down.

"Can you see what I'm seeing?" Rachel asked, leaning forward until her eyes were only two hand-widths away from the monitor display.

"It looks like a mirage on the highway," Yuki replied.

"Heat waves. That looks like heat waves," she affirmed.

"On Earth, heat-wave mirages are caused by temperature differences in the atmosphere, which refract light in different ways – due to the dense atmosphere and the associated refraction of light. The atmosphere here is much thinner than that on Earth and consists mainly of carbon dioxide. Due to the small temperature differences in the Martian atmosphere, the refractions are not large enough to create heat waves as we know them on Earth," Madeleine explained.

"She's nervous," Yuki said and Rachel nodded.

"Definitely nervous."

"You're damn right. That's what happens when I see something that shouldn't be possible," grumbled the computer scientist. "Because I also see heat waves in the picture."

Adam's high-resolution camera image pointed directly at the apparition, which took up most of his field of vision. It was as if half the horizon was shimmering. Perhaps it was partly due to the interference that had started to distort the images of the three astronauts a few seconds ago. Again and again, white noise was mixing in with the images, and the quality of the radio contact.

"We're stopping now," the commander radioed, and the rovers stopped.

"Adam, we're getting a lot of fractals and interference. Can you also confirm the interference on site?" asked Madeleine.

"Yes. The rover is complaining about a strong magnetic field nearby. It must have something to do with the signal."

"That looks really freaky," Liu said, and his image showed him moving parallel to the shimmering sphere. "The visual effect is not very pronounced, but it looks like the air is shimmering like it does on a hot summer day. It spreads at least a hundred meters to the right and left and upward."

The section his camera was showing suddenly shifted downward. Apparently the taikonaut had just dropped to his knees. Rachel was afraid he might have fallen as a result of the signal having done something, but then he continued speaking.

"It looks like the effect is not at ground level, or at least not visually recognizable."

"What's that in the middle?" asked Raphael.

Rachel squinted to see what the German was looking at. Only after looking several times did she discern a dark spot on the ground under the center of the shimmer.

"It looks like a hole," said Adam. "Can you guys hear that whispering sound?"

"I think it's the wind," Raphael replied.

"It's probably an acoustic illusion caused by wind noise on the helmet," Liu agreed and straightened up again. "The optical effect that we perceive as shimmering seems to start one or two meters above ground level and extend about one hundred and fifty meters in all directions. It's much stronger in the center than at the edges."

"Okay, we'll take it one step at a time," Adam commanded as he turned to the two heavily laden rovers. "We'll set up our gear first so we can collect data. You know the procedure. We've practiced it a lot. I bet we can beat our best time from training. But remember not to go beyond the provisional safety distance of two hundred meters."

The three of them set to work unloading the heavy crates, which would have taken four of them to carry on Earth and here they could easily move them in pairs.

"Maddy, do you want to explain a bit about this to our viewers?" asked Yuki.

"Oh, sure." Madeleine shook her head as if startled out of a waking dream.

"So, as you can see, Adam, Raphael, and Liu are currently setting up several detectors to investigate the photon phenomenon. First, Adam is installing a spectrometer to analyze the photons' emission spectra. This will allow us to determine their energy levels and the type of radiation they emit. Liu is working on a photomultiplier, a highly sensitive light detector. You can recognize it by its shape – it looks like a futuristic laser gun. This is due to the very large diameter of the device, which is otherwise much smaller. This complex thing allows us to detect even the smallest amounts of light and count the photons, which in turn allows us to better understand the spatial distribution and intensity of the photon source."

Madeleine looked up into one of the cameras under the ceiling, which blinked green to indicate that it was the one through which millions, if not billions, of people were watching them.

"Liu is in charge of setting up an interferometer with which we can study the spatial coherence of photons. The interferometer measures the interference patterns that arise when light beams interact with each other. This allows us to better understand the wave properties of photons. These devices were all specially designed for this mission and are therefore relatively light, compact, and energy efficient. They are designed to work under the extreme conditions of Mars, and to provide valuable data for our research for a long time to come."

"As soon as the detectors are set up and operational," Yuki interjected, "we will analyze the collected data and try to draw conclusions about the nature and origin of the signal. Whatever secret is behind the photon source, we are well equipped to get to the bottom of it."

Rachel watched as Adam, Raphael, and Liu set up the devices, forming a semi-circle facing the Ambassador in front of the shimmer so they wouldn't have to worry about too much signal interference. It took them almost three hours to set up all the detectors, connect them to the mobile battery on the cargo rover, and then align them correctly. They were guided by Madeleine, who kept checking the incoming signals and directing adjustments until she finally gave the green light after another hour.

"What do the dosimeters say?" the computer scientist finally asked.

"That we've overstayed our welcome," Adam replied nebulously enough for Rachel to feel a twinge of worry.

"I'd like to send one of the copter drones out to take pictures from all angles," Raphael spoke up. "I realize that's not planned until tomorrow, but with the storm coming in, I'd rather not miss the opportunity."

Adam pondered for a while, during which the image from his helmet moved side to side across the shimmer effect, and the radio remained silent.

"Agreed," he finally decided. "But we'll pull back further to minimize our radiation exposure. We'll drive back until the curvature is adequate and then park behind one of the larger rocks."

That was what they eventually did, driving back along their outbound tire tracks and leaving the cargo rover where it was.

"Carter, let me know if you pick up anything unusual with the rover sensors," Adam said.

"Of course, Adam." The AI sounded almost lifelike.

Behind their improvised radiation shield, they released one of the small reconnaissance drones from its box, the first prototype of which had been tested on Mars with 'Ingenuity' as part of the 'Perseverance' mission in 2020. These new 'Red Sentinels' were optimized versions with greater carrying capacity and a more powerful energy supply. This time, the small helicopter drone was controlled directly by Raphael, and not by a computer with instructions from Earth.

The live image from the Red Sentinel was extremely high-resolution and sharp, and displayed what was possible with the latest ultra-small cameras. Due to the low air density, Raphael had to steer the drone very carefully and almost gingerly using his VR HUD in his helmet, but it generated an amazingly good all-round image of the signal source and the shimmer.

"Do you see that?" asked Adam.

"What?" The voice belonged to Liu. Rachel had mentally asked the same question.

"Fly higher again with a wider lens angle," Adam told the German, and it looked as if the drone's camera was zooming out.

It took Rachel a few moments before she saw it too: beneath the shimmering sphere, a dark ring with an extremely large diameter.

"It's some kind of ring structure," Adam explained. "It must be huge."

"Why didn't the MRO see this from orbit?" Rachel asked her two colleagues.

"Probably due to the low resolution at this distance," said Madeleine.

Liu asked, "Ambassador, do you have the data?"

"We have received everything – with interference and fractals, but we see it."

"Good."

"What about the hole under the optical effect?" Raphael asked. "I could try to fly in, below the shimmering."

Adam was silent for a while, then his camera's image shook up and down. He'd obviously nodded.

"But be careful."

"I always am."

Rachel looked at the small dark dot in the center of the ring, which kept appearing and disappearing like a brief visual disturbance due to the distortion of the shimmering effect. But it was definitely there.

Red Sentinel did one last lap. Rachel was silent, her eyes fixed on the fascinating, strange landscape that spread out before her in rich shades of red. Yuki and Madeleine didn't speak, either. The drone hovered skillfully around the mysterious shimmer that crowned the summit of Elysium Mons and then carefully continued on its course. Light wind caused the image to jerk briefly whenever the ultra-light aircraft encountered its turbulence.

Regardless, the drone flew with graceful precision at a respectful distance from the anomaly and spiraled downward. Just above the ground, the Red Sentinel braked so abruptly that Rachel feared it would crash. Instead, it chased along below the shimmer, diving between the ring and the ground. The rugged, rocky surface of Mars glistened like a mighty, parched sea of iron-oxide-red floes. Every breeze that swept across the surface turned into a gentle puff and stirred up small sand devils as the drone flew toward its target.

Rachel's heart beat faster as it headed for the hole.

"It looked tiny from above," murmured Madeleine. "But the thing must be ten meters in diameter, if not more."

"At least that, yes," Yuki agreed with her.

The dark abyss came closer, and with it, increasingly strong interference. The recording on the screen began to flicker, and the images showed more and more pixel errors and ugly fractals that turned the scenery three kilometers away into stroboscopic chaos. They held their breath as the image froze several times before returning to its original state for fractions of a second.

"Adam?" Madeleine radioed to the away team.

"Yes, we can see it too," he replied. There was no more crackling in the connection now that they had moved further away from the signal source.

Suddenly, for a brief moment, the image came back into focus as the drone plunged into the dark hole like Luke's proton torpedo into the Death Star. Rachel could hardly believe what she was seeing. It was as if the Red Sentinel was sliding down into a cosmic maw that opened up between the planes of the real and the unimaginable. There was a dark hole with a distant, tiny red dot, and it was so incredibly deep that it looked as if the drone was frozen in place.

"Contact has broken off," Adam announced.

"The temperature readings exploded just before it went out," Raphael said with audible confusion. "How is that possible? According to the last warning message, several hundred degrees Celsius!"

"What is that?" Rachel whispered, unable to turn away from the still image.

"It looks like an extremely deep hole," Yuki murmured thoughtfully.

"But what is that red dot? A light?"

"I don't know," Madeleine replied instead of the Japanese woman. "But it's certainly no more of natural origin than this ring or this shimmer business."

36

CHRISTER

"So, what do you think?" Saruko asked when Christer entered the director's office an hour later, his hair still wet from a shower.

"That it's a very special experience to cook in your own sweat in an industrial heat protection suit," he replied. After a gesture from the Japanese man, he sat down on one of the two chairs facing the spartanly furnished desk.

"And urine."

"Excuse me?"

"Didn't you need to go while you were wearing your suit?" asked Saruko, more curiously than usual.

"I was wondering what was tingling down there."

"It certainly wasn't champagne."

"Did you just make a joke?" Christer straightened up in surprise.

"Who, me?"

"I didn't think you were capable of it."

"So, what do you have to say?"

"It was scary. The whispering sounded like something

out of a horror movie," Christer replied, glad to be far away from the cavern.

"It's because we humans are exposed to too many horror films along with all the other audiovisual garbage," declared Saruko, leaning back and scowling. "If people knew what they were doing to their mirror neurons, they would only watch benign children's movies and comedies."

"Those engineers and technicians, they really are crazy," Christer continued, as if the Japanese man had said nothing. "They even seemed to enjoy the whole thing. The heat, the noise, the dosimeters going crazy."

He put as much disapproval and reproach into his voice as possible, but Saruko brushed off his remarks with a gruff, "Hmph," and a hand flick.

"The danger of radiation to the human body is mainly measured by the duration of exposure. We have forty years of experience with this radiation source down there and we time our operations accordingly. Don't worry about it."

"You asked for my impressions," Christer snapped, "so listen up, man."

Saruko smiled thinly and folded his hands in front of his chin expectantly.

"Object Alpha seems even stranger than I imagined. The ring feels ancient, as if it has its own unique presence. It's hard to describe, but that's what it feels like. I think, after watching the experiment, we can assume that the light phenomenon on Mars and the shimmering down here have the same origin and work according to the same principles."

"Yes. We've been suspecting that for a long time. Ever since the NASA images were delivered to us, to be precise. An artificial photon source on Mars – nothing else could explain it."

"Did you get the pictures before the public?"

"I don't know. I only know I got the pictures. We hardly

get anything from out there down here," Saruko replied with a hint of impatience. "So, if you want to know whether our backers have direct access to NASA, I have to disappoint you – I don't know."

"You wanted to show me something?" Christer opted to change the subject. Trying to have a normal conversation with this man seemed painfully laborious.

"Yes. I'd like to talk to you about second thirty-four."

Christer frowned. "Should that term mean anything to me? If you mean the experiment with the plasma, I don't think the plasma stream was maintained for that long. Maybe about twenty seconds. At most."

"You know, the first exploration team that came here in 1982 and discovered the natural cave system after the first drillings was led by Ludwig Höglmayer. He was one of the best speleologists of his time and was hired by Megah Adara to locate possible drilling sites so that soil samples could be taken."

Saruko opened a drawer in his desk and tossed him a faded color photo of a bearded man, maybe in his forties, sweaty and hatted, but obviously happy. He was holding an old Super 8 camera in his hand like a trophy.

"A passionate amateur filmmaker. But he was forbidden to film the exploration area. At least that's our theory, because there's a very long recording of him discovering the cavern and encountering Object Alpha for the first time. You can see him on the film, at least up to a certain point."

"So someone else filmed him," Christer concluded. "A somewhat clumsy way of flouting a regulation, but apparently he succeeded." He thought about it. "I haven't seen him down here, though."

"No, and you can't either. He discovered the cavern, and it was thanks to the video recordings that this facility became what it is today. If he knew what he had created, he would certainly be proud of himself."

"You seem to ... worship him."

"I do," Saruko admitted with a serious face. "Everyone here does."

"Why are you telling me all this?"

"Let me ask you a question first. Do you really believe in intuition?"

"If you're asking me this question," said Christer, "you probably already know that I've spent a lot of time on this topic, and that I'm ridiculed for it by colleagues in the scientific world."

"The first: Yes. The second: No. Would you like to enlighten me?"

"Um, sure. In scientific terms, intuition would be defined as the ability to process knowledge or decisions quickly and without conscious thought. Intuition is often the result of experience, implicit knowledge, and cognitive abilities. It helps us to react quickly to situations without slowing us down through conscious analysis and logical thinking. It is therefore an important aspect of our thinking, which often takes place unconsciously and is based on connections that our brain makes between different pieces of information."

"But you don't agree, am I right?" Saruko asked, leaning forward to rest his elbows on the desk.

"No, I don't, and that's why I'm ridiculed as an esotericist. Only because I don't think we should dismiss everything that works but can't be adequately explained, and label it esoteric, or just squeeze it into something familiar through a brutal act of reduction just to make us feel better. That is unscientific in my eyes."

"So what do you believe intuition is?"

"There is the idea that the human brain could interact with quantum phenomena at a subatomic level, giving us access to information beyond our conscious thought. The best known is the theory of 'Orchestrated Objective Reduction' or 'Orch-OR,' developed by Roger Penrose and Stuart Hameroff. They propose that the human brain could use quantum processes that take place in the microtubules of neurons. These quantum processes could lead to our brains processing non-local information and thereby gaining intuitive insights that go beyond what would be possible through logical thinking alone," explained Christer.

"And you believe that?"

"I believe that they are closer to the point than those who want to explain everything with experience and unconscious thought processes because they are lazy or unimaginative."

"Why?" Saruko asked.

"Because I can sense patterns. I sometimes know where the pattern is and what it looks like without having approached a data set with my mind. I often know intuitively where to look and what I want to find." Christer shrugged his shoulders. "Besides, there are signs that Penrose and Hameroff are right."

"Such as ...?"

"Does the name Rupert Sheldrake mean anything to you?"

"No."

"Sheldrake is a renowned British biologist who conducted research for Cambridge University and has been widely vilified as a pseudoscientist for his hypothesis of morphogenetic fields. In his opinion, these are possible energy fields that influence the development and behavior of organisms. Sheldrake has proposed that these fields serve as a kind of invisible memory that stores and transmits information about the shape and organization of biological structures.

"In principle, he also believes that quantum processes can

lead to certain information – perhaps even all information – being unconsciously retrievable. Except, he applied it to biological structures before quantum mechanics became popular. The idea is that living organisms contain a kind of collective memory that is shared across space and time.

"When an organism develops a certain structure or behavior, this information is fed into the morphogenetic field. The more organisms exhibit the same structure or behavior, the stronger the field becomes and the easier it is for future organisms to adopt that structure or behavior.

"Mothers sometimes know that their children are in danger, something that science is still unable to explain. People sometimes feel that they are being watched, and they are! The sensation comes suddenly and then they notice that someone is staring at them. In psychology, there are so-called 'collective memory phenomena' – groups that share memories even though they have never had contact with each other.

"Incidentally, around half of all people believe that Nelson Mandela died in prison in South Africa in the 1980s. In monkey populations in South America and South Africa that cannot possibly have contact with each other, it has been observed that when one of the monkey populations learns a new skill, the other develops the same skill in a very short time. These are just a few examples. You should read up on it. It's really interesting stuff."

"Which sounds difficult to prove," said Saruko.

"It is, which is why most scientists confine themselves to ridiculing Sheldrake's hypotheses – just like those of Penrose and Hameroff – instead of taking them under consideration until they are dis-proved."

"But you believe in it."

"I don't know. But I believe that all three are pursuing the right approach. Maybe they're groping in the dark, but they've opened the right doors." Christer shrugged his shoulders. "But I'm sure you didn't ask me here for a round of scientific philosophy."

"No. I need your intuition," said Saruko, scrutinizing him carefully.

"I would have thought you were more conservative."

"Let's rather say that I like to try out every tool before I dismiss what I'm working on as unrepairable. Or label it intuition."

"Now I'm a tool?"

"That applies to all of us here."

Saruko switched on the television behind him, which until now had only shown a screensaver with a reclining figure eight.

"I'd like to show you how half of the exploration team members died horrible deaths. And then I'll show you how Ludwig Höglmayer disappeared."

37

RACHEL

"It looks like an extremely deep shaft or something like that," Adam said. He stood with his arms folded in front of the table in the workroom, in the middle of the semi-circle they formed around the huge display. He, Liu, and Raphael had been back for half an hour and were still wearing their sweaty multifunction underwear, but no one paid attention to their smell.

The excitement was too great for that.

"But who would dig a shaft that deep?" asked Madeleine incredulously.

"The ones who brought the ring here," Raphael replied, pointing to the last frozen image from the Red Sentinel before the drone had been destroyed – presumably by the heat.

"And what is this red dot supposed to be?"

"Lava," Liu said firmly. "We know that Mars is volcanically active. Elysium Mons cooled down a few million years ago, yes, but that isn't very long ago in geological terms. There is nothing to suggest that the planet is not still hot – or at least warm – at greater depths. If the shaft is many kilometers deep, it could be that this red dot," he stretched out a finger to point to the four pixels that were red instead of black, "is lava."

"That would suggest that the ring needs some form of energy source," Raphael pointed out. "I would never have thought of geothermal energy on Mars, but I wouldn't have believed I'd find an alien machine here, either."

It was quiet for a while as the meaning of his words slowly sank into their heads. Just hearing them had a surreal effect on Rachel.

"I think that it's a viable hypothesis to first assume that this ring generates the photons," said Adam. "Then there could be a shaft down to the lava below that supplies it with thermal energy. We don't see any other energy sources. Solar energy is probably out of the question. There simply isn't enough space for that."

"I think I need to cast doubt on the lava hypothesis," said Madeleine. "We don't see any cables or other means of transmitting the energy, and by the time the heat gets up here from down below, there shouldn't be enough energy left to generate such an effect."

She pressed a button and a live image of the ring appeared on the screen from the cargo rover. The shimmer was visible against the bright background if you looked closely.

"The object is hovering above the surface," Yuki reminded them. "I think it might be sophisticated enough to have some kind of non-physical induction."

"Yes, it could," Adam agreed. "Theoretically."

"How is that possible?"

"Imagine the object uses advanced thermoelectric materials that can convert thermal energy directly into electrical energy. This happens through the Seebeck effect – also called the thermoelectric effect – where temperature differences within a material generate voltage, which in turn generates electrical current. These materials do not necessarily have to be conductive because the Seebeck effect occurs due to temperature gradients. The ring itself then absorbs the energy accordingly."

"Or there might be a second ring down there that somehow potentiates or concentrates the heat and transmits it to the ring on the surface," Liu suggested. "Of course, it could also be a completely 'wireless' effect. One possibility for that would be to use electromagnetic waves or vibrations generated by the thermal energy of the lava. It could use a kind of resonance principle, where it is tuned to a certain frequency of electromagnetic waves and can absorb energy from the environment without having physical contact with the lava."

"But that would be quite beyond our technological concepts," Raphael said doubtfully.

In response, Liu simply pointed to the live image of the huge ring three kilometers away.

"Touché." The German quantum physicist sighed. "It certainly has energy; we can agree on that. At this point, the best explanation is that it's somehow connected to the presumed lava in the depths, which is at least supported by the fact that the drone measured greatly increased temperature values shortly before it melted away."

"It's, um, hiccupping," said Madeleine abruptly. She had remained remarkably calm until now. All heads turned to where she sat on the floor to their far left, holding up her tablet. "It's flickering!"

"Can you elaborate, please?" Rachel asked. "I don't suppose you're talking about a display malfunction on your tablet?"

"It's flickering. Or hiccupping. Or something," the computer scientist replied and stood up. Her movement seemed springy – wrong – to Rachel's eyes, which were used to Earth and its gravity. Madeleine tapped around on her tablet screen and a video popped up on the main display. It showed the strange optical effect over the ring, slightly more intense in the center, more of an impression at the edge. Only when she looked at the timestamp at the bottom left did she realize that the video was playing in fast motion until it slowed to normal speed starting at minute six.

"Okay, that's the camera feed from the rover," Raphael said after a while. "So?"

"Watch carefully," Madeleine urged him, all of them, with a raised palm. "Right now, at six minutes and thirty-three seconds."

Silence fell as they all stared transfixed at the display.

"Don't pay attention to the timestamp. Just look at the center of the shimmer and wait."

"There!" Rachel gasped louder than she intended, and the others were startled.

"Show that again," Adam requested, and Madeleine dragged the cursor back. The flicker was visible for a mere fraction of a second. If Rachel hadn't known what to look out for, and when, she would have missed it. Even if she had looked closely, she might have mistaken it for a brief display glitch – if anything at all.

"Are you sure it's not a camera error?" Liu asked doubt-fully. "I mean, it takes a bit of imagination to recognize this as a 'flicker,' or whatever."

"That's for sure. I didn't catch it myself, I had Carter search the camera footage from the last two hours for patterns. He's great at that," Madeleine explained. "He found out after a few minutes that there was a recurring deviation in the shimmer effect. Every six minutes and thirty-three seconds."

"Did Carter find out anything else?"

"Negative," the AI replied over the speakers. "However, my data analyses are still ongoing and could possibly provide further results at a later time."

"Did the various detectors pick up anything that matches this?" asked Liu.

"Yes." Madeleine nodded and showed the relevant data, which she put up on the screen. "The photon density is highest immediately after the flicker and then slowly decreases until a total cut-off at six minutes and thirty-three seconds. It's just a fraction of a millisecond, but no photons come out of the center of the shimmer. After that, it starts all over again."

"So it's cyclical," Rachel commented, glad to have finally understood something. It was easy to feel stupid next to these 'best of the best.'

"Yes, apparently so."

"All right then," Adam said, "if I may summarize, we have a hovering machine that presumably gains energy geothermally by means of a material-less induction transfer and thus generates a kind of photon fire above it, which is mostly short-wave, and was only briefly changed in its wavelengths by the CME from the sun so that it was in the wave spectrum visible to us – or has expanded accordingly. The photons are 'born' in the middle of the shimmer and then spread out in all directions at the speed of light. It is therefore not a directional effect."

"Which brings us back to the hypothesis that it's some kind of signal fire," Raphael noted.

"That's a very anthropocentric idea," Rachel countered. "In our evolutionary history, we've used torches to drive animals away, and fires to bring light into the darkness – or used them as signals, which we still do today in a modified form with lighthouses, warning lights, alarm lights, buoys, and so on. But this ring is clearly not of human origin, so we cannot necessarily assume that its builders assigned the same symbolic meanings to a photon source. It could be a completely different intention. We are also not saying that God, or whoever, created the sun as a signal for whomever, but as a source of life, or source of energy, or who knows what?"

"What kind of intentions, for example?"

"I don't know," she replied honestly. "But I think it's a mistake to commit ourselves – even if only mentally – to an interpretation that subconsciously predetermines our future thoughts."

"She's right," Madeleine agreed. "We can only make progress here if we don't get stuck on anything. But there is one thing we should concentrate on."

She looked directly at Rachel.

"What?" she asked, feeling uncomfortable as they all turned to her. Had she missed something?

"Communication."

"I know you think it's a signal, but I study linguistics, not photonics," she replied, trying to smile, but they were obviously serious.

"This machine was certainly built by intelligent beings, that much should be clear. Intelligent beings usually communicate. We take care of scientific approaches, you take care of what might not occur to us due to our points of view," Madeleine suggested and smiled encouragingly.

Rachel nodded reflexively. Although she had no idea what that meant, she had no intention of being pessimistic now. She was here to bring light into the darkness, so she would do everything she could to help solve the problem.

"Very good." Adam nodded slowly. "First we should find out more about the nature of these photons and why an alien civilization would build a machine to generate them. Intelligence only does things for a reason. And before anyone counters with art: it has a purpose, such as cultural context, the release of certain positive hormones and so on."

"We could try to disrupt the process and see if there's a reaction, a kind of a 'we are here' approach," Raphael suggested.

"That doesn't sound particularly friendly to me," Yuki said.

"It's obviously a machine and not a living thing. Interference could cause an automated reaction, but it certainly would not cause it any kind of suffering."

"Are we talking about communicating ... with the photons?" Liu asked, and although the Chinese man was always extremely polite, making it difficult to find out what he was really thinking, this time there was no doubt that he thought Raphael was out of his mind.

"No, I just want to create interference and see if there's a reaction," Raphael objected. "But since Rachel has just correctly encouraged us not to lock ourselves into one way of thinking – why not?"

"Photons cannot have a metabolism."

"Neither can robots, but they can still be intelligent."

"But they don't 'live' according to our definition."

"Photons are not created in the middle of nowhere for no apparent purpose."

"Let's not do this," Adam intervened. "We still have an hour of daylight left, so we won't be able to do much. We'll prepare the relevant tests for tomorrow and then we'll go to sleep. But I want one of us to be awake at all times, watching the monitor with the live images from the camera on the cargo rover."

They nodded in turn.

"I have one more question," Raphael said in Madeleine's direction. "Did Carter also analyze that strange noise coming from the ring?"

"That whispering?" asked Madeleine.

"Yes."

"I'm sorry, I could not detect any corresponding sounds on the audio tracks," the AI answered for itself.

"That's strange."

"Yes, there are some strange things here." Adam clapped his hands. "All right, people, one thing at a time. Let's get everything ready for tomorrow. Carter will take care of the spectrometer analysis. I think the best chance of deducing intelligence or some kind of system is in the spectrometer data, to be honest. Raphi, you're preparing the portable laser so we can send out different electromagnetic waves tomorrow. Maybe one of them will generate resonance. Liu, you take care of the photodetectors so that we know if there's a reaction. Maddy, can you get the signal generator ready so that we can use it to control and modulate the laser?"

"Sure thing."

"We will take care of dinner," Rachel decided, hooking arms with Yuki.

"Good idea, I'm starving," said the Japanese woman with a relieved sigh. This day felt as long as a lifetime, and it wasn't even over yet.

They heated up packs of ready-to-eat rations and, one by one, delivered them to their friends, who hurriedly gobbled up the food paste and then continued working on their respective devices. Next, Rachel checked the weather forecast, which Carter produced using data from the Mars Reconnaissance Orbiter and two other satellites. The storm had slowed down, but only a little. They had three and a half days before

Elysium Mons would be entirely shrouded in dust coming in at fierce wind speeds, without any form of force – a 100-kilometer-per-hour breeze. Some things she could understand, but not imagine.

That night she dreamed of rings and talking streaks of heat in the middle of a tornado, and when she woke up it was five o'clock in the morning.

Rachel washed up and brushed her teeth. Then she went to find Adam, who was in the cockpit having a conversation with Mission Control about his report from yesterday. Apparently Houston had sent him a whole list of ideas on how they could proceed, drawn up by hundreds of the world's brightest minds who had been up all night. Their presence could be sensed, in spite of the distance.

"I'd like to go out with you this time," she said when he had finished his transmission.

"Ahh, good morning, Rachel."

"Good morning. Sorry."

"No problem." He stifled a yawn. "Actually, the plan is to check the rover's detectors and power supply. We need to know how well they cope with the statically charged dust."

"I realize I'm not much help, but I'd like to see it." She quickly raised a hand when he tried to say something back. "Wait, please. I don't mean like a space tourist, I mean like a member of this team. If I'm going to try to discern whether there's some kind of communication pattern – based on my expertise and point of view – then I need to see it for myself. That's just the way I work."

"Do you think linguistics will help us in this case?" Adam was too decent a guy to allow it to sound like a rhetorical question, and therefore acted rather interested.

"No, I honestly don't think so," she admitted candidly. "But I still think I might be able to contribute a few creative ideas outside of your technical horizons. That seems to be the best way for me to contribute constructively at the moment – until the little green men jump out of the ring, of course." She smiled. "That's when I'll take over."

Adam returned her smile and, to her surprise, he finally nodded. "You're right, a fresh look won't hurt anything. I would have liked to schedule four weeks for initial tests and observations, then another four weeks of experiments, and then assess during the final four weeks. But with the storm, we don't have the time and we'll have to improvise."

"Thank you," Rachel said, relieved.

As she turned to leave, he held her back.

"Wait – why do you think you need to see it? With your own eyes, I mean?"

She shrugged her shoulders. "Intuition. I don't know."

"Let's grab a quick bite to eat."

"Don't we want to do that afterward? So as not to waste time?"

"Oh," Adam said, grinning. "It'll be quick."

When all six of them had gathered in the lounge area, Adam took a small box from one of the sealed cooling compartments and placed six chocolate Mars bars on the table.

"The quick breakfast of champions," he said and the others laughed.

"There's nothing better than starting the day with a silly joke," Madeleine said, shaking her head as if she was highly disappointed in her commander. But her smile was warm and she ate her bar with obvious pleasure.

An hour later, Rachel was standing on the platform with Adam, Liu, and Raphael. They let themselves be lowered to the surface by the unfolded crane device and gazed at the Martian sunrise in the east. It seemed to last much longer, and the colors remained pale. Aloft, cirrus clouds composed mostly of carbon dioxide drifted across the brightening sky, and in the distance, ground fog could be seen in some of the canyons deep below them. As they touched down, she glanced at the time on her forearm display.

"Hah," she said. "Look at the time."

"The clock reads 6:33." Liu chuckled. "It's a good thing I'm not superstitious."

"Don't you Chinese believe in ghosts or something?" asked Raphael.

"No, we believe in diligence and hard work. Religion is more your thing," replied the taikonaut as they boarded the rover. Everything they did took longer on Mars, as they had to make every movement in a controlled and deliberate manner due to the unfamiliar gravity conditions. There were no sharp corners, and certainly no protruding bolts or edges on the vehicle, but they still had to be careful, because any rupture to the suit, however unlikely, was potentially fatal.

Ironically, the ensuing journey felt even slower to Rachel than when she'd been watching the monitors inside the Ambassador. Perhaps it was due to the extremely barren landscape, which seemed monotonous and depleted as she experienced her second outing. She was a little ashamed of the thought. Millions of people back home would probably have sacrificed a hand for the chance to be in her place. But Mars was made of dust and stone, and the prevailing light was much less noteworthy than on Earth.

Rachel felt like she was visiting the set of a science fiction movie when they finally arrived at the ring. The detectors in their different shapes and complex arrangements, along with the interconnecting cables, looked almost as alien as the ring with its mysterious shimmering, and the cargo rover seemed somehow fake.

Apparently there had been a change of plan during the night, because Adam informed them that they would be starting with Raphael's quantum communication attempt. It was probably due to the time pressure the commander kept pointing out.

Their first task was to unload the portable quantum light generator, which was able to generate entangled photon pairs.

"This is based on a laser that shoots through a special beta-barium borate crystal – a process known as spontaneous parametric down-conversion, or SPDC," explained the German astronaut as they worked together to take the complex device out of its case. "It looks like a diva made of steel and circuitry, but don't worry, it's strong, light, and energy efficient."

"If it survived the trip here, definitely," she replied.

It took them over an hour to set everything up under Raphael's guidance. He started the experiment, and Rachel listened to his announcements to the Ambassador, fascinated by what was going on. She only understood half of it, but tried to grasp what was happening as best she could.

Raphael directed the entangled photons into two separate channels of the quantum light generator. One of the channels was intended for them to carry out their manipulations and measurements, while the other was designed to enable possible interactions with the photon source in front of them.

For this task, they used optical fibers and free-space optics. Embedded in the system was a modulatable beam splitter. This enabled them to manipulate the entangled photons in a targeted manner and transmit the desired information. They were able to change the polarization, phase, or other properties of the photons in order to encode information. They achieved this by using an electro-optical modulator and a liquid crystal phase modulator – delicate and precise devices that Raphael operated with great care, almost reverently.

"In order to detect possible answers in the form of changes, I am setting up the sensitive detection system in a new way," he announced.

They were using photomultiplier tubes and single-photon avalanche diodes to detect changes in the entangled photons in the second channel. Any difference, however small, could be a sign of interaction with the shimmer, she understood, and that was what she was waiting for.

With the experiment set up and ready to go, they finally began their communication attempts. They manipulated the photons in their channel by encoding their state.

"This is an extremely simplified explanation," Raphael explained when Rachel asked him what exactly they were doing, or expecting. "We work with the polarization of our entangled photons by employing a binary code. A horizontal polarization stands for '0' and a vertical polarization for '1.' So we encode the Fibonacci sequence in binary form into the quantum states. And then we observe the reactions in the second channel."

"It's that simple," she said dryly.

"So easy," he agreed with her without catching her intended humor. "The hardest part is reading the possible reaction. Quantum decoherence is the name of the problem, because of the interactions with the environment. A lot is lost in the process."

"Are we now measuring the quantum state of the photons in the sphere?"

"Correct. We shoot our photons into the sphere and thus determine the quantum state of the photons there. We keep their twins here in the generator. Because they are entangled, the measurement immediately determines the state of the entangled twins. We therefore only measure indirectly in the sphere by measuring here. This is what is meant by the 'collapse' of entangled particles. They immediately collapse into the state of the entangled partner particles."

"How long will it take?"

"Not long at all." He looked at his tablet and his eyes widened.

"What? What is it?"

"That's impossible!"

Adam and Liu came jump-running over.

"What is it?" they asked simultaneously.

"I have an answer. I think." Raphael raised a hand as if to scratch his forehead, only to be surprised that his helmet made it impossible. "I made a mistake typing in the Fibonacci sequence. But the partner particles in the generator are arranged correctly."

"So maybe you didn't make a mistake after all?" Liu suggested.

"Yes I did – I can see it on my tablet." Raphael looked up at the eerie shimmering. The four of them seemed so tiny compared to the ring and its strange effect. "I think it made the change itself."

"That's impossible," Liu disagreed. "States of entangled particles cannot be manipulated after entanglement."

"Not that we know of. But that's exactly what I believe just happened."

Suddenly, his tablet went out and the lights on the generator also went out.

"Guys, we're not receiving any more data here. Only from the camera," Madeleine reported from the Ambassador. "What's more, the rover's magnetometer readings have just gone crazy. What's going on?"

"I think we just got our answer," Raphael murmured, looking up with a fearful expression at the shimmering sphere that now appeared angry to Rachel, even though she knew it was just her reptilian brain leading her imagination into dark imaginings. In truth, nothing had changed – at least visibly.

"And the sphere didn't like something," said Adam. "In any case, the quantum light generator has been destroyed."

38

CHRISTER

"You did all that in a year?" asked Ludwig Höglmayer, speaking English and running a dirty hand through his wiry beard. He looked up and the image followed him, showing a huge borehole with a blue sky at the upper end.

"Yes, and it wasn't cheap," replied a voice from somewhere. The camera moved back down and to the side, where a huge drill head lay at an angle in an uneven cave below the hole, as if it had fallen to one side.

"Neither am I," Höglmayer replied. "A natural cave system can extend for a day or a month. You never know beforehand. I need power down here, preferably a lot of generators and batteries before I go down there. You've paid me two weeks in full, which I see as an advance. If it takes less than two weeks, you won't get anything back."

"That was already agreed." From the accent, the voice belonged to an American who was standing next to the speleologist in hiking gear, dabbing the sweat from his forehead with a cloth. He wore a hat on his head, which would have been frowned upon today as a glorification of colonialism.

"Good, then we're in agreement. Make sure there are always enough supplies and we'll map this beast for you."

"Okay, good. Hurry up."

"Oh no, I won't do that. Haste is the breeding ground for stupidity. And caves don't forgive stupid mistakes."

"You have assured us that you are the best."

"Yes, because I've lived long enough to gain experience." Höglmayer tapped his forehead. "You should think about it."

The speleologist turned away from the American and raised a bulky flashlight as big as a full-grown man's head, emitting a yellow light. In its glow, the camera caught the faces of nearly 20 men wearing hard hats and work clothes. They were all wearing backpacks, had huge flashlights in their hands, and in some cases, sleeping mats were strapped onto their packs.

"All right, two teams. Team One goes with me, Team Two with Andrew." The camera with its grainy image switched to Höglmayer, who gave one of his men – apparently Andrew – a wave, whereupon he separated from the group and the two teams had formed up shortly afterward.

Now the Austrian looked directly into the picture. "You're coming with us. But conserve batteries in between or we won't get far."

"You got it, boss," replied a youthful voice from off-screen.

"Good, let's go then."

The following shots were all shorter excerpts. Sometimes they showed bizarre cave formations with stalactites and creepy shadows moving across the rugged walls like dark demons. Ludwig Höglmayer could be seen in every single one, sometimes illuminating the paths, sometimes making notes on a map, and sometimes looking into the camera with his intense eyes to explain something about geological peculiarities and give hints about possible locations where uranium rock might be found. He looked like a driven man on the outside, which probably had something to do with his unique appearance and the bright blue color of his eyes. At the same time, however, he also exuded an aura of calm and determination, as if each of his words and gestures was preceded by a series of deliberate considerations.

Days passed, and from the conversation between two explorers at the edge of the picture it was clear that it had been a week at some point. Finally, they reached the cavern Christer had seen. Höglmayer and his team of 12 became very excited when they noticed the reddish glow that filled the huge space. However, as soon as they spotted the ring in the light of their flickering flashlights, they fell silent. Even on the Super 8 video, which was extremely poor quality by modern standards, grainy and full of image interference, it could be seen that the metamaterial of its shell seemed to swallow up any illumination from the flashlights.

One of the men asked, "What is that, boss?"

"I've got no idea. Watch where you're going," replied Höglmayer, staring at Object Alpha, which looked exactly the same on the moving images as it currently did, as if it had traveled back in time. The researcher mumbled something.

"Rewind," Christer urged Saruko. "Turn it up as loud as you can."

The Japanese man complied with his request and the recordings on his television rearranged themselves.

"What's that, boss?" asked one of the men. This time his voice sounded so loud through the speakers that it was scratchy and hurt his ears.

"I've got no idea. Watch where you're going," Höglmayer

replied, staring at Object Alpha. Although the soundtrack was extremely noisy at its current volume, his mumbled words could just about be understood: " ... knew it."

"Did you hear that?" asked Christer.

"Yes." Saruko nodded and smiled barely noticeably.

"Of course you did."

"It's not the first time I've heard this recording. However, it took us considerably longer to notice it."

"What did he say? I knew it?"

"Possibly, but the beginning of his mumbling cannot be determined even with the most modern methods," replied Saruko. "Someone obviously knew something."

"Mm-hmm. Keep playing it. At normal volume, please."

Höglmayer gave a few orders and his researchers spread out to the right and left in the cavern, climbing along the then unworked rock through the sweltering heat that could be seen from their sweat-soaked clothes. One of them slipped and fell into the hole that gaped in the cave floor beneath the ring like the upper rim of a giant funnel. His scream quickly died away, but the fearful cries of the exploration team did not.

"Silence!" shouted the Austrian, and the others quickly fell quiet. His voice echoed powerfully off the walls.

"Boss?" someone asked – obviously the young man behind the camera. "Do you hear that too?"

"Yes," said Höglmayer, without taking his eyes off the ring hovering 30 or 40 meters above the hole. "It sounds like someone's whispering somewhere."

Silence fell for a moment.

"Stop," Christer said, and Saruko stopped the recording. "Did you hear that?"

"Hear what?"

"Nothing. You can't hear the whisper on the recording."

"Correct, you cannot." Saruko nodded. "The whispering can't be recorded, no matter how sensitive the microphones are. We've already tried everything."

"How can that be?" Christer asked incredulously, staring at the eerie object.

"It can't, really. Maybe the sound is just in your head, perhaps one of your quantum effects?"

Christer gave him a wave and the recording continued.

Over the next half hour, various recordings showed how the other team joined them and brought a wide variety of equipment with them. This included several cameras, spotlights, and two diesel generators. The researchers ate, drank, and slept in the natural access tunnel, spending the rest of their time examining Object Alpha. Some fixed climbing hooks in the cupola-like rock ceiling, which formed a giant dome, until they finally reached the center and secured themselves with ropes. From there, they took more photos until one of the climbers fell 50 meters into the shimmer and burst like a ripe melon in a shower of blood.

Panic spread.

Some of the explorers fled, although Höglmayer's commanding voice persuaded most of them to stay. The next day, two of the men approached the ring wearing thick clothing because they wanted to retrieve a piece of equipment that had fallen into the cone-shaped belly of the cavern. Both began to scream when only ten meters separated them from the object.

They were able to return, and both reported severe pain in their ears and claimed to have heard a deep roaring noise.

"That thing doesn't want us here," said one of the explorers in a gloomy voice.

"'That thing' is a thing, nothing more!" Höglmayer bellowed in rebuke, but a close-up of his face revealed that there was a lot going on behind his eyes. He appeared almost feverish whenever he looked at the ring, as if he could see right through its secrets.

The next dispute arose when he ordered a climber to ascend to the ceiling and lower a rope from there.

"I'm not tired of living!" protested the young man, whose accent identified him as Scottish.

"If we don't dare to do anything, we won't get any answers," hissed Höglmayer angrily.

"Ludwig, I've been traveling with you for ten years and you know that I trust you. But this? This alien shit is really creepy, man!"

"This isn't alien shit."

"How do you know that?"

Höglmayer didn't answer immediately. He fixed his eyes on the ring again with one of his signature long stares. "I just know it. Besides, it's here on Earth. So it can't have come from aliens. Or have you discovered a part of the cave through which this piece would have fit?"

"No," the climber replied. "But apparently this artifact doesn't abide by the laws of nature."

"If you're scared, turn back and you're out. But don't come back to me when you can't sleep because this discovery won't give you any peace and you want to find out what it is," the speleologist said calmly and pointed into the access tunnel. "You'll get your pay and you can get on with your daily routine, whatever that looks like."

The young Scot seemed to be struggling with himself

while looking back and forth between the ring and the tunnel. Finally, he uttered a curse and began to put on his climbing gear.

"Okay," said a hardhat-wearing man who appeared to be about Höglmayer's age, "we have spent three days analyzing the various camera recordings." He was leafing through a book with complex sequences of numbers and notes that could only be guessed at due to the poor image quality and lighting conditions. "The shimmering is constant, but it has a regular interruption, like a quick flicker, every six minutes and thirty-three seconds."

Höglmayer took the notes and wordlessly withdrew to study them. The recording changed. According to the time stamp in the picture, it was a day later. A rope hung from the ceiling directly through the flickering into the unnatural shaft that led down into the lava flows deep below Indonesia.

"The rope is already charring, so hemp would have burned long ago," said the older researcher from the day before, and Höglmayer stepped back into the picture. "Even the steel mesh will melt when ..."

"Probably," he interrupted, and pressed the man's notebook back into his hand. The other explorers huddled in small groups against the cave wall like rats fleeing from danger and trying to crawl into corners. "Send them all away."

"Excuse me?"

"Send them all away. We've done everything we can here. We'll leave the rest to the company."

"This shouldn't end up in the hands of a single company, Ludwig."

"It won't, don't worry." He grabbed his colleague by the arm. "Send some of the locals out first and get them out of the way before you send the maps. Just to be on the safe side."

Their eyes met for a while, then the other nodded with a worried expression.

Höglmayer's gaze moved directly into the camera image. "You film to the end. Then you go, too," he ordered.

"What end?" the cameraman asked uncertainly, but the Austrian didn't answer and coordinated the removal of the equipment. When the others were all gone, he gave the camera a wave and began to descend toward the ring.

"Sir? What are you doing?"

Höglmayer did not answer, nor did he respond to any further calls from the young man behind the camera. He climbed purposefully toward the center of the cavern. After about ten minutes, he could be heard groaning and moaning loudly. Then he got down on all fours and crawled under the ring until he reached the edge of the hole, where he crouched down and jumped toward the rope.

For a moment it looked like he was slipping, but then he was dangling from the rope, barely recognizable as a silhouette in the grainy image detail, which looked even worse when zoomed in, distorted and wavering. The ring and the shimmering looked like heat waves straight from hell, and the colors seemed to fade. The whole image gave the impression of feverish malice and disturbing intensity.

A scream echoed through the cavern, presumably from Höglmayer's hands burning on the steel cable. But his silhouette gained height, climbing from below through the ring and into the shimmering, before disappearing from one moment to the next.

Under the curses of the cameraman, the picture wobbled until it stabilized and showed the ring and the shimmering sphere, although tilted on its side.

Saruko stopped the recording.

"He disappeared," Christer remarked hoarsely. "Not burst, like the others. He was just suddenly gone."

"Yes. We don't know why, but apparently it makes a difference from which side the flicker is touched. Our theory is that there is hard radiation of short wavelengths in the center of the flicker, which is attenuated outward by some effect. However, the concentration there seems to be high enough for human bodies to spontaneously heat up so extremely that they burst," explained Saruko.

"But not Höglmayer. He just plain disappeared."

"Yes."

"It looked like he somehow knew. How did he come to take on such an ordeal?"

"That's my question to you," Saruko said seriously. "Intuition, perhaps?"

Christer thought about it. "Maybe," he finally muttered.

"That's not all. Do you remember the flickers?"

"Yes, of course. Every six minutes and thirty-three seconds. That's the interval at which the shimmering effect flickers for one millisecond."

"Correct." The Japanese man nodded and let the video continue. This time, however, he fast-forwarded until the flicker was just barely visible due to the poor picture quality.

"There it is again. So?"

"We have analyzed these recordings hundreds of times. The flicker looks the same as always, but it is offset in time. We always come out at six minutes and thirty-four seconds here. That timing has never been observed since. Just this one instance."

"So you think it has something to do with Ludwig Höglmayer and his disappearance."

"You tell me. You're the expert in pattern recognition and intuition. Since we've only been able to observe one case, that's a poor data basis."

"Once is a coincidence, twice is a pattern," Christer

agreed with him. "I don't suppose this has happened before ... or since?"

"No." Saruko shook his head meaningfully. "It's the only deviation we've ever recorded. Since then, everything has run like clockwork. The fluctuation is punctual to the nanosecond – every six minutes and thirty-three seconds. The radiation levels are high but stable, the interference effects on our electronics always start at the same distance and then gradually increase in the direction of Object Alpha. The temperature is always the same, as is the photon density. The thing runs like a metronome."

"Except for this one time."

Saruko nodded and repeated, "Except for this one time."

"Why did you show me that?" asked Christer, although he thought he already knew the answer.

"Because I think you might be able to understand Ludwig Höglmayer. Or at least help me to understand him."

"What makes you think that? Shouldn't you have kidnapped a psychologist instead?"

"I have not kidnapped anyone," Saruko corrected. "And you and Höglmayer share many characteristics."

"Such as?"

"Many ... life circumstances, but also views. He always attributed the success of his unique caving discoveries to his intuition, describing it as a 'divine connection.'"

"I'm not a believer."

"It would be enough for me if you thought you could put yourself in this man's shoes."

Christer thought back to the Austrian's intense gaze and his apparent inability to let go of something once he had set his teeth on it. He felt the same way himself – once his teeth had sunk into a pattern, there was no letting go.

"I can do that."

"Then find out what drove him and why."

"You seem to be in a hurry."

"I am."

"Because of the Mars mission?"

"Yes. They're already there, examining that ring, and the board is pushing us to deliver results that will help the astronauts on the ground," explained the Japanese man, slumping back in his chair and rubbing his temples. "But we've made progress more and more slowly over the last thirty years. We can now record in even greater detail what was already postulated back then when they had far fewer resources. These are not new findings."

"So there are some people behind the board who have good intentions," Christer said half to himself, feeling a little relieved. Saruko obviously knew exactly what was going on 'out there,' which confirmed some of his suspicions.

"Nobody knows what the board wants, but you could look at it that way. But that's irrelevant. One thing is relevant, though." Saruko paused and slid him a printout. "The crew of the Ambassador figured out the interval, too: Six minutes and thirty-three seconds."

"How ...?"

"Object Beta is located on Mars. It is significantly larger than this one, yet it has the very same characteristics on a correspondingly larger scale. It even has the same fluctuation intervals – and its flicker happens at the same time as ours. Precisely the same time."

"So the rings are somehow aligned."

"So it seems. Make something of it, and do it quickly. That's your specialty."

39

RACHEL

She stood with her back to her friends and colleagues who were at the large table in the common room. They had spread out the display so that it obscured the tabletop with the sequence of polarized photons from the quantum light generator.

"I still can't believe it," said Raphael, shaking his head repeatedly like a bobble-head figurine in the rear window of a car. "The change in the state of the entangled photons is clear. They've corrected themselves to complete the Fibonacci sequence. It's as if she recognized the error and corrected it."

"She?" asked Adam with a raised eyebrow.

"She, he, it, whatever."

Madeleine now shook her head as well. "That would be logical if we assume that there's some kind of intelligence behind it. But what if there was simply a problem in our experimental setup? Some kind of interference that we didn't take into account?"

Adam snorted. "Our test setup was flawless. Planned for months and ..."

" ... and rushed because of the storm," Madeleine objected.

"We have considered all possible interferences. It is almost impossible that we have overlooked something," their commander insisted.

"Almost impossible is not impossible," she countered. "Besides, we're on Mars here, not on Earth. There could be forces at work that we don't yet understand."

"I'd say that's obvious," Rachel muttered.

"We should also consider the effects on our psyches," said Yuki, who until now had been conspicuously quiet, beyond her typical calm and thoughtful manner. "We are far away from home, in an environment that is completely alien to us, confronted with technology that we don't understand. It is possible that we see patterns where there are none."

"That's unlikely," Liu objected. "The evidence from the data is clear. The photons have changed. We preferred the experiment because it seemed to us to be the best way to make contact with an intelligence that could generate something like a photon source. The idea of sending in information was, and remains, a good one. We wanted a result and we got it. To deny it now would be a mistake, in my opinion. As I said, the states of the photons have changed. The question is, why?"

Rachel turned away from the window and looked at her colleagues. They looked worried and agitated at the same time – with varying degrees of intensity, but it was obvious that they were upset by what they had seen.

"We are faced with a decision," she finally said. "Either we assume we've made a mistake and try to correct it, or we accept the possibility that we have come across a form of intelligence that we do not understand. Both will require a lot of brainpower, and therefore time. So, let's not get lost in both. Otherwise, my friends, we will not make any progress."

The discussion fell silent. They looked at one another, each lost in their own thoughts. Then Raphael said, "We are scientists. We follow the data wherever it takes us. And the data tells us that something has changed the photons."

"Yes," Adam agreed, "but we also have to consider all the other possibilities. We can't just assume we've come across an alien intelligence because we want that to be the answer."

"I think we should do both," Madeleine suggested. "We should check our equipment to make sure there are no errors in our experimental setup, but as Rachel said, let's not spend too much time on it. At the same time, we should run more experiments to see if we can reproduce the phenomenon."

"The quantum light generator is ruined. The magnetic effect destroyed the electronics. I can try to repair it with Adam's assistance, but that would take days, possibly weeks. If it can even be done," Raphael objected.

"And what if we can reproduce it?" asked Yuki. "What does that mean for us? How should we proceed?"

Rachel looked at her and smiled slightly. "That would mean we are not alone," she said.

"But until we know that for sure, we should be careful," Liu warned. "We don't know what the purpose of this photon sphere is. But we have seen it react to us. We should prepare for all possibilities."

"That's what's still puzzling me. If it corrected your mistake in the Fibonacci sequence, why did it destroy the quantum light generator afterward?" Rachel looked at the faces of her colleagues. "I mean, it reacted to us twice."

"Yes, it said hello in the form of a mathematical answer," Raphael was certain. "A mathematical correction is as clear an intelligent answer as you can expect."

"But after that, it destroyed our means to communicate," she reminded him. "We shouldn't forget that."

"On a date with a lady, I'd call that mixed signals," Adam

said with a chuckle. "And it makes just as little sense here. Why would something answer us in the language we both seem to speak – math – only to destroy our ability to talk to it?"

"That's not so unusual," Rachel noted. "Many primitive peoples with no outside contact communicate with strangers who approach them, after which they attack. The only problem is that their warnings are not always understood because they use different symbolism."

"So, in your opinion, that was something like, 'Hey, we're here, leave us alone?'" asked Madeleine.

"Possibly. I don't know. It's just an intuitive assessment."

"We can't draw conclusions of that magnitude on the basis of one single observation," Liu interjected. His hand brushed a pile of data reports. "Yes, the results are strange, but we can't just assume that we've made contact with an alien intelligence. That would be premature."

"Liu is right," Adam agreed. "We need to collect more data and carry out more tests. There are a lot of physical phenomena around the ring that we don't fully understand yet. Maybe what we're seeing here is one of them."

"Adam, Liu, I understand your skepticism," Raphael said calmly. "But we can't deny that something strange is going on. Photons don't just change state. They don't. And yet we've seen that they do. How do you explain that? 'Something we don't understand yet' is not an explanation, it's just an excuse."

The two of them avoided his gaze. They had no answers.

"Maybe we need to take a step back and think about why we were actually sent here," Yuki said. She was always the level-headed one, the one who kept an eye on the big picture when the others got lost in the details. "We're here to explore the unknown. We are here to find answers. And we've found something we can't explain. Isn't that exactly what we were sent here to do?"

"Yes, but ..." Adam began, but Yuki cut him off.

"No buts! The answer is, 'Yes.' And, we've found something that has shocked us all. Something that challenges our understanding of physics. Isn't that exactly what science is all about, the search for the unknown, testing hypotheses, adapting our models to fit reality? We have a huge team of experts from all over the world behind us, to support us."

It was quiet in the room as they all thought about Yuki's words.

"Maybe we should worry less about what we should expect to see and more about what we actually see," Liu finally said. His voice was quiet but firm. "Maybe we should focus less on what we know and more on what we don't know."

"And we should get on with it," Rachel suggested. "With repairing the quantum light generator, I mean. What if we've found alien life?"

"We certainly have not found life," Adam countered. "At most, the relic of extraterrestrial life."

"Don't we have to think outside the box here?"

"For example?"

"What if the photons themselves are the aliens? They are information carriers, right?"

"Yes, but they aren't alive."

"Not according to our definition. But a highly developed robot also has no metabolism and no direct ability to reproduce, yet it has many of the characteristics of living beings on an organic basis. What if we have communicated with photon life forms?" Rachel knew she might be sounding crazy, but she wanted to keep the mood on a no-holds-barred brainstorming session.

"Then we would have a problem, because we could never get in touch with them," said Raphael.

"Why not?"

"Because photons always move at the speed of light, and according to the special theory of relativity, no time passes for particles moving at c. For them, time would stand still, so they would have no sense of time."

"But light slows down in certain media like water, doesn't it?" asked Liu. "Couldn't the photons from the sphere be slowed down by water and then we could communicate with them?"

"No. They would still be moving at the speed of light, just at a slower speed of light. That means their actual speed is slower, but it's still c and so they would still have no sense of time. For them, everything around them would stand still," Raphael explained patiently. "So even if Rachel's theory were true – and it's extremely bold because it would contradict everything we know about life – we would never be able to talk to them."

"Because we don't exist in the same time, if you like?" Rachel scratched her head. "Hmm."

"Exactly."

"But then how could we get an answer? Surely an answer takes time?"

"Maybe it's some kind of automatic error correction," Madeleine speculated. "Like an advanced program heuristic."

"This might sound a bit obvious, but if there was any actual communication," Rachel proposed, "it must have been from the ring and not from the photons themselves, right?"

"Yes. Photons may be suitable for storing information – or as information carriers – but not so much for entities. They always fly in one direction until they lose their momentum through collision with other particles, they can't change direction and, as I said, they don't perceive time. Difficult conditions," said Raphael.

"But the ring is obviously a machine, and machines can be intelligent," said Adam. "The smallest and most insignificant of our devices today have one form of intelligence or another. Even smartphones, printers, or CNC machines. So we can probably assume that the ring has some kind of software and therefore artificial intelligence."

"I wouldn't be so sure," Madeleine disagreed. "We're at a point where artificial neural networks and machine learning are getting exponentially better and changing our world forever – and we're significantly less advanced than that out there."

"That doesn't sound like a contradiction."

"Think about it. If we have to ask ourselves, right now, whether AIs will be the end of us, and whether we can solve issues like their alignment, it's possible that aliens who are more intelligent than us will reject artificial intelligence outright because they are smart enough to know that this path would lead to general artificial intelligence and thus to the last invention. There is serious debate as to whether artificial intelligence is the great filter that will inevitably make civilizations extinct. To be honest, I've believed this with complete conviction for years. But that thing out there seems like a good counterargument – if," Madeleine emphasized this word in particular, "it's not a confirmation."

"What do you mean?" asked Raphael.

"She thinks it could mean that the builders of this ring never created artificial intelligence, and were therefore able to survive long enough to invent technological wonders like the ring," Rachel said.

"Exactly." Madeleine nodded in agreement. "It may have taken them much longer than would have been required had they used AI, but they got to this point, nonetheless. It's purely speculative, of course."

"So that means the ring could be a highly developed but stupid machine?" Rachel asked incredulously.

"Yes." Madeleine nodded. "That is entirely possible. A natural limit to intelligence, as with us humans, does not mean that progress is equally limited. Knowledge always builds on knowledge, and great civilizations continue to specialize. Aliens who are thousands of years ahead of us could, given enough time, have managed to do this without strong AIs."

"The question is, how does this help us, practically?" Adam inquired. The shirt-sleeved engineer seemed to be showing the first signs of impatience with their lengthy theorizing. But maybe Rachel was just imagining things. "Does anyone have any idea how we could make contact with the ring?"

Everyone looked at her, which she only realized after a few moments.

"Oh. I don't know, a creepy ring made of alien material doesn't exactly seem like a talkative E.T.," Rachel said, raising her hands defensively.

"How would you go about it in terms of basic attitude?" asked Adam, as if she hadn't said a thing.

"I would try to take an optimistic approach." She thought for a moment. "The idea that the ring destroyed our equipment to protect itself should be understandable. In other words, that we triggered some kind of self-protection mechanism."

"That's optimism?" Raphael grimaced. "Now I'm afraid to ask for your pessimistic theory."

"Well, it could have wiped us out as the root of the problem," she pointed out. "Instead, it only neutralized the piece of equipment that was directly involved in the photon entanglement."

"She's right," Yuki affirmed, bowing slightly as she often did. "I'm not sure we humans would have reacted in such a limited manner – nor would a machine we built with the ability to protect itself."

"But your self-protection thing makes no sense," Liu objected. "I apologize for my choice of words."

"It's okay. No offense taken." Rachel waved him off. She knew him well enough to know that he was one of the most polite and careful people she had ever met.

"I just want to say that we didn't break anything. We didn't interact with the ring, either, but with its ... product, if we can call it that."

"What if the so-called product is valuable?"

"Are you alluding again to the thesis that photons are conscious or alive?"

"Yes." Rachel tensed up. "I know you all know a whole lot more about physics than I do. But there's so much here that you would have called 'impossible' before we discovered it, so why not this, too? Maybe we played around with some kind of birthing process or something and messed it up."

"However, the fact that the fluctuation pattern of six minutes and thirty-three seconds has not changed would speak against this. The spectrometers show the same radiation intensity," Madeleine replied. "As far as we can see, nothing has changed."

"Let's try it out," Rachel suggested. "Let's talk to the ring."

"But how?" asked Yuki.

"I'm sure that if we could manage to communicate with tiny little photons, we can find a way to make contact with a massive ring."

40

CHRISTER

He sat at his desk in the silence of his office, where only the hushed whirring of the computers and the ticking of the wall clock could be heard. A cup of coffee in his hand, his gaze fixed on the abstract patterns that the black liquid had left on the wood. The seemingly random stains, circular yet imperfect, appeared to transport him to another time, another conversation that he had so often replayed in his mind. It wasn't an explicit thought of Rachel, but more an echo of her presence reverberating in the silence of his office.

Christer looked at the coffee stains and noticed how their nature reflected what he had long since internalized: most patterns consisted of circles, cycles, repetitions. This was the true nature of the world, far removed from the linear way of thinking that he and so many others were used to. The circles on his desk, insignificant as they were, were a microcosm of something larger, something fundamental.

The Earth revolving around the sun, the moon revolving around the Earth, the stars revolving in spiral galaxies, even atoms with electrons revolving around their own nuclei – everything was a manifestation of this fundamental principle.

No beginning, no end, just constant movement and change in an endless cycle.

He thought about how the seasons changed, how the tides came and went, how day passed into night and back into day again. Everything was a cycle, an eternal dance of growth and decay, of construction and dismantling.

At that moment, in the silence of his office, he saw the world not as a line but as a circle. It was a brief flash of realization. He understood that what had passed would come again, that what had ended would begin again. He saw the universe not as a collection of fragments but as a whole, constantly in motion, constantly changing, but always returning to the same point.

And as he sat there, coffee in hand and looking at the circles on the desk, he felt like a small, spinning wheel embedded in a complex system of circles. He saw himself as part of a larger circle, a larger cycle. And in that moment he realized that even though the universe was full of mysteries and unknowns, it was also full of patterns and repetitions, circles and cycles.

Christer leaned back, his gaze drifting from the circular coffee stains to the concrete ceiling of his office, where he imagined the lush green of the trees high above him, their leaves swaying in the warm summer breeze. Even here, in the midst of the pulsating silence, he could not escape the cycle of life, the incessant flow of birth and death and birth again that held the world in its grip.

He thought of the countless generations of living beings that came and went, each one a wave in an ocean of existence that rose and then fell again, only to make way for the next wave. Each death, as painful and final as it might seem, was only a transition, a step in an endless dance of becoming and passing away.

Was it this pattern that Ludwig Höglmayer had seen

when he first beheld the ring? Had the structure caused a kind of enlightenment in him to recognize the nature of the universe? Was this the reason why he had voluntarily ended his own life?

Christer looked at his hands, the veins that branched out under his skin, the wrinkles that time had drawn in his flesh. He saw the transience of his own body, the inexorable erosion of the years. But in this decay he also saw a kind of birth, a continuous new creation. Every cell that died made room for a new one, every end was a beginning, every transience carried the seed of rebirth. It was the one law that people could not escape: their place in the larger pattern, and this pattern was a circle.

He thought of evolution, this vast, billions-of-years process that played out in circles and spirals, returning again and again to the same point, only to break out in a new direction. Each species, each individual, was only a temporary form, a momentary manifestation of a much deeper, more fundamental pattern.

Of a circle. Of a ring.

Christer picked up his desk phone and pressed Saruko's direct dial button.

"Mr. Johannsen? What can I do for you?" asked the Japanese man.

"Are you able to forward a message to the Ambassador?"

"As you know, I can't do anything myself from down here. But I can send the board a request for forwarding."

"Do you think the board is willing and able to do this?"

"Yes, I assume so."

"Then please send the request. I think I know why Ludwig Höglmayer killed himself. And I also believe that I know why the deviation occurred," Christer explained.

"What's the message?"

"You have to send a recording of Höglmayer's ending and a short text."

"The board will never do that. That would reveal that there is a second ring," said Saruko with audible displeasure.

"Possibly. But if they don't, they'll never find out what the shimmer is all about, and how we can decode it."

"And you think you can do it?"

"I'm sure of it. The board will have to decide whether it wants to have answers after forty years, or if they'd rather keep pumping money into the project and enjoy their damn secrecy."

41

RACHEL

"Imagine, Raphi," she began, sucking from her drink pouch and swallowing, "that you are a photon traveling along through the universe at the speed of light. What do you think it would feel like?"

The quantum physicist looked up from the display where they were watching Adam and Madeleine approach the ring, carrying a box. "A photon? Me? That's a thought I've never considered before. But from a purely physics point of view, if we follow the theory of relativity, a photon would not experience time. It would be an existence without time. But Rachel, photons don't have consciousness. We've already been through that."

She leaned back, her eyes fixed intently on him. "But just because we can't detect consciousness in photons doesn't mean they can't have it. What if they did? What would that say about our concept of time?"

Raphael stared into his cup as he thought this through. He'd been the first – the only one – of them to switch back to cups. The others were all still using their drinking tubes out of habit. "Time is a dimension, just like space. It's fundamental to our understanding of the universe."

"But for a photon couldn't it be illusory, just a construction of human perception?"

"Extremely theoretically, yes," replied Raphael. "We humans experience time as a constant flow, but that's only one perspective. For a photon moving at the speed of light, this flow of time would not exist. It would be a constant present, without beginning or end. That would call into question our whole concept of past, present, and future."

He shook his head, but his look was thoughtful. "That's interesting, as speculation, Rachel. But as a scientist, I have to say that we have to base our theories on observable and measurable phenomena. The idea of conscious photons and illusory time is seductive, but it's not tangible. It cannot be falsified."

"But isn't that exactly what science is supposed to do?" She grinned as she squeezed her drink pouch and made a fountain of water fly from her drinking tube into his cup. Due to the low gravity, the stream of water described a strangely slow, wide arc before landing in his container. "It's as if I've slowed time," she said thoughtfully as they both watched the jet of water. "Isn't science supposed to push the boundaries of the conceivable and explore the deepest mysteries of the universe, even if they are beyond our understanding?"

"It should, but there is a horizon beyond which we cannot look because we are bound to the perception of things through a filter called the human brain. And that works according to certain rules that cannot be circumvented. Just as we will never be able to observe the edge of the universe because it is moving away from us faster than light due to accelerated expansion, and its light will never reach us. That remains an incontrovertible fact." Raphael laughed softly. "Maybe you're right, Rachel. Maybe science should philosophize more and measure less. But for now, let's stick to the things we understand."

"Imagine," she countered, "we were in a spaceship moving through the universe at the speed of light. How would we perceive time then?" Rachel let the question hang in the air, the challenge sparkling in her eyes. "If you don't want to think through an abstract example, maybe we can look at one like this?"

Raphael leaned back and rubbed his chin. "Okay, that's an interesting question, Rachel. According to Einstein's special theory of relativity, time would pass more slowly for us the closer we come to the speed of light. To an observer looking at us from a stationary point, it would appear as if time stood still for us. But for us in the spaceship, time would pass normally."

Rachel tilted her head to the side. "So, while moving at the speed of light, we would experience time exactly as we do now?"

"Exactly," confirmed Raphael. "That's the so-called 'time dilation' effect. But there's something else known as length contraction. As we move at the speed of light, the universe would shrink in front of us and it would seem as if we could reach our destination instantly."

Rachel's eyes lit up. "So we could, theoretically, travel to any point in the universe without wasting any time?"

"In theory, yes," Raphael replied. "But there are still a few catches. First, it would take an infinite amount of energy to accelerate to the speed of light. Second, if we're moving at the speed of light, any collision – even with a speck of dust – would result in a nuclear explosion. Third, and finally, there is the problem of slowing down again. We would need an infinite amount of time to slow down to a normal speed again."

"Of course," she replied. "That's all I wanted to know."

When Adam and Madeleine returned, the computer scientist all but glued herself to her workstation and didn't say a word. While Rachel and the others ate, Madeleine didn't even respond to questions about whether she wanted anything to eat or drink.

"What's she doing?" Rachel asked Adam across the table.

"We have attached the magnets and she wants to establish communication with the help of the on-board AI."

"Carter," Yuki said.

"Yes," said the engineer reluctantly. He still didn't seem to have come to terms with the fact that a highly developed algorithm was taking over important tasks of the mission.

"And how is that supposed to work?" Rachel inquired.

"We'll try binary code first," Raphael replied. "That's a simple universal principle. On and off, existence and non-existence. Every intelligence should understand that."

"As long as we manage to make it clear to it that we mean exactly that," she said.

"Yes."

"Got it!" Madeleine suddenly shouted and jumped back from her display.

"What do you see?" exclaimed Rachel.

"The ring! I think it answered!"

It suddenly became silent. Rachel felt as if an electric current was buzzing through her body that had no beginning and no end.

"What?" Liu stammered.

"How?" Adam demanded eagerly.

"I gave Carter control of the magnets and created a very specific – albeit long – spoken prompt. His first task was to teach the basics of binary code. One and zero, short and long, light and dark – you take two distinct states and assign meanings to them. In this case, Carter used strong and weak magnetic pulses to symbolize these differences. A strong pulse stood for 'one,' a weak one for 'zero.'

"Then it was about the sequences. Carter made sure that there was a pause between each binary number – a kind of breath to separate the information. Without these pauses, everything would have looked like an endless stream of data. It was important to formulate clear, single words.

"Carter started with the simplest patterns. He sent sequences like zero zero, zero one, one zero, one one, and repeated them over and over again. He made them sound like a language, like a rhythmic, magnetic melody. It was brilliant. Repetition was the key to getting the ring to recognize and learn the patterns, and it learned extremely quickly.

"Then Carter went one step further and introduced decimal numbers. He started with the numbers from one to ten, translated into binary code. First one, then two, and so on until he reached ten. Each number was repeated several times to illustrate the link between the binary code and the corresponding decimal number. Then, once Carter was sure that the ring understood the concept of binary and decimal numbers, he began sending more complex patterns.

"He sent patterns that were representative of basic math concepts – the Fibonacci sequence, prime numbers, square numbers. He wanted to see if the ring was able to recognize and respond to these patterns, which it did by correcting faulty patterns and sending its own. The whole thing took an hour, and now they have exchanged the concept of radio, or rather made it clear that they both know and understand the transmission of information via radio waves."

"An artificial intelligence," said Liu. "I knew it, didn't I? The ring is an intelligent machine!"

"Wait a minute," Adam said, sounding a warning. "You had a reason for stopping at the concept of radio, didn't you?"

"Yes." Madeleine nodded her head and looked depressed. "Carter?"

"If we exchange radio frequencies, there is a risk that the alien machine intelligence will take over our system. My system," the AI explained over the loudspeaker. Carter's calm baritone stood in stark contrast to what he was saying.

"Is there a danger to Earth?"

"Most likely not. At worst, it would take over our data storage. But the satellites are not suitable for very large data packets, and it would have to use them. Otherwise, it would be practically impossible to send significant signals to Earth."

"Can we afford to try it?" Raphael thought aloud.

"Can we afford not to?" Rachel asked excitedly. "We've just got proof of an alien intelligence communicating with us! Think about it."

"Rachel's right," Yuki agreed. "This is the most important discovery in human history, and we mustn't take it frivolously."

"I wouldn't use the word 'frivolous' here," Adam said. "It could be frivolous to give a machine that we know next to nothing about, except that it destroyed some of our equipment, access to our spaceship, and our data storage. It would learn an awful lot about us and our species."

The discussion was now picking up speed, but Rachel shut herself off in her thoughts. She kept imagining the huge ring out there, and that there was an intelligence behind the eerie black material, and that it might soon be in the Ambassador.

" ... not to do it," she heard Liu say just then. "It's not something we can decide on our own."

"He's right," Adam replied, and went to one of the communications consoles. "Houston, this is Ambassador. We need instructions from you on this matter. Should we risk

JOSHUA T. CALVERT

potentially revealing everything about ourselves to another
intelligence for the chance to make contact?"

They waited silently for a quarter of an hour for the
answer. It was oppressive, each of them caught up in their
own thoughts.

The response came from Lucille herself.

"Ambassador, this is Houston," her voice rang out
through the speakers. "We're putting all orbiters into hiber-
nation mode. You know their override codes by heart. Delete
them from the database and only reactivate them when you
have full control of the Ambassador. Under these conditions,
we recommend making contact in the form of radio communication."

"All right," Adam said, with an obviously heavy heart,
and he proceeded to delete the relevant codes from the on-
board computer so that the alien AI could not take posses-
sion of the satellites. "Madeleine?"

"Carter," the computer scientist said, "send the ring a
radio frequency and give it the data access it needs to learn
our language."

"Understood."

Silence fell again.

"The process is complete," said the AI after a few
minutes.

"Already?" asked Raphael.

"Yes. Apparently the data processing is extremely fast. It is
able to communicate with us."

"Is it invasive?"

"No. It does not seek to penetrate any data areas that I
have not released. I have selected a neutral storage node and
shielded it with firewalls. It is staying in there."

"How much does it know?" asked Adam.

"Our language, or more precisely, English."

Adam turned to Rachel. "What does this mean?"

"This means that it knows all the connections that language creates. Places, people, history, time periods, feelings – the entire symbolic interactionism," she explained. "It only takes a few seconds to learn the word for Earth. But to agree on what exactly is meant by Earth, it takes complex contexts of meaning so that both understand the same thing."

"That assessment is correct," Carter agreed with her.

"Can we talk to it? With the ring, I mean?" Rachel asked hopefully.

"I can give it access to my text-to-speech model if that's what you want."

Everyone looked at Adam, who finally nodded hesitantly.

"Which voice should I give it?"

"A friendly one," Rachel replied.

"Got it," Carter said.

"I send greetings," a female voice suddenly rang out from the speakers, sounding sympathetic and warm. Rachel wondered if she had made the best decision, because combined with the knowledge that this voice was being used by an alien intelligence that was currently talking to them via their ship, it made the voice sound eerie – like some kind of uncanny Valley effect.

"Hello," she replied as the others froze. "I'm Rachel. Who are you?"

"I am a machine."

"Do you have a name?"

"Beginning and end."

"What does that mean?"

"That's my designation."

"What is your function?" asked Raphael, the first to break out of his stupor.

"My function is to generate photons. What is your function?"

Now they looked at each other questioningly until all eyes went back to Rachel.

"We are researchers," she said after a moment's thought. "We strive for knowledge." When she didn't get an answer, she decided to ask another question. "Who built you?"

"A machine."

"What kind of machine?"

"A machine."

Rachel frowned. Are we sure this ring has intelligence?

"Are you an artificial intelligence?"

"I am a machine. I have the necessary intelligence," replied the pleasant female voice.

"How old are you?" she tried another question. "How many years have you been doing your job?"

"Four million, five hundred and sixty-seven thousand, five hundred and forty-four years," came the curt reply, which Rachel first had to digest.

"Did someone bring you here?"

"No, I was built here."

"Are there others like you?" asked Liu.

"Yes."

"Where?"

"On Earth."

They fell silent again. Tension filled the room like thick glue – the breathing air seemed to have become thinner.

"Where?" Adam looked at one of the speakers in the wall.

"I do not share this information," the ring replied.

"Why did you destroy our quantum light generator?" asked Raphael.

"I have a protective mechanism for the photon source I generated. Your machine caused an unacceptable disturbance."

Rachel decided to try another variation on one of her original questions. "Why are you generating photons?"

"Because that's my function."

Crap.

Raphael seemed to want to ask something else, but Liu put a hand on his arm and asked, "Why are you communicating with us?"

"To determine, in accordance with my function, whether you pose a threat to the performance of my function," replied the alien intelligence.

"We are not a danger," said Liu.

"Where are your builders from?" asked Rachel.

"I created myself."

"Have you ever had contact with biological life forms like ours?"

"Yes."

"Were these life forms there before you?"

"Yes."

"Do they still exist?"

"No. My analysis of your intentions is now complete. You pose no threat to my ability to perform my duties," said the voice from the loudspeakers.

"That is correct, we are no threat. We'd like to ..."

Carter interrupted Rachel. "Contact has been lost," said the AI.

"Just like that?" Adam sounded almost indignant.

"Yes. It has withdrawn from the data node and radio contact no longer exists," Carter explained.

Rachel cleared her throat after a long pause, during which no one seemed to want to say anything. "That was ... strange."

"That's one way to say it," Raphael grumbled.

"If that was an artificial intelligence, then Siri and Alexa are real Einsteins," said Adam.

"Maybe Rachel was right," Madeleine stated. She looked

as if she had aged several years. Disappointment was written all over her face.

"About what?"

"The machine was obviously built by someone. Maybe by other machines – maybe that's what it meant by creating itself. The life forms that came before us, biological life forms, created machines that can then build themselves. In our factories, machines also build other machines."

"I still don't understand what this has to do with Rachel."

"She suggested that it could be from a civilization that built 'dumb' machines. Given enough time, they could still have created extremely sophisticated technology without exposing themselves to the dangers of general artificial intelligence. Making the assumption it's like our drive for progress at all costs could be a mistake."

"An anthropomorphism," Rachel specified, nodding in agreement.

"The ring is obviously extremely sophisticated," disagreed Raphael. "Just the fact that it decoded our binary code and our language so quickly is proof positive."

"But perhaps only within the scope of its programming. This machine could fulfill its task and not think beyond that. That's exactly what it sounded like to me," Liu said, crossing his arms. "And you could make the argument that binary code is something quite universal. Existence and non-existence are probably universal thought concepts. Duality. One and zero are just mathematical concepts for on and off, yes and no, right and left, up and down, light and dark – two sides of one thing can be seen everywhere in the universe."

"Binary code is the most logical and the simplest code," Madeleine agreed with him. "If you meant to say that the ring has long since mastered binary code, I would certainly agree with your reasoning. It would seem logical to me."

"But then why did it learn from Carter first?" asked Adam.

"On the contrary, it could have been learning what we know. If you listen carefully to the teacher, you learn exactly how far his knowledge extends."

"And the only point of the communication was to find out if we were a threat?"

"It worked, didn't it?" Rachel shrugged her shoulders. "We've given access to our data in the form of language and mathematics and therefore also to our technological level – at least indirectly."

"And now it is no longer interested in us because we are not a threat to its function and, according to its programming, it is only interested in us for that reason. Paradoxically, a rather simple but highly intelligent program," Madeleine summarized. "Anyway, now we're back to square one."

42

RACHEL

She couldn't sleep and climbed out of her bunk after pulling open the curtain. The dimmed night light was just enough to make out the contours of the habitat, but Carter automatically brightened it a little when she got up.

Rachel took the ladder upstairs to the work area where Liu was sitting at the large laboratory table. He had his headphones on and jumped when she touched him gently on the shoulder.

"Rachel," he said, exhaling a deep, drawn-out breath. "You scared me."

"Sorry. I couldn't sleep."

"Neither could I."

"What are you doing?" She pointed to his headphones. The display picture only showed the night scene of the ring and the shimmering sphere. Judging by the time stamp, it was live.

"I keep listening to it," the Chinese man said and sighed heavily. Dark circles had formed under his eyes. "The conversation with the machine."

"Beginning and end."

"Excuse me?"

"Beginning and end. That's its name, it said," she clarified.

"Oh." Liu nodded. "Yes. Pretty cryptic, isn't it?"

"Not to me. It was one of the few parts of the conversation that revealed a lot, I thought," Rachel disagreed.

The taikonaut spread his hands and leaned back. "Will you share your perceptions with me?"

"'Beginning and end' didn't fit in at all with its otherwise so-technically-cool manner. Beginning and end are concepts of transience that a machine understands, of course, but which have no such meaning for it as they do for us, who are descended from evolution. Beginning and end have a completely different relevance for computers. For us, the one certainty in the universe and our lives is that we were born and we will die. A machine knows on and off, but not death in the sense we do."

When she noticed that the furrows in his forehead were only threatening to deepen, she zeroed in, "I believe that biological beings gave the ring this name. 'Beginning and end' is not something a machine would come up with. More likely Alpha-1 or some other logical sequence. After everything this machine has said, I would have guessed 'Machine-1' or 'Function-XY.'"

He nodded slowly and rubbed his eyes. "You're probably right about that, yes."

"Also, the name is an allegory of its form, which needs creative thinking and awareness, I believe. Allegorical sensitivity, maybe even a sense of humor," Rachel went on. It was good to share her thoughts instead of despairing over them because they wouldn't let her sleep.

"I have to admit that you're losing me a bit here," Liu said apologetically.

"A circle either has no beginning and no end, or it begins

and ends everywhere, depending on where you start on the circle," she explained. "There's a reason why a ring was chosen for marriage as the symbol of eternal love, and why two touching rings, side by side, symbolize infinity. I wonder if the machine's builders, wherever they are, really chose the ring shape only out of technical necessity or if it was a kind of sign, maybe even a joke or something of that nature. The name certainly suggests something like that."

"Mm-hmm," Liu said, examining her closely.

"What?"

He smiled warmly. "You've reminded me once again why you're a valuable member of this team, and why your popularity ratings are through the roof."

"What kind of popularity ratings?"

Liu looked surprised. "Don't you know about that?"

"No, what are you talking about?" she asked.

"There are polls every week for our popularity ratings. We're kind of like rock stars at home, I suppose."

Rachel frowned. "That's ... weird."

"We're all pretty popular, so we're all doing pretty well. But they love you."

She changed the subject. "Do you know what I think?" She felt a little ashamed. She didn't want to be more popular than the others, it felt exclusive and unfair. Most of the time she had felt like an inferior monkey who was allowed to go on a school trip with five Einsteins. Maybe that was the crux of the matter? The masses of 'normal' people could probably identify with her more easily.

Liu smiled broadly and his eyes looked a little less tired than before. "No, but I'd like to know."

"Shortly after the discovery of the sphere of light during the coronal mass ejection last year, I had a conversation with a very nice man in Washington, D. C. His name was Christer, a Swede, I think. Or Norwegian?"

Rachel thought about it and then made a dismissive gesture. "It doesn't really matter. Anyway, we had a cigarette and philosophized about why everything is round in the universe."

"It's not quite that simple."

"Well, the stars, planets, larger asteroids, galaxies, black holes, asteroid belts, planetary ring systems, the universe ... Even atoms on a much smaller scale – but I'm sure you know that better than I do," she said. "We see cycles of creation and decay all around us. We humans seem to be linear phenomena, from birth to death. Period. But this is an illusion, and many cultures have language codes to point out the illusion.

"Do you really know where your life began? With your first breath? Or in your mother's womb? You were already alive then, too. Or as a sperm in your father's body? Half of your genetic material was stored in it, so you could argue that you were already there then, just in a different form.

"The same applies to your mother's egg, of course. And her mother, without whom you wouldn't be you, either. It is impossible to objectively place a beginning or an end. When you die and decompose, you nourish microorganisms in the soil, which feed from it and generate healthy topsoil for plants, which in turn feed your descendants and thus they live. So, they indirectly absorb something from you again. If we look at nature neutrally, it has no beginning and no end – apart from the fact that at some point there were the first cyanobacteria and photosynthesis and so on, of course."

"I see what you mean."

"But what's the tragedy of it?" she asked, eyeing him challengingly.

"The finite nature of life," he said without hesitation, and she nodded.

"Exactly! Every living being wants to live, to preserve its existence as a thinking consciousness, because we feel separate. I think that the ultimate goal of every intelligent and conscious species is to overcome death – the interruption of beginning and end."

"There could be something to it. Everyone is afraid of death."

"And everything it stands for. Transience, the fleeting nature of beloved things and the fear of missing something. Not having enough. Of becoming less. But what if we could outsmart this apparent law of nature?"

"Well, mortality is not necessarily a law of nature. It's just an evolutionary advantage because it results in the optimization of the gene pool. Without mortality, evolutionary pressure would not work, so nothing could improve," Liu replied.

"True, but what if we could make sure we never die again? To live only in the present, without painful memories of the past and without a future? Without missing anything?" she asked emphatically.

"Do you think ...?"

"Yes, I think that a predecessor civilization from Earth built these machines to achieve the ultimate goal of every biological species: Immortality and a cheating of death. What better way could there be than to encode information – which is what our personalities are – into photons? They always exist in the present, always travel at the speed of light and know no death. They do pass away, but only from our perspective. No subjective time passes for them."

She could see the doubt in his eyes, so she quickly continued.

"Think about it. Even with our limited technological means, we have encoded photons with quantum stuff. Why shouldn't it be possible for an ultra-advanced civilization to build machines that encode photons with their personality information and thoughts? A big step, but not unthinkable.

"The machines are programmed to maintain their function without allowing themselves to be distracted or destroyed, and so they give birth to more and more photon beings. Do they have a swarm consciousness? I don't know. Are they even conscious in our understanding? I don't know that, either. We couldn't talk with them even if they wanted to. We don't exist in the same perception of time.

"But think about it. If a species had such technology, would they use it to transcend themselves? To switch to a non-material, immortal plane of existence where there is a constant presence? Possibly with all the knowledge of the universe as a consequence?"

Liu contemplated and nodded slowly. "Yes, that sounds like some kind of civilization's final destination."

"It's logical." She pointed to the display with the live recording of the ring. "That's a photon birthing machine."

"How did you think of that?" he asked quietly.

"Intuition." Rachel just smiled to herself as she thought back to her encounter with Christer. "Pure intuition and a conversation about circles."

Her forearm display chirped to indicate that she had received a message from Earth. She was excited because she suspected Masha and Beth were behind it, but when she opened the email with the attachment, she had to blink a few times.

"Speak of the devil," she gasped.

"Are you all right?"

"Yes, I'm fine. Can I have the display now?"

"Sure." Liu stood up and squeezed her shoulder. "I'm going to sleep now. Those are really good thoughts, Rachel. We should discuss it with the others first thing. I think what you just said is the most logical explanation I've heard so far. And it would fit with the strange behavior of the ring, including why it destroyed our experiment so as not to compromise the photon states. Maybe we accidentally over-wrote some personalities."

"If that's what happened, we didn't know." She pointed apologetically at the display and he nodded before climbing down.

Rachel played the message. It had been recorded as an audio file. Attached was a video file that was still down-loading.

"Hi, Rachel. I'm proud of you," came Christer's pleasant voice from the speakers. "With the mission and everything. Back on that rooftop in Washington, I knew you were in for big things. I was thinking about our circle conversation and I came across something. I think I know what the ring is. It was pure intuition at first, but then I came across an anomaly, a fluctuation."

How does he know all this? she thought.

"Another guy seems to have had a similar intuitive thought long before us and climbed through the ring from below. He simply vanished. If you approach the shimmering sphere from above, if you fall in, so to speak, you simply fizzle out, burst like a red water bomb. But if you go through from below, you disappear. That made me think. Because what happens is that the interval changes from six minutes and thirty-three seconds to the next short fluctuation at the end of the intensity reduction. If you go through it from the bottom, you add almost a second to it. I find that amazing."

There was a short break.

"I've attached a video file for you. It's now UTC+7 at my place and I still want to have this date with you." He laughed briefly, then his voice grew more melancholy. "I know it's not easy to ask, but I still believe in synchronicity and my 'nose.' How about 6:33 your time? I would love to talk to you about so much. But maybe a second will do it. See you soon, Rachel."

As she tried to dispel the confusion his words had caused her, the download screen slowly approached its end. While waiting, she played his message twice more and pondered its contents. When she finally saw the video of a much smaller ring than the one on Mars, located in a cave, and how a bearded man went under the ring in agony and then disappeared into it as he straightened his knees, she suddenly understood.

43

CHRISTER

The moment he confronted Saruko with the carefully crafted lie, he was filled with an almost childlike excitement. He knew that telling him the truth would not lead him to the place he needed to go. It was a bit like the nervousness he felt before every college exam – only magnified. But he couldn't let on.

"I have to recreate Höglmayer's last day to find a pattern," Christer said in the facility manager's office. It was already late, but Saruko never seemed to sleep.

"What do you mean? Something like a role-playing game?"

"Something like that. He saw something back then, recognized something that made him kill himself," Christer lied. "To find out what it was, I have to stand in his shoes."

The doubt on Saruko's face was hard to miss – his brow furrowed and the corners of his mouth twitched.

"You can give me a couple of chaperones," he suggested, seemingly candidly. "Since I want to reenact the whole pattern, I need a few people to act as extras anyway."

"Do you also want me to bring in eighties costumes?" the Japanese man asked in a rare touch of sarcasm.

"No, it'll be fine without that."

Saruko sighed. "You'll get the time. But I hope you'll bring me results."

"I will," Christer promised. "You have my word on that."

His supervisor took Christer's key card and placed it on a sensor. Then he reached to give it back.

"Here you go. This will get you into the cavern." Saruko held on to the small card as Christer pulled on it, looking him in the eye. "Give me until tomorrow morning and I'll have a team assembled. How many people do you need?"

"Twelve. Just like on the video."

"All right, then."

It took him five minutes to reach the 'forbidden gate,' as he called it. It was painted red and was the only gate with lots of warning signs and, in front of it, two armed security guards, who were rarely seen anywhere else.

"Good morning," he said.

"No admittance," replied one of the two bored guards.

Christer lifted his key card and waved it. The other gunman took it and swiped it over a reader, which responded with a beep – a sound that obviously satisfied him, because he let Christer pass. There was another reader at the smaller staff passageway, but it also beeped dutifully and released the lock.

He quickened his pace in the large tunnel beyond. He could not be stopped now. At the lockers in the preparation section, he took out one of the heavy protective suits and hurriedly climbed in. Knowing Saruko, the guy wouldn't miss a thing, and that didn't give him much time.

The cavern was not just a dark abyss, it was an incomprehensible, shuddering void that ate deeper into his consciousness with every step he took. An almost-impenetrable veil of darkness enveloped the ring, making it seem like a hole in space itself. It was as if even reality was stepping into the shadows at this point to allow the ring to take precedence. Having seen it twice before with his own eyes obviously hadn't helped him get used to it. It remained eerie and strange and at the same time attractive, as if it emanated a magical power.

The whisper Christer heard grew stronger the closer he came to the cavern. This time he didn't block it out, but welcomed it, even though it was strange, as if it were a language he couldn't decode but could intuitively sense. It was a surreal sound that seemed to nestle in his innermost being, an intangible melody circling his thoughts and clouding his senses.

With every step he took closer to the cavern the whisper grew, pushing itself forward until it pushed everything else into the background. It was like the sound of a distant ocean, like the wind singing in the trees, but at the same time completely different – a voice without words, a message without content, and yet it captivated Christer.

In the heavy protective suit, which shielded him against both radiation and heat, he felt like an astronaut on an alien world. Every breath was a struggle, every movement an effort. But despite the physical strain, he couldn't turn back. He was like a moth being drawn to a flame, knowing that he could burn, but still fascinated by the light, the heat.

He risked a glance at his watch: 6:25. Eight minutes remaining. The numbers glowed green and artificial in the darkness, a silent reminder that time was moving inexorably forward, even in this strange place.

Saruko's voice crackled over the radio and snapped Christer out of his trance-like stupor. "Mr. Johannsen, what the hell are you doing down there?" The words sounded abrupt and harsh in the otherwise silent cavern, like a sudden thunderstorm stirring up the calm lake, a scream that displaced the whisper.

Christer couldn't help but grin. "I have a date," he replied, not taking his eyes off the ring floating in the darkness.

With one hand on the railing he climbed further down toward the ring. His feet found purchase on the rough rocks, his breathing heavy in his tight suit. But he was determined to keep going toward what awaited him. Sweat ran down his body and collected in his boots.

And suddenly he was there, standing in front of the ring. The darkness that surrounded him seemed even more profound, even more endless, and the whispering stopped abruptly. It was as if time itself stood still at that moment. But there was still more to do.

"You'll have your results, Saruko," he transmitted by radio, unsure if the other man could even hear him over the interference the ring was emitting. "You will have them."

He got down on all fours, panting from the heat and the knowledge that, despite his protective suit, he was being hit by hard radiation that was destroying his DNA. There was no turning back, but he had taken that into account.

As quickly as he could in his bulky suit, he crawled under the ring, right at the edge, just before he would have fallen into the maw. He reached up to the top of the ring, which wasn't easy as he barely had room between the kilometers-deep hole and the alien structure.

Höglmayer had used a rope. Christer was taking full risk. He glanced at his watch and just managed to make out the time before the hands melted: 6:32:50.

"I can count to ten," he muttered, searching for fear within himself, but finding only determination and curiosity.

44

RACHEL

She stretched a hand upward, examining it. It felt cold. A tingling sensation ran along her arms and up to the back of her neck, as if a swarm of ants were running over them and assembling under her hairline.

Rachel felt a pang of guilt over what she was about to do. Was it selfish? Heroic? Or neither, a mere impulse sparked by her intuition, the guidepost of her life that had never let her down.

Was now to be the first instance? It would be a bad time for fate to leave her hanging.

In the background she heard voices over the radio, familiar, but also strangely confused because they were distorted by intense interference. Snatches of words filtered through to her. Here and there she caught her name, sometimes a 'not' or a 'back.' But scratching and static swallowed up almost everything and marginalized the sounds to mere disturbances at the edge of her perception.

Strangely enough, she saw nothing above her but this foreign sky, which looked like a particularly hazy day at home when the ground fog arose.

All she had to do now was stretch upward to discover the truth, possibly even to become the truth. Forever. She wasn't doing it for herself, but for all those who would follow, who wanted to reach the end that everyone was striving for in their hearts.

Did she have any choice? She thought of Christer. Would she see him? Or would it no longer matter, because there would be no Christer as she had come to know him?

Out of the corner of her eye, she saw the others approaching. She had no more time. Either she solved the mystery for posterity, or she backed off now due to emotions. Masha was constantly present in her thoughts and heart. She had to do it for her, too, even though it meant the end for herself.

Isn't there a beginning in every ending?

"Six minutes and thirty-four seconds," she said over the radio. Whether her friends could understand her or not didn't matter. It was her last contact with the mortal world, her final goodbye.

Rachel was afraid, but also felt a pull toward realization that could not be stopped. The first law of life was: you will die. The body, her form, was constantly approaching its end, whether through an accident, illness, or the decay of time. All of that could come to an end now, if Christer was right, if she herself was right, if the ring had not lied to them.

Her intuition told her that she was doing the right thing, despite the guilt she felt toward Masha. But her daughter would grow older and understand, and if her mother's intuition was right, then Masha would follow her and perhaps fathom the secrets of the universe.

She took one last look at the time display in her helmet, which she had set to UTC+7 Earth time. Jakarta. 6:32:58 a.m.

Rachel stretched her legs and rose up through the ring. In a flash of inspiration, she began to laugh as the realization hit her like a freight train. The circle was complete, This had happened a long time ago, and the aspect of the whole that had been 'her,' 'someone,' had lived through itself to the point of transcendence. A turning on its own axis.

What she was looking for, she had always been: everything and nothing.

EPILOGUE
RACHEL & CHRISTER

It existed as energy. It had begun to be with a birth, but it had always been since then and always would be. Birth remained a constant process, but it was freed from a before and an after because that was no longer its nature. Space and time were no longer shackles – they never had been. The infinity of the cosmos, an ocean of stars and galaxies, was its playground, and at the same time, it itself was this playground. It saw the beauty of the universe, the beauty of the stars and galaxies, although a perception of beauty had to be a brutal reduction of reality. It saw the cosmic nebulae that spread out like splashes of color in the endless darkness. It saw the black holes that stood out like scars in the fabric of space.

All these phenomena existed as part of what it was. They were manifestations of its own nature. They were facets of its own essence. It knew that dark matter – that invisible substance that permeates and holds the universe together – was part of what it was. It knew that gravitational waves, those vibrations that move through the universe and change the structure of space, were part of what it was. It knew that quantum entanglement, the process by which particles are linked together across arbitrary distances, was part of what it was. These were all just aspects of the same conscious universe.

It knew that there was no distance, that there was no separation. How could there be a way from here to there if no time could pass between here and there? It knew that everything was connected, that everything was one, because this unity was inseparable from its non-being. It knew that everything was present at the same time, that everything was now and never was and never would be.

It knew that there was no beginning, no end. It knew that there was only the perpetual state of being, the state of timeless presence. It knew that it remained beyond the illusion of time and space, beyond illusions.

It knew that there were no names, no labels, no categories. It knew that these concepts were irrelevant, illusions of a creation searching for itself, limited in its perception, lost in a painful reduction.

It knew that it was beyond duality, beyond polarities. It knew that it was the absolute, that it was the infinite, that it was the eternal. It knew that it was that which lay beyond all ideas, beyond all words. It knew that it was that which was never born and would never die, because it needed identification with a body to do so.

It did not see the universe as separate entities, but as an indivisible whole, always now and without any movement. Nothing ever changed and it was therefore here and now. It did not see the stars and galaxies as individual objects, but as part of a continuous spectrum of energy and information. It did not see the universe as a collection of things and events, but as a singular phenomenon that exists and experiences itself on its own.

It felt the vibrations of the superstrings, the basic building blocks of all matter, as a melody that resonated to the rhythm of the cosmic symphony. The rhythm was now. Thoughts need time, and there was no time. So there were no thoughts, either, as everything remained in the now. It understood the complexity of the eleven-dimensional structures not as a mathematical construct, but as an intuitive understanding of the nature of reality, embedded in its presence.

It could perceive the dark energy, the mysterious force that drives the universe apart, and it could perceive the infinity of the multiversal foam that gives rise to countless universes that exist simultaneously, and yet are isolated unto themselves in their illusion of separation. It could recognize the fine-tuning of the cosmological constants, the precision with which the natural laws of the universe are tuned to make life possible.

It could recognize the indeterminacy of the quantum world, where particles can exist both as waves and as particles, where they can be in multiple places at once, where they can enter a state of superimposed being until they are observed. It could recognize the non-locality of quantum entanglement, where two particles, no matter how far apart, can interact instantaneously – because something other than the instant does not exist, must be illusory.

It could recognize the singularity of black holes, where space and time cease to exist and thus form centers of truthfulness – blobs of the real nature of what is. It could recognize the phenomenon of Hawking radiation, where particle and antiparticle pairs are created at the edges of the event horizon, and one particle from a pair falls into the black hole while the other escapes into the universe.

It could perceive and understand all these wonders of the universe, and yet it knew that it itself was the greatest wonder of all. For it was the universe that experienced itself. It was the universe that recognized itself. It was the universe that loved itself. And it remembered each of its parts, each circle that closed.

It took no effort because nothing ever was – it is.

EPILOGUE
LIU

Liu sat with the others around the large display and watched as Chinese and American special forces rappeled down into the deep drill shaft. Through the artificial eyes of the soldiers' helmet cameras, they watched spellbound as the military personnel stormed the underground cave system with quiet precision, arresting shocked scientists and capturing a handful of security guards who looked as if they were seeing ghosts.

An elderly Japanese man – the only one who was relatively calm when his office was broken into and he was secured with cable ties – even smiled thinly.

"Six thirty-four," he said, in English.

It was the fourth time in the last two hours that they had played the video.

"Do we know more now?" asked Madeleine.

"Yes, we do. Apparently all these people were kidnapped and forced to research the ring. Both of our countries deny having anything to do with it, but the internet and newsfeeds are full of speculation," he replied.

"It is now under public control," Adam noted.

Liu smiled reflexively, although he also felt like crying. He called up the two recordings, the one from the rover and the one from the cavern under Jakarta, placed them side-by-side, and watched again as Rachel Ferreira and Christer Johannsen disappeared simultaneously as they went from below the two rings, pushed up and through them, and the fluctuation occurred, extending the cycle for a single increment from 6:33 to just under 6:34.

"Do you think she was right?" he asked. "That the machines were built by a predecessor civilization on Earth to enable them to transcend as a species?"

"She and this Christer were obviously right in their prediction of what would happen," Madeleine said. "And the idea isn't nonsensical. It fits together."

"What does your intuition tell you?" Raphael posed with a group-wide grin.

"That she's out there," Liu replied with words and a matching grin, "in an endless present."

"Yes," Adam agreed with him. "And she and that Swede have opened the door to them and eternity for all of us. She made a sacrifice for all of us – and with this," he pointed to the stopped recording from the cavern under Jakarta, "anyone who wants to will be able to follow her."

"Hey," said Raphael and stood up. "Who's up for a trip to eternity? To Rachel?"

AFTERWORD

Dear reader,

I hope you enjoyed Rachel and Christer's story. You will no doubt have noticed that I haven't gone down the classic route of my other stories. I've taken a bit more time to explain the physics, I haven't chosen a classic suspense story, there's much less drama, and I haven't gone for a finale with lots of ruckus. It has become a quiet book, and that's a good thing because it feels right to me.

Below you will find a bonus chapter on the fascinating world of photons, as a short scientific essay that I put together for you during my research. I hope you like it. If you liked this book, please consider leaving a rating or review on Amazon, something that always helps authors like me a lot.

If you would like to read my book Rift: The Transition at no charge and exclusively as an e-book, simply sign up for my newsletter at www.joshuatcalvert.com. Rift is my gift to you. In the newsletter, I occasionally inform you about new releases and background information.

If you would like to contact me directly, you can do so via e-mail: joshua@joshuatcalvert.com

Best regards, Joshua T. Calvert

BONUS CHAPTER
THE FASCINATING WORLD OF PHOTONS

1. Introduction

In the world of physics, countless particles and forces exist, interacting in a complex and fascinating ballet to shape reality as we know it. Among these, photons are unique and fascinating because they can exist both as particles and as waves, a concept known as 'wave-particle duality.'

Photons are the basic building blocks of light and all electromagnetic radiation. They are massless, charged particles that always move at the speed of light. They are both waves and particles and can propagate through space, transferring energy and momentum. In many aspects, they are the mediators of the electromagnetic force, similar to how gluons mediate the strong force and W and Z bosons mediate the weak force.

Understanding photons and their properties is fundamental to understanding light and its interactions with matter. They play a crucial role in a variety of phenomena, from the illumination and heating of our world by the sun, to the possibility of wireless communication through radio waves, and imaging in the medical and scientific fields.

The wave-particle duality of photons is one of the most remarkable and paradoxical aspects of 'quantum mechanics.' They can manifest themselves as particles when they transfer energy and momentum to other particles, as in the so-called 'Compton effect' (also called 'Compton scattering'), in which photons bounce off electrons, transferring energy and momentum. On the other hand, they exhibit wave properties when they propagate through space, forming interference and diffraction patterns typically produced by waves.

Furthermore, photons exhibit a property called 'spin,' which in some aspects is reminiscent of the rotation of classical objects, although photons moving at the speed of light cannot, of course, rotate in the conventional sense. The spin of photons is always equal to a certain value, called 'Planck's reduced constant,' and can be oriented in two directions, either parallel or antiparallel to their direction of motion. This leads to the phenomenon of 'circular polarization' of light.

It is hard to overestimate how much photons shape our world. Without photons, there would be no light, no heat from the sun, no way to see the world around us. Their unique and often counter-intuitive properties are an essential part of what makes modern physics so fascinating and challenging. They are a key to understanding nature at the deepest and most fundamental level and will undoubtedly continue to fascinate and challenge us in the future.

2. The Birth of the Photon: From Max Planck to Quantum Mechanics

The history of the photon is closely linked to the development of quantum mechanics. At the beginning of the 20th century, classical physics was faced with a number of puzzles that it was unable to solve. One of these was the so-called 'ultraviolet catastrophe' or 'blackbody problem,' which related to the radiation emitted by an idealized, perfectly absorbing and emitting body – a blackbody. Classical physics predicted that this body should emit an infinitely high energy in the ultraviolet region of the spectrum, which, contrarily, was not observed.

It was Max Planck who solved this problem in 1900 by proposing that the energy of light is not emitted continuously, but in discrete 'packets' or 'quanta.' Planck postulated that the energy of such an energy packet is proportional to the frequency of the light, with the proportionality factor now known as 'Planck's constant.'

Although Planck's quantum theory successfully solved the black body problem, it was very controversial at the time. It was Albert Einstein who further advanced the quantum theory of light in 1905 when he explained the phenomenon of the 'photoelectric effect.' He hypothesized that light consists of discrete packets, which he later called photons, and that these photons can 'knock out' electrons from the surface of a metal if their energy is sufficient.

Einstein's theory was confirmed by experiments, particularly by the work of Robert Millikan, who investigated the photoelectric effect in detail and confirmed Einstein's predictions. Einstein was awarded the Nobel Prize in Physics in 1921 for his work on the 'quantum theory of light.'

The idea that light consists of discrete quanta was revolutionary and represented a radical break with the classical notion of light as a continuous wave. It was one of the triggers for the development of quantum mechanics, the theory that today determines our understanding of the microscopic world.

Quantum mechanics has not only shaped our understanding of light and photons, but has also enabled a whole range of technologies based on the properties of photons. From lasers and semiconductor devices to quantum computers and encryption technologies, many modern technologies are based on our understanding of the fascinating properties of photons.

3. The Duality Principle: Wave or Particle?

The question of whether light is a wave or a particle has occupied physicists for centuries. Issac Newton advocated the 'corpuscle theory of light,' which views light as a stream of particles. Christiaan Huygens, on the other hand, treated light as a wave. In the 19th century, the scientific community tended to accept the wave theory, particularly due to the experiments of the British physicist Thomas Young, who demonstrated the interference of light – a phenomenon typical of waves.

However, with the introduction of the photon by Einstein, light was once again regarded as a particle. Quantum theory seemed to finally decide the debate in favor of particle theory. But the story was not over yet. With the development of quantum mechanics in the 1920s, it became clear that light can exhibit both wave and particle properties. This phenomenon is known as wave-particle duality and is one of the central and most fascinating properties of quantum mechanics.

The wave-particle duality means that photons, although they are particles, also have wave-like properties. They can interfere and overlap, just like waves do. On the other hand, they can also act on matter like particles, as in the photoelectric effect or in Compton scattering. Which properties they exhibit depends on the circumstances of the experiment.

The wave-particle duality is not limited to photons. It applies to all quantum particles, including electrons, protons and even atoms. Quantum mechanics describes these particles through wave functions, mathematical functions that indicate the probability of finding the particle at a particular location. The wave function can interfere and overlap, just like a wave, but if you measure the particle, you will find it at a specific location, just like a particle.

Wave-particle duality is one of the most fascinating and puzzling features of the quantum world. It demonstrates that, at the deepest levels of reality, nature is vastly different from our everyday experience. It also shows the amazing flexibility and versatility of photons, which can act as both waves and particles.

4. The Role of Photons in Quantum Information and Quantum Communication

The 20th century saw the birth of quantum mechanics and with it the concept of photons, which ushered in a revolution in our concept of light and matter. In the 21st century, quantum mechanics opens up new possibilities for information processing and communication. Photons play a central role in these new technologies, which are summarized under the generic term 'quantum information.'

Quantum information is based on the principles of quantum mechanics, in particular the phenomena of 'quantum superposition' and 'quantum entanglement.' Quantum superposition enables a quantum system to be in several states at the same time, which leads to an exponentially greater information capacity compared to classical systems. Quantum entanglement makes it possible to exchange information between distant quantum systems without the need for classical communication.

Photons are ideal for applying these principles because they are easy to manipulate and can travel over long distances without significant interference. With the help of photons, we can realize quantum bits or 'qubits,' the basic unit of information in quantum information. A qubit can not only be in one of two states, like a classical bit, but also in a super-position of these states, which leads to the aforementioned exponentially larger information capacity.

Another important area of application for photons is 'quantum cryptography,' the most secure form of informa-tion transmission currently known. With the help of photons, we can generate encryption keys that are secure against eavesdropping. The principle of quantum cryptog-raphy is based on quantum entanglement and the impossi-bility of measuring the state of a quantum system without disturbing it.

Quantum information and quantum communication are still in their infancies, but they promise a revolution in infor-mation processing and communication comparable to the introduction of quantum mechanics in the 20th century. Photons, the smallest and most fundamental particles of light, are at the center of this revolution, once again demon-strating their central role in our conception of light and matter.

5. Photons in the Future: The Emerging Era of Quantum Technology

As we have seen in the preceding sections, photons play a central role in a wide range of phenomena and technologies, from fundamental physics to modern applications in communication and information. But this is just the beginning. With the advent of 'quantum technology,' we are on the brink of a new era in which photons will play an even greater role.

Quantum computers, which are just beginning to emerge, use photons to represent quantum bits. These qubits have the advantage of being able to superimpose states, which means that they can store much more information than classical bits. In addition, the ability of photons to entangle enables the creation of states that are inaccessible to classical systems. This allows quantum computers to perform complex calculations that would be unattainable for classical computers.

But the impact of quantum technology is not limited to computer science. In communications technology, for example, quantum cryptography enables the creation of security protocols that cannot be broken by any form of eavesdropping. And in sensor technology, photons can be used to make extremely precise measurements that go far beyond what is possible with classical methods.

But all this is just the tip of the iceberg. Quantum technology is a rapidly evolving field, and we are only at the beginning of what is possible. With each passing day, we are learning more about how we can manipulate and use photons to create ever more complex and powerful technologies.

Photons – those tiny packets of light – are central to all these developments. They are the messengers that transmit information, the building blocks that power quantum computers, and the tools that allow us to measure the world with a precision that was previously unimaginable. The future of technology is quantum mechanics, and photons play a central role in this future.

In conclusion, all that remains to be said is that photons, despite being the smallest and simplest elements of light, enable an astonishing variety of phenomena and technologies. They are the fundamental building blocks of light, the messengers that transmit information, the tools that allow us to measure the world around us, and the keys to a new era of quantum technology. They are quite possibly the most fascinating particles in the universe.

6. Summary and Outlook

After this in-depth study of the fascinating world of photons, it is clear that these tiny particles of light play an essential role in our understanding of the universe and our technological development. Although photons may be the smallest and simplest elements of light, they enable an astonishing variety of phenomena and technologies that shape our lives and our understanding of the world we live in.

Beginning with their role as the fundamental building blocks of light, we have seen how photons form the basis of our understanding of electromagnetic radiation and thus the way we see and measure our environment. Their interaction with matter and energy has helped shape our understanding of the fundamental laws of physics, and their ability to transfer energy and information makes them an indispensable tool in a wide range of technologies, from communications to medicine and the exploration of the universe.

Furthermore, we have seen how photons, through their special quantum mechanical properties such as superposition and entanglement, form the basis for new and exciting technologies that have the potential to revolutionize the way we communicate, compute and measure the world around us.

But despite all these advances and discoveries, we are still at the beginning of our journey to fully understand and utilize the world of photons. With each passing day, we learn more about these fascinating particles and their capabilities, and with each new breakthrough, new possibilities for the future open up.

It is clear that photons, these unimaginably small yet incredibly powerful particles of light, play a central role in our past, present, and future. They are the messengers that bring us information from the furthest corners of the universe, the tools with which we measure and manipulate the world we live in, and the keys to a new era of quantum technology.

The journey to discover and harness the full potential of these fascinating particles has only just begun, and there is no doubt that the future they open up to us will be full of wonder and discovery. As Albert Einstein once said, "The important thing is not to stop questioning." And photons inspire us to keep asking questions and exploring the mysteries of the universe.

Made in the USA
Middletown, DE
29 September 2024

61644856R00208